Penguin Books

MODERN INTERIORS

Andrea Goldsmith was born in Melbourne in 1950. She has worked and travelled in the United States and Britain. Her first novel, *Gracious Living,* was published by Penguin in 1990.

Also by Andrea Goldsmith
Gracious Living

Andrea Goldsmith

MODERN INTERIORS

Penguin Books

Penguin Books Australia Ltd
487 Maroondah Highway, PO Box 257
Ringwood, Victoria 3134, Australia
Penguin Books Ltd
Harmondsworth, Middlesex, England
Viking Penguin, A Division of Penguin Books USA Inc.
375 Hudson Street, New York, New York 10014, USA
Penguin Books Canada Limited
10 Alcorn Avenue, Toronto, Ontario, Canada M4V 1E4
Penguin Books (N.Z.) Ltd
182-190 Wairau Road, Auckland 10, New Zealand

First published by Penguin Books Australia, 1991
10 9 8 7 6 5 4 3 2 1

Typeset in 10/12 Andover by Midland Typesetters, Maryborough, Victoria
Made and printed in Australia by The Book Printer, Maryborough, Victoria

National Library of Australia
Cataloguing-in-Publication data:
Goldsmith, Andrea, 1950- .
Modern interiors.
ISBN 0 14 014726 8.
I. Title.
A823.3

The author gratefully acknowledges permission to quote from I, ETCETERA, copyright © 1978 by Susan Sontag. Published by Farrar, Straus and Giroux, Inc. and reprinted by permission.

$6-50

It's not our faults that trouble me.
It's our virtues.

SUSAN SONTAG

ONE

After a meal of rare roast beef, potatoes au gratin and green beans, George Finemore poured himself a Scotch, settled in front of the television and died. A premature death on a wet June night – although tidy enough, the doctor said, diagnosing a massive and efficient stroke. But tidy or not, it was clearly too much for his wife. Philippa Finemore, formerly so dignified, changed overnight; and while a husband's death is a terrible thing, Philippa's reaction was judged as extreme, even perverse, and quite unacceptable for a woman with position to maintain and name to consider.

People tried to be kind. Eccentric, they called her, Philippa Finemore has become quite eccentric since George's passing. But in private mutterings they mentioned senility, in crackling whispers they said she had lost her mind.

'Crazy. Mother's gone crazy.' It was Melanie Pryor who was speaking, and she was definitely not whispering. 'I simply don't know what's got into her, and if she's like this now, just a few months after Dad's death, what can we expect in a few years time!'

Evelyn Finemore, Melanie's sister-in-law, sat shaking her head. What indeed? And, for the first time since marrying Gray, was grateful for her own utterly ordinary parents, such dismally genteel people whom she knew would never cause embarrassment.

'And we thought Dad would be the one to crumble if Mother went first.' Melanie clenched her jaws and tightened her fists. 'She used to be so dependable, now it's as if none of us existed.'

Evelyn agreed. Philippa had lost her senses, and, along with them, any thought for the family. Her behaviour had been atrocious, beginning with the trip to Japan less than a month after George's death. George had refused to visit Japan; nothing to do with the war, he said, rather he disapproved of the Japanese attitude to alcohol. Surely there was more to a nation than the drinking habits of its people, Philippa had protested, to which George Finemore, managing director of Finemore's Fine Wines and Spirits, had replied, that to know a man's drinking habits was to know his character. But with George dead, there was nothing to stop Philippa from going to Japan. So off she went, and while that had been bad enough so soon after the funeral, it was her going with Lorraine Pascoe, head of Finemore's retail division and George's long-time mistress, that was truly indelicate. Then, on her return, she had resigned her voluntary work at the nursing home (too close for comfort, she said), taken up yoga and joined Friends of the Earth. The Mercedes had developed a farrago of stickers advertising her new interests: ONE NUCLEAR BOMB CAN SPOIL YOUR WHOLE DAY, THE AMAZON FORESTS ARE THE WOMB OF THE EARTH, and, worst of all, SAVE A GAY WHALE FOR CHRIST.

'You can't have that on your car!' Melanie protested.

'Be sensible,' Gray pleaded.

Only Jeremy, the second son and middle child, approved, and not merely of the gay whales but of his mother's whole new orientation; but, unfortunately, Jeremy carried little weight in the family circle.

Even Philippa's conversation changed. Suddenly she seemed more interested in fluorocarbons than family, in the homeless rather than her own hearth, and when the Society for the Handicapped approached her for the three dozen aprons she always made for their annual fête she politely refused. Of course, they said, they understood, her terrible loss . . . But it was not her terrible loss, she said, rather her priorities had changed and aprons no longer claimed favoured status. The charity work went, the lunch parties ceased, and so, too, the nice little biscuits long associated with Philippa Finemore's home. Now, when the grandchildren asked for a snack they were given biscuits from a packet. Melanie was not impressed and said as much. Philippa explained again that her priorities had changed; besides, she had never liked all those sweet things.

'But we did,' Melanie said.

'Good darling, I'll give you the recipes.'

And so she did.

But in the light of her latest aberration all the previous ones were as leaves in a storm. Exactly five months after George Finemore's death, Philippa announced she was leaving home.

'Leaving home! A woman her age!' Melanie helped herself to the coffee pot and another piece of Evelyn's home-made almond bread. 'Leaving *our* home, the place where we grew up, for an inner-city hovel where no one in their right mind would live!' Melanie paused for a mouthful, patted her lips with an embroidered napkin, breathed deeply and began again. 'She has a responsibility, and I don't mean just to us, although that's not irrelevant, she has a social responsibility. She's not just anyone, people look to her, to people like her to show an example.'

What Melanie meant, but considered it in poor taste to say, was that wealth brings responsibilities, wealth sets one apart, and there could be no doubt that Philippa was very well off. Both Melanie and her brother Gray had been pleasantly surprised at the reading of the will to discover their father had been an extremely wealthy man. Melanie's husband, Selwyn, had looked similarly surprised, although he was, in fact, the only member of the family to know the exact extent of George Finemore's fortune. Indeed, Selwyn Pryor had acquainted himself with George's worth more than fifteen years before when evaluating Melanie's credentials as a future wife, and ever since had maintained a careful watch over his inheritance. Selwyn knew the value of Finemore's Fine Wines and Spirits, and a fine business it was, knew too, of George's investments in prime real estate - only a dozen properties but all very prime. Selwyn knew it all, had known all along.

'A responsibility,' Melanie was saying to her sister-in-law, 'and her present behaviour is simply unacceptable.'

Evelyn went into the kitchen to make fresh coffee. She felt very sorry for the family and hoped she was managing to show it. Hers was a passionless, inert sort of face – she was too self-conscious to show very much – and while Melanie had been talking, Evelyn had tried to mould her features into expressions of sympathy: to purse the mouth, frown, raise the eyebrows at the nose end only, and while the tiny facial muscles were among the body's most recalcitrant, the fact that Melanie was still sitting in Evelyn's lounge room, suggested that the concern Evelyn felt had percolated through her naturally bland features. And feel it she did. Philippa was disrupting the family; Melanie was distraught and irritable, Gray was short-tempered, and unless something were done soon, there would be one of those dreadful Finemore family dinners seething with silent accusations and Jeremy would be there and he always made Evelyn feel so uncomfortable.

'So what's to be done,' she said, as she took up her place on the leather two-seater. 'We can't forbid Philippa to leave home, it's her money after all.'

'Personally, I think she's certifiable, but that would mean an awful fuss.' Melanie watched Evelyn pour the coffee. 'Just half for me, I'm trying to cut down.'

'Oh?'

'Wrinkles. I heard somewhere that caffeine causes wrinkles.'

'Are you sure you don't mean nicotine?'

'Of course I'm sure. If it had been nicotine I wouldn't have bothered to listen.' She paused for another bite of almond bread. 'We have to be firm with Mother, give her guidance. We mustn't forget she's used to Dad making all her decisions, so it's not surprising she's floundering now.'

'Do you think this might only be a passing phase?'

Melanie shook her head.

'A short-term reaction to your father's death?'

Melanie shook her head again.

'Perhaps she just needs to spread her wings a bit and then she'll return to her old self.'

'No, Evelyn,' Melanie said. 'Mother's had five months of spreading her wings, and now it's time she was brought back to the nest. It's time for her to settle down.'

Philippa Finemore had no intention of settling down. She had been settled for the forty years of her marriage and was now ready for a change. Not that George had been a bad husband, but as the years passed, Philippa found she had little need of him, and as the children grew, she had little need for them either. As children that is. She had tried to steer them into realms more interesting than the usual mother-child relationship, but her children had resisted, preferring she remain exclusively in the maternal role – with the exception of Jeremy, always the exception of Jeremy. But now, by her calculation, with only twenty good years left, she wanted more than mothering, more than grandmothering too, and was determined to begin anew.

The need for change, while lurking for some time, had emerged clearly on the day of George's funeral. After the cemetery, family and friends had returned to the Finemore home to drink to his memory. Philippa had managed to escape solicitous pats and sympathetic sighs and was standing on the landing at the top of the stairs watching the crowd of chattering mourners below. Her thoughts were of George as she watched his friends in his house drinking his liquour recounting his stories. How he would have loved this! And the very fact of his absence at a gathering of his friends marked his death more forcibly than the sprawling emptiness of his reclining armchair, the brazenness of the coffin, the dirge of a service and the hole in the ground. Here was a party in George's own home and George was not playing convivial host, so George must be dead.

George would not have been happy dying so young. Such a lively man with so many plans, Philippa was sorry he would have to miss out. But she was not sorry for the loss of a husband. Theirs had been a marriage frayed by familiarity, a faded relationship with occasional patches of brilliance; but like an old neglected tapestry, patches of brilliance cannot reclaim the parts already lost. And lost they were, long before George's death. It wasn't his women or his devotion to football, it wasn't even his long absences from home, rather it was his indifference to everything that was important to her, and consequently his indifference to her. He was kind and generous as men of his ilk were, and polite and sociable, but he regarded his wife as he would a pretty bird, and talked with her only to hear the sound of his own voice; if ever he noticed she needed a little air to breathe, a little music to sing by, he did nothing about it. So she pared her desires back, stripped them down until their original colours were faded even in memory; but while they became distinctly threadbare, she never discarded them. Under the dust of years they lay, years of doing the same things, seeing the same people, years when the passing seasons did little more than change her clothes, her hairstyle, inject new words into her conversation and remove some of the old, and still the ambitions lay quietly, and a small voice insisted there was still time. And at twenty there was still time, similarly at thirty, even forty and fifty, but at sixty-one, time is on its knees, and, in a burst of impatience, the dust of years is brushed away to reveal, still fresh and buoyant, the expectations and desires of a hopeful youth.

Which was not to suggest her marriage had been unsatisfactory, or, for that matter, unusual. It had been calm, George hadn't interfered, he had been a good provider. It was the repetition that had been so trying, the long days gripped by habit. And while there had been occasions when she waved a hand in protest, the movement was always small and the direction invariably ambiguous. She seemed to lack the courage to protest with conviction until now, as if George's passing had given her the strength to make her own move; or perhaps it was more simple, that, with George's bulk no longer obstructing the view, Philippa could better plot the way ahead. There were things she would miss, his boisterous laugh, the powder on the bathroom floor, but overall, the passing of the marriage was long overdue, it was just a shame it had taken George's death to bring it about.

She felt herself smile, so many possibilities, so much to look forward to, and then, just as quickly, the smile vanished as

Lorraine Pascoe's neat figure entered her field of vision. If anyone had lost a husband it was Lorraine.

Philippa had known about George and Lorraine ever since a dinner party about fifteen years before, when she had stooped to retrieve a piece of nineteenth-century silverware from beneath the table, and had seen Lorraine's hand kneading George's thigh. Kneading his thigh but precariously close to other parts. Philippa had never minded about Lorraine, indeed, disinterest in sex coupled with enjoyment of Lorraine's company meant the affair quite suited her. But not so George's other secrets, those heavy silences that occasioned a surprise gift – jewellery, a leather handbag, once even a new car – offered with a smile twitching over his great blond face and apologies clotting in his throat. At such times, Philippa would wonder at the secrets that could render him so coy. In the early days, she had interpreted the gifts as expressions of love, but it was not long before she realized that for men like George, gifts were nothing more than prettily-packaged apologies or anodynes for guilt. For men like George, love of a wife was implied, unspoken, axiomatic; love was caught in the emblems of marriage, in the shared house, the sons and daughters, the family breakfasts.

It might have been different for Lorraine, perhaps in the absence of marriage and its accoutrements, George had affirmed his love. And if so, how much worse for her now he was gone. Philippa wondered whether she would stay on at Finemore's. An unofficial visit from the family lawyer the previous evening 'to save Philippa any embarrassment at the reading of the will,' revealed that Lorraine Pascoe would not need to work. George had bequeathed to her one of his real estate holdings, a warehouse, and the first piece of property he had ever bought; it yielded a sizeable rent and a more than comfortable living. While Philippa registered her relief that George had done the right thing by Lorraine, the lawyer was apologizing for bearing such distressing news. George had rejected all his suggestions of how best, and discreetly, to provide for Miss Pascoe; 'Your husband refused to listen,' the lawyer kept saying, 'he simply wouldn't listen.' Philippa had patted the poor man's arm, poured him a short brandy and finally shown him the door. As for George, Philippa recognized that the manner of the bequest was his way of acknowledging that Philippa had known about Lorraine all along, and that he had appreciated her tolerance and forebearance. Always a stickler for propriety was George, a man who wouldn't have wanted to leave any loose ends, any favours owing. Again, she looked at the trim figure of Lorraine Pascoe and wondered how she would manage without George. Sensing the scrutiny, Lorraine looked up to the landing and smiled, an open, warm smile, and returned to her discussion.

A burst of laughter arose from a group near the den. Philippa saw Selwyn Pryor standing with a few of his friends; Melanie, too, was part of the group, her large features carefully monitored even while joining in with the laughter. Melanie had inherited her father's appearance, although, unlike George, would never capitulate to fat. She was tall and strong-framed, with a broad face and abundant mouth, a big woman who strove to convert her handsome features to petite femininity. And she was, in large part, successful. But in rare moments of spontaneity, she would throw back her head and open the large mouth and utter a joyous bellow that did her father proud. As a large woman she was extremely attractive, but as a large woman trying to shrink there was less to please the eye. Indeed, to someone like Philippa who was small and olive-skinned, with dark hair and almost black eyes, the large blond features of her daughter were something of which to be proud.

Philippa watched as Selwyn took a bottle from the sideboard and refilled his friends' glasses. Throughout the exercise he did not stop talking; he chewed his words and spat them out, and with a mouth so muscular and a neck so anguine he had a distinct advantage over most other people. Philippa had never liked her son-in-law and was convinced that with a different man Melanie would have blossomed. Instead, since her marriage, the bright, outgoing girl had become a mask of social convention. Melanie responded to the dictates of fashion; she believed the current beliefs, purloined from the editorial of the daily newspaper, and was horrified at the latest horror campaigns – drug abuse last year, child abuse this; she did aerobics when aerobics were the rage and was now devoted to power walking; she wore her hair short three years ago, but shoulder-length today. Melanie seemed devoid of any interior and Philippa laid the blame squarely at the feet of her son-in-law. George had seen it differently. Selwyn Pryor was an astute businessman with the ability to transform an ordinary business into something special. Selwyn Pryor, said George, had the makings of a rich man.

'But surely there's more to a man than making money,' Philippa had said.

Of course there was, George had replied. Hadn't Selwyn already proved himself as an academic? And hadn't he been offered the safest conservative seat in the country? Selwyn Pryor could do anything, George said, but he'd chosen business, he'd chosen Finemore's. Not that Philippa needed any reminding, for it was clear to her that business, or rather making money, had long been Selwyn's major interest. George said she was too hard on her son-in-law, that creative flare in business suggested other virtues that would, in time, reveal themselves. But they had not. Selwyn's was a personality of stucco, impressive enough, but hard and superficial; he was a man bereft of positive qualities, or so it seemed to Philippa. Others regarded him differently; even now, at his father-in-law's funeral, he had a solid following; his friends were gathered around, content to let him talk, laughing when required, apparently happy to be included in his circle. People found him handsome, but not Philippa, he was too tall and angular, and his thick brown hair was styled too self-consciously and his nails manicured too carefully, and despite shaving twice a day, the beard always got the better of him. Then there were the silly blue eyes, Selwyn's major vanity, two bright blue blisters set at the bridge of his proudly patrician nose. The appearance fitted the man, Philippa had long ago decided: he was driven by self-interest and looked the part.

It occurred to her that with George now gone, Selwyn's self-interest would gain momentum. Not that George had ever deliberately confined him, but the fact of George's running a large business he had built from nothing, had placed clear limits on Selwyn's ambitions. No such restrictions remained now. Immediately, Philippa's thoughts turned to her oldest child: poor Gray, it would not be easy for him. Gray took a doctrinaire approach to life; long after Selwyn had raided the tomb and disposed of the loot, Gray would still be planning his strategy. As George used to say: Gray would make a living but Selwyn would make a fortune.

She found Gray in the crowd and was pleased to see him with Finemore's personnel manager. Not that a father's funeral was an appropriate place to do business, but times ahead would be tough for Gray. Like Melanie, Gray had inherited his father's appearance, but something had gone awry. He was tall, over six feet, but the shoulders were too narrow and the paunch too prominent; the blond hair was nondescript sandy, and the eyes were pale and limpid within a large pink face. He was thirty-nine, but had looked the same at twenty and would probably be no different at fifty. Except for the moustache. This narrow strip of vanity was the sort of decoration that required constant and delicate care, a moustache that was less a moustache and more a statement of character. Philippa had begged him to shave it off when it first appeared some five years ago and still hoped for its removal, but, so far, Gray had remained firm.

And that was Gray, firm and solid, although a deficit in natural ability did not make him always reliable. Not that he was aware of any such deficit; Gray had an opinion about most things and was not shy in giving it. Like his brother-in-law, Gray was saddled with a bulky arrogance and a driving ambition, although was quieter about both than Selwyn. Gray was also entirely without humour which merely added ponderousness to pomposity. He would have made an exemplary Victorian, Philippa had often thought, but as a man of the late twentieth century he tended to try one's patience. Children complain about having no choice in their parents, but parents don't choose their children either, and can be extremely surprised at what they've produced. Philippa had never told anyone of the disappointment in her oldest child. It was not that she didn't love him – what mother doesn't love her children? – but Gray's bloated sense of his own importance made him disinterested in others and insensitive to their needs.

She watched as Gray shook hands with the personnel manager and moved off towards the bar. The crowd seemed to be swelling, although, as a liquor merchant's wife, she was well-acquainted with the effects of free-flowing alcohol, the raised voices, the exaggerated gestures, people occupying more space. Death's a party, Philippa thought, what a shame George had to miss it. As for Philippa, she wished they would all leave; after forty years with George and four crowded days preparing for his burial, she wanted to slip off her navy blue wool dress, wanted to let down her hair (wanted, in truth, to cut it off, the whole greying auburn mass that George had liked so much, despite having not touched it in years), remove her makeup, the stiletto shoes, the stockings, and sit quietly by herself in the empty house. After that, the years stretched ahead, empty of obligation and rich with dreams. She smiled at the thought and noticed Gina Ballantyne smiling back. A party, that was all. Gina had not spoken to George for months, not since George had commented on her facelift, in company, at a dinner party arranged by Gina and Barry to display her new face. George, usually so tolerant of his liquor, had drunk too much, or so he explained to Philippa afterwards, and out it had slipped: 'Love your new face, Gina.'

Having a dinner party to celebrate your new face is one thing, acknowledging this is what you are doing is quite another; Gina would have liked to do George damage. What she did, however, from her position at the head of the table, was smile her new-look smile and respond with a brittle thank you. Everyone else fiddled with their food, except Barry Ballantyne, an old friend of George's and a man devoted to his wife. 'What a rude bastard you are George,' he said. 'You're the last person to be casting aspersions at someone else's appearance,' and he puffed out his small man's chest and blew up his cheeks in an imitation of George's bulk.

Nothing to imitate now, Philippa thought, poor George's bulk was being bloated by morbid gases and bountiful bacteria hungry for human flesh; as for Gina Ballantyne, she looked like a smiling cadaver. Her skin, so tight and smooth, appeared to be squeezing the substance from her; the skull so defined and the body pared back by exercise and diet was a welded sculpture of angles and joints.

Philippa would have to go downstairs soon and join them. She had learned over the past four days that a bereaved wife was permitted only limited time alone, too much was considered unhealthy. Even now, she saw Evelyn, her sweet, dull daughter-in-law, approach Melanie and whisper to her. The two of them looked up at Philippa, Melanie nodded and moved towards the stairs, while Evelyn collected another plate of savouries for the mourners. But Philippa was not ready to be collected, not yet. She left the landing and slipped into her bedroom and from there to the bathroom and closed the door. She heard Melanie's 'Are you all right, Mother?' and replied with a cheery 'I'll be down shortly.' She slipped off her shoes, loosened her belt and sat on the enamel lid of the toilet. George's toilet. For that matter, George's bathroom and George's house. All of it now Philippa's: the six bedrooms, the four bathrooms, the three large entertainment areas, the servants' quarters, the clinker brick, the swimming pool, the tennis court, the terraced gardens. Yet somehow it jarred in a life without George, and as her gaze passed over the marble and gold of George's bathroom, Philippa knew she would sell the lot.

Exactly five months later, soon after her sixty-second birthday, Philippa Finemore announced to Gray and Evelyn, Melanie and Selwyn, and her younger son Jeremy, that she was leaving home. It was a Friday night and they were lingering over coffee and port at the huge mahogany dining-table George had bought soon after he and Philippa were married. The grandchildren were either in the sitting-room watching television or asleep in the cots that Evelyn and Melanie kept in one of the spare bedrooms. Philippa passed the coffee pot around, waited for a lull in the conversation and made her announcement.

'I've decided to sell the house.'

In the silence that followed, Jeremy smiled and reached for his mother's hand, while the others looked to Gray for a response.

'Don't be ridiculous,' he said. 'If it's help you're needing we can easily organize that.'

'Of course,' said Evelyn, looking at her husband, 'we'll organize that. Melanie and I can do the shopping, and we'll arrange for a cleaning service to help Julia with the housekeeping. And we can increase John Slowe's hours in the garden, perhaps hire someone else for the lawns.'

Evelyn was clearly warming to the task, but it was not help that was on Philippa's agenda, it was change. Selwyn leaned over and patted his mother-in-law's knee.

'Now Philippa, we know how difficult these past months have been, but what's required is a little more time, a little more patience.' And patted her knee again. Selwyn spoke in earnest; he had plans for the property, located as it was in a prime residential suburb and ideal for a substantial town house development. 'You mustn't rush into a decision you might later regret.'

'Besides, it's our home,' Melanie continued, 'you can't sell our home.' For Melanie, too, had plans. The house was just the right size and in just the right location for her own family. The house was Finemore property as far as she was concerned, and Philippa had no right to dispose of it.

'Perhaps it's only a passing phase,' Evelyn suggested a few days later as she and Melanie sat in Evelyn's lounge room drinking coffee and eating home-made almond bread.

But it was not. The auction notice went up, six weeks later the house was sold for a respectable 2.1 million and two months after that Philippa moved into a single-fronted Victorian terrace, fully renovated, only a short walk from the centre of Melbourne and a long drive from the rest of the family. Except Jeremy.

'I think it's perfect.'

It was late afternoon and Jeremy had come straight from the university 'to wet the head of the house,' as Philippa had so neatly put it. After a day spent cleaning and unpacking and discovering the secrets of her new home, Philippa had retired to the couch while Jeremy opened the champagne. Now she watched him, enjoying the warm distance that tiredness often creates, seeing his dark skin and eyes, noticing how the heavy, almost-black hair fell over his forehead, the deft gestures, the compact body whose slightness had always worried his father, and knew he could be mistaken for no one's son but her own. He felt her gaze, looked up and smiled, and with the bottle now open and the drinks poured, came and joined her on the couch.

The summer sun was still high in the sky, yet, due to certain architectural feats in the renovation of the terrace, the room was still cool. Philippa sipped her drink and sighed. 'I'm going to be very happy here. I love the area, the house is extremely comfortable, and it's just the right size.'

'Which is what the others find so disturbing. Where can the children play? Where can they take their naps? Where are we to have our family dinners?'

'At their places.' Philippa stood and walked to the galley kitchen at the end of the lounge. She rummaged in a box for some rice crackers, returned to her chair, took a handful and passed the dish to Jeremy. 'Do you think I'm being unfair? Do you think I'm being selfish?'

Jeremy smiled. 'I'm absolutely the wrong person to ask. But,' he held up his hand to deflect her interruption, 'you do have a life to live, your own life and not simply that of grandmother and babysitter. Selfish? The word has a bad reputation. What you're doing is looking after yourself. I think you're being responsible.'

'It's not that I don't love them—'

'I know.'

'Nor is it that I don't want to see them—'

'Of course not.'

'But I don't need to see them all the time. The fact of the matter is, Jeremy, I've got other things to do.'

'I know, and I'm pleased.'

'Only vague ideas at the moment, but a host of them. This,' she raised her arms to the room, to the little house, 'is only the beginning.'

TWO

Philippa went into the front room to finish unpacking. She was pleased for Jeremy's visit and grateful that at least one of her children understood her need for change. Which was fortunate, for the inclination was gathering momentum; each day had its share of new hopes and possibilities, some so bizarre they might have been borrowed. As the months passed, Philippa was discovering aspects of herself that were strange and unfamiliar, yet, at the same time, invigorating and curiously seductive. The discoveries did not help clarify her plans, but they did provide for a burgeoning array of options. Jeremy seemed to understand this mysterious alchemy that had, in such a short time, transformed his mother, not simply into a more lively person, but into a woman unknown.

Philippa smiled: an unknown woman with an unknown future, what a luscious prospect! And set about putting the house to order.

The front room had originally been designed as a second bedroom, but Philippa, determined never again to need a second bedroom, had converted it to a study. The cupboards intended for clothes, housed much of the Finemore finery, that reservoir of silver and crystal and linen and lace once so essential to Philippa's lifestyle. Later, all of it would go to the children, but with her plans still so unformed, premature distribution seemed imprudent. She had installed book shelves along one wall, and, in front of the window with a view to the street, had placed George's leather-top desk, a beautiful piece of furniture in dark, aged wood that George had inherited from his father, although it had been George's mother, Dora, who had truly occupied the desk. Unknown to the rest of the family, Dora had written poetry throughout her married life. In the middle years of Philippa's marriage when the days had dragged by in dreary repetition, Dora had taken Philippa into her confidence, and, until her stroke, Philippa had been Dora's first reader, privy to the tentative pleasures of a new poem as well as the capricious joys of publication. And while Philippa admired the poems, and would return to them over and over again, what she valued most in those days was Dora's choice of her, Philippa, as confidant.

When Dora died and her possessions were sorted, the family had been surprised to learn of Dora's poetry, and not understanding it, had belittled it, referring to 'Mother's little secret' as one might a bottle of brandy concealed at the back of a cupboard. Philippa had been furious, feeling the affront not only on Dora's behalf, but as an insult to herself. Dora's poems had taught her that in a life reduced to the basics, any foreign elements must be protected, that in a life already diminished, further reductions leave permanent scars. Philippa maintained her silence while George and his brothers passed their snide remarks, but she wanted justice. And three months after Dora's death she got it. One evening, a rare solitary evening when Philippa was alone in the house, she stole all of Dora's papers, her poetry, correspondence, recipe notes, even a few shopping lists, she stole the lot. And when, many years later, George wondered what had happened to 'Mother's jottings', Philippa said they must have been thrown out. Now, from one of the cartons, she withdrew the folders containing Dora's writings and placed them on the desk, out of hiding and safe in Philippa's house.

Philippa's house: she savoured the thought. For forty years of marriage, Philippa had never had her own space, despite the huge Finemore home. It had always struck her as iniquitous that children had their own rooms, and husbands had studies or workshops, but wives, who spent most of the day at home, rarely had a place of their own. It was a theft of privacy, she now decided, for if you define someone always in relation to others, define her exclusively as wife and mother, then the need to be alone is rendered otiose. Philippa had taken to visiting St Kilda pier for her solitude, secret trips, as if there were something shameful about wanting space for herself, wanting more when she already had so much. She would sit on the pier, together with the crusty old fisherman, a few truant boys and a couple of women whom she guessed were fugitives like herself, sit with her line cast over the side, listening to the waves breaking against the pylons. She would wrap herself in Dora's afghan rug, pull on a hat against the winter wind (she never went to the pier in summer, the noise, the pestilential crowds were no better than home) and stare out to sea. She never caught anything, but that wasn't the point, neither did she use bait. All she wanted was to sit quietly and allow her thoughts their itinerant fancies. The fishermen got to know her, would grunt an acknowledgement as she walked past them to her spot further down the pier. One old fellow used to talk to her, would regale her with tales of the old days when the 'flatties were as long as yer arm' and 'yer could feed a family in less than an hour.' She would sit quietly listening to his stories, watching the limp, stained cigarette dangling from his lower lip, and would suck in the scented wind of salt and seaweed and, from the kiosk at the end of the pier, the pungent smell of hot oil and freshly cooked fish and chips.

The incongruity of her sanctuary never escaped her; she had been forced to leave a large house to find a piece of territory that was neither the children's, nor George's, nor the housekeeper's, nor the gardener's. And it was not as if she hadn't tried. Of an afternoon, she would perch on her side of the bed, feet firm to the floor, reading a book or writing a letter, but the effort of keeping to her own side simply reminded her she was trespassing. As for the laundry where she kept her sewing table, this was Julia's domain, and although Julia was a kind person who was fond of her employer, she made it clear that, unless there was sewing to be done, it was best if Mrs Finemore stayed out.

Which brought her to another problem: the servants. In all the years with George, Philippa had never become accustomed to them. Her own background, while far from poor, certainly did not include housekeepers and gardeners and a clutch of cleaners. But from the very beginning of life with George, there had been 'help' in the house, and from the very beginning Philippa was on uncertain ground. As the years passed, she did learn to make her requests, to ask for rooms to be cleaned or silver to be polished, but what she never managed to do, and what appeared to be essential for harmonious cohabitation with servants, was become immune to their presence. For it seemed that only in that way could one go about one's business, dress and undress, leave hair in the bath, soiled clothes in the basket and not feel the shame of exposure. It was absurd but true: servants were only compatible with one's sense of privacy if one pretended they weren't there – as human, as *like oneself*. In this, Philippa had failed; at the end of her marriage she was no more inured to servants handling her soiled clothes than she had been as a young bride, neither, for that matter, had she ever learned to erase the fingerprints of strangers from the garments that touched her body. With servants in the home and nowhere to hide, she was, at the same time, trespasser and trespassed upon.

But no longer. She patted Dora's poems, stood a moment inhaling her solitude and left the room. Dusk had entered the narrow passage; grainy lightbeams shot through the stained glass panels beside the front door and another stronger shaft stretched like a pyramid from one of the skylights. Philippa leaned against the wall, the plaster cool through her blouse. That she was happy was undeniable, such an odd sensation, more consonant with the shallowness of youth than the insights of age; George was dead, her family were furious and Philippa was happy.

And, she realized, very hungry. She walked down the passage to the kitchen and prepared some food. She ate standing at the bench, looking across the lounge through the glass doors to the courtyard beyond, and, as night absorbed the tiny garden, saw, ever more clearly, her new life reflected in the glass: the smallness of the room, the old furniture from the den unrecognizable in a pale floral print that George would have dismissed as insipid, the black bundle that was Peach asleep on her sheepskin rug, the beige carpet so impractical with young children, and, in the middle of it all, Philippa Finemore, a widow of sixty-two, who had shirked her duty and deserted her home, a short woman with a gentle figure, greying hair now comfortably bobbed, and a face that with its high cheek bones and angular jaw, its olive skin and dark eyes, and the mouth, most of all the mouth, full and prominent with lips that pursed when she spoke as if her first language were French, had always distinguished her from the blonde, pale-eyed women of her acquaintance.

The face had changed in the past few months. She now resembled more closely the fifty-year-old she had once been rather than the ageing widow at George's funeral; she felt better than she had in years. Tedium takes it toll, she thought, and habit shrivels the imagination, and if she were less than lively in those years, should she have been surprised?

How she envied today's young women with their swag of choices, and how sad she was that her own daughter had taken so little advantage of them. Poor Melanie, so many opportunities discarded for so little, and now, after fifteen years with Selwyn, it was impossible for her to admit that, in choosing him and his ambitions, a bargain had been struck.

Philippa poured herself a fresh glass of champagne. Ever since Selwyn Pryor had entered Melanie's life Philippa had worried about her daughter; now Melanie was thirty-six and still Philippa was worrying. Not that Melanie asked for her concern, on the contrary, she made a point of appearing satisfied; she was always surrounded by people, held successful dinner parties, was a regular guest at the parties of others, raised money for worthy causes, was demonstratively adoring of her husband. Yet she seemed to be wasting away; her large frame was pinched and her once expressive face was locked into a few essential masks, her voice was sharp and her smile increasingly rare; and still she insisted she was happy. Although wasn't this the bargain struck by all wives? That, like Sisyphus, they would push their burden through the years, their brows creased with hope, their hearts bursting with anticipation, their minds forever closed to the futility of the task? Isn't this what Philippa herself had done? But there was one fundamental difference between Philippa and Melanie and that was Selwyn Pryor: how anyone could even pretend happiness with a man like that was beyond comprehension.

The sense of having failed her daughter was still strong, even after all these years, and yet Philippa didn't know what else she could have done. And it was not only Melanie, all her children condemned her as a less-than-successful mother; Gray, her oldest, was a sententious bore, Melanie had chosen a life of artifice, and Jeremy was a homosexual. She shrugged, a bad mother? Perhaps, and yet the extent of her children's demands – not Jeremy's, but Gray's and Melanie's, suggested they were satisfied enough. They were quick to ask her to mind the grandchildren, to cook, run messages, to lend her home for large functions – the old one not the new – still they wanted her to be their mother, and were reluctant to regard her in any other way. In all the months since George's death, neither Gray nor Evelyn, Melanie nor Selwyn had expressed any interest in her well-being (with the exception of their irritatingly regular exhortations to 'keep busy'), they simply added 'widow' to 'mother' and 'grandmother' and expected her to continue as before. Which annoyed Philippa, who believed she had earned the right to some consideration. It was as if she were invisible to them; Philippa Finemore, widow, mother, grandmother and a person who had finished with being an extension of other people's lives, was outside their purview.

For several minutes, Philippa had been staring at the windows at the end of the lounge room, glancing across her new life as if it didn't exist. Family is like that, she thought, it insinuates itself where it doesn't belong and blocks out everything else. She brought the room back into focus, made a cup of coffee, and, with Peach at her heels, walked along the passage to the front door and out to the verandah. She leaned against the wrought iron railing and sipped her drink. Her children accused her of being selfish, but what about them? They only wanted her as bedrock to their own lives. Families could be such shabby cells of deceit, Philippa decided, and yet she'd devoted most of her life to hers. Was she a hypocrite then, or merely stupid? Because she had not been miserable, or at least not often. Had she confused stability with boredom? Satisfaction for a lack of choice?

From her first meeting with George, Philippa's life had been set on the solid rock of his certitude. 'Don't worry,' he had said on their first date when she had tripped and torn her stocking. 'Don't worry,' he had said when he proposed to her and she told him she didn't love him. 'Don't worry,' he had said when the children started school and she complained of her empty life. 'Don't worry,' George had said throughout the years of their marriage, because he would take care of things. So she didn't worry, but neither did that remove the pain and the irritation and the fatigue, she had to learn to live with those. And, in the process, they acquired highly specific labels – life, marriage, motherhood – labels more acceptable than misery, habit and disappointment.

Which is not to suggest there hadn't been a struggle to keep misery at bay. She had silenced her youthful dreams because they made her dissatisfied, and searched instead for a little sparkle amongst the blandness of her days. She came to notice the first spring buds and the subtlety in the sun's shadows, she heard the dry autumn leaves, felt the hesitation of a changing wind. She saw the new hairstyle of the dressmaker and the pallor of the butcher, the smile of the grimy fellow with a full bottle of plonk, the ageing man at the wheel of his gleaming red Porsche. And only later, after George was gone and there was time to think about such things, did it occur to her that the common belief in women's natural disposition for detail was quite wrong: when you are tethered to routine you need to notice the ordinary in order to stay alive.

There had been occasions when her vigilance had flagged and

she would find herself in a prowling darkness that sent her reeling, but no one ever noticed – except, of course, Jeremy who noticed everything; George was always happy, Gray too, and so was Melanie in the years before Selwyn came along.

From the moment Selwyn entered the Finemore home Philippa had not liked him. He was unctuous to a degree rare in one so young, dispensing flattery with an extravagance incompatible with sincerity. Then there was his smile, so plastic, so utterly nauseating that Philippa had been convinced within five minutes of meeting him that this was a man bereft of integrity. Like most arrogant people, Selwyn lacked any deep feeling towards anyone other than himself, or rather himself and his father, a hard, mean man whom he adored. When it came to his mother, a shrill, nervous woman, Selwyn paid more attention to his neckties. As for love, Philippa was sure its very immateriality made him doubt its value.

Selwyn was, however, deeply interested in authority. Several years as an academic and a lifetime of ambition had taught him everything that could be known about authority, and while he knew that the bigger the pool the more seductive the power, he also knew that even a small amount of power could be highly rewarding. From the beginning then, Selwyn was intent on changing Melanie, pressing her to make what he called 'personal improvements'. He suggested less weight so she lost several pounds; he was critical of boisterous women so she dampened her laughter; he liked bright colours so Melanie wore oranges and yellows which made her look sickly. And while Philippa knew that such actions were part of the disturbed syntax of marriage, the old Melanie ran the risk of disappearing altogether.

These days, Philippa would look at the shallow, judgemental woman Melanie had become and strive to remember the outgoing, joyous girl she had once been, and if this was what was required to love her daughter, then so be it. Although it was not always easy. Since George's death, Melanie had become more overbearing than ever, issuing demands and dispensing directions, yet, at the same time, being curiously absent – or perhaps she was simply becoming less familiar to Philippa. Melanie seemed to be fully acquainted with the appropriate posture of a wealthy widow, and when Philippa was seen to veer from the right path, would swoop down and correct her. Melanie clearly had much invested in Philippa's doing the right thing, but whether it was for personal gain or fear of nonconformity, neither of which was particularly palatable, Philippa did not know. But of all Melanie's changes, it was her loss of warmth that was Philippa's greatest sorrow. Melanie failed to distinguish between people; she used the same demeanour for her closest friends as for the electrician, and none of them was given any affection; like Selwyn, it seemed she had identified emotion as an inessential commodity. Only with her children was she different; she channelled all her love into these two young things, and, being young they lapped it up, but when they were older it would be a different story, and what would Melanie do then?

Philippa looked up at the night sky. It was cramped with clouds and only a thread of moon, a murky sky with neither pattern nor direction. It reminded her of her family-cluttered mind. Mind cluttered with *her* family. For no matter who they had become, her children were still her children, and the grandchildren more precious than anyone alive. Philippa sat on the cool bluestone of her front step and Peach jumped into her lap. She rubbed her face against the woolly fur and breathed in the dog's familiar smell; soon Peach settled down and went to sleep and Philippa was left staring into the darkness, determined to clear her mind of the family but unable to think of anything else.

THREE

Evelyn Finemore pulled into the curb to consult her street directory. It was bad enough that Philippa had left the home where she belonged and the family who loved her, but how much worse to have chosen this particular area with its rows of identical houses and its network of closed and one-way streets, euphemistically called 'traffic-controlled'. The family would have come to accept a nice villa unit or a high-rise apartment, but a tiny inner-city Victorian terrace was beyond the pale.

And it was impossible to find! For the past fifteen minutes, Evelyn had been driving towards floral fences and bluestone barriers that, according to her ageing street directory, did not exist. And all the while the Finemores were falling apart and there was Evelyn's usual appointment at three o'clock with Brother Trevor and she didn't want to be late for that.

Ever since Philippa's eccentricities had become too embarrassing to ignore (and over the years plenty had been ignored, including the ridiculous St Kilda pier business with all those smelly old men), Evelyn knew she would be the one to speak with her. The others, Gray, Melanie and Selwyn, were all so furious that when they weren't biting their anger, which was their preferred approach in Philippa's company, they were so caustic, so utterly condemnatory that productive discussion was impossible. It would have been far better if, instead of their private ragings, they could have confronted Philippa, but this was not the Finemore way. When in the presence of the offending party, Finemores would, with a polite skirting of the edges and a scatter of smiles and niceties, pretend that nothing was wrong; it was only behind the person's back that true feelings could be aired. So, not a night would pass without a bitter tirade from Gray: how his mother had deserted her responsibilities, how her actions were an economic disaster and a betrayal of family, how it was unnatural not to want to spend as much time as possible with your grandchildren, how his father would turn in his grave if he knew what she was doing. Every night the same litany of complaint – made to Evelyn, not Philippa where it rightfully belonged. And the days were not much better. It had always been Gray's practice to telephone Evelyn from work 'to keep in touch with the home front,' but now his phonecalls had become just another opportunity to rail against Philippa, and only in closing would he make a perfunctory inquiry about Evelyn's day. Melanie's calls had been similarly spoiled; Evelyn, different to her sister-in-law in so many respects, appreciated Melanie for those very qualities she herself lacked; Melanie's phonecalls, spiced with an enticing blend of chat and gossip, had long been a source of pleasure. But now, because of Philippa's behaviour, they were filled with hostility and resentment and blame and anger, and if Melanie were still privy to society gossip, her phonecalls to Evelyn gave no indication.

Finemore family life was in tatters and it was Philippa's fault; her defection (for no matter what she might call it and irrespective of the frequency of her visits, a defection had in fact occurred) had far-reaching repercussions. Worst of all was the effect on the children, who loved their grandmother as she had seemed to love them. Once an exemplary model for impressionable young minds, Philippa now, by example, was promoting values and attitudes that could do the children no good. This appalling neighbourhood for a start. It wasn't its humble mien that was so worrying, it was the perverts and foreigners and drug addicts who were the real problems; and while Philippa had, since the move, come across town to see the children, that might not always be the case.

If only they could have it out with her or, better still, all of them, Philippa included, swallow their pride and let bygones be bygones. Melanie and Selwyn, Gray and herself wanted Philippa back where she belonged – not back home, it was too late for that, but in the locality, a villa unit, or an apartment, the area was full of suitable places. 'And at reasonable prices too, what with the current down-turn in the property market,' Gray had been quick to point out. But they would not beg Philippa to return, Gray had added, for it was not up to them to instruct their mother how to behave.

But it was, Evelyn had decided, because while Philippa's need for the family might have diminished, the family's need for her had not. Philippa had always been a point of stability; she was dependable, sensible, and the only person Evelyn really trusted to look after the children. Philippa needed to be reminded of her duty. And it had to happen now, before the situation deteriorated, for while her desertion had made family life difficult, there was worse trouble looming in the executive offices of Finemore's Fine Wines and Spirits. It was the boys, Gray and Selwyn, nothing new, but without George's restraining presence, the distrust they had always felt for each other had been left to grow unchecked. Distrust, and, if the truth be known, dislike, but being family, the dislike was carefully put to one side. Poor Gray was exhausted, working twelve-, fourteen-hour days, and spending most weekends at his desk. Selwyn couldn't be trusted in the office, Gray said, so as long as Selwyn was there, Gray had to be there too. Each evening, usually as a preface to his Philippa tirade, he would recount, or rather assess, Selwyn's daily movements, and each evening, Evelyn brooded on the image of her husband traipsing after Selwyn from office to office, warehouse to loading bay, listening in to telephone calls, eavesdropping on conversations.

With so much time devoted to Selwyn, it was not surprising Gray's own work was suffering. His figures were down and two of his best men had joined the main opposition. As for the satisfaction that had been so much a part of Finemore's in George's time, it had all but disappeared. These days, Gray pondered his drink, his evening meal, the darkness at the end of the bed with a face pale and heavy as a bull-terrier; these days, Gray was not a happy man. One time, and in all seriousness, he had described the problems between him and Selwyn as 'an irreducible mathematical concept' a sort of prime number of commerce; George's death, he said, had left the managing director's chair vacant, only one chair, he said between grim lips, and two large men.

One chair and two large men. Was it any wonder that Gray was not himself? He was sleeping badly, switching on the light in the early morning to make notes, and, as he wrote, he sighed and grunted and thanked God that George wasn't alive to witness the rumblings at Finemore's. Evelyn did her best to calm him with hot whisky drinks, massage to his tense muscles, even oral sex, but worry followed worry, complaint followed complaint, a veritable avalanche of words that was doing Gray no good. There were inconsistences too, today's opinion would contradict yesterday's; Gray, always so sure, always so predictable, was becoming confused. Evelyn thought it best to let the inconsistencies pass; she would listen silently as was her custom, concentrating her features into various expressions of sympathy, until Gray finished. And it was always at the same point:

'Selwyn's not a Finemore,' he would say, 'he does not understand liquor.'

But Evelyn feared that might not matter, after all, George Finemore had not understood liquor, or not in the way Gray meant, and it hadn't stopped him. George always said that the liquor business was about business first and liquor second; after fifty years in the trade, George couldn't distinguish a Riesling from a Chardonnay, a burgundy from a Shiraz; even with Scotch, and he had been a Scotch drinker all his life, one was much the same as the next. Oenology, or the 'connoisseur bullshit' as George was wont to call it, was the buyers' area, his concern was merchandising which was, George said, the nub of a successful business. And he must have been right, for when he died, George was eulogized in the financial pages as the Leviathan of Liquor; as for Finemore's Fine Wines and Spirits, it was the nation's largest, privately-owned, wholesale liquor trader and, with its expansion into the retail market, was variously described as diverse, aggressive, exciting and visionary.

Now all of it was under threat. No, Evelyn was being dramatic, not under threat, for Finemore's was as sound as a rock, rather the Finemore family lifestyle was under threat, and, having taken more than a decade to adapt to the Finemore way of doing things, Evelyn wanted nothing to change. She wanted Philippa to see sense and the boys to hide their differences, and while her preference would have been for Gray to take the necessary actions, she knew her husband was not the man for the job. Gray was a man of words; he would make nightly proclamations from his side of the bed: 'Selwyn wouldn't know a good claret if he were swimming in it,' or 'Mother should have more respect for the Finemore name,' a welter of allegations and declarations that might calm Gray's offended nerves but did nothing to rectify the situation. In the months since George's death, although Gray's tirades had increased both in force and frequency, they had done nothing to keep Philippa at home or Selwyn in his place. While Gray talked, others acted, while Gray accused, others accomplished. Philippa had sold the house, packed her belongings and moved miles away, while in the office, the staff were looking to Selwyn for direction. Selwyn might not be a Finemore but he was, nonetheless, very clever, and his manner, although oozing with thin-blooded sincerity, mobilized the Finemore staff far more than Gray's sure, steady ways.

Selwyn and Gray, thrown together by George's death and the clumsy fusions of family, could not have been more different. There was the matter of character: Selwyn was a greyhound while Gray was more draughthorse; and personal manner: Selwyn brash and Gray sombre; and the future direction of Finemore's: rapid expansion according to Selwyn, selective development at the top end of the market from Gray. The only quality the two men had in common was a thriving ambition, but ambition is a light sleeper and it was clear the men were becoming restless.

Evelyn had raised the problems with her sister-in-law, but while Melanie was happy to elaborate on the value of conflict, happy, too, to advise on how to deal with Gray, she refused to hear any criticism that might reflect badly either on Selwyn or the Finemore name.

'You don't understand the Finemores,' she had said in words that could have been borrowed from Gray. 'We're tough, but we're private, and we don't like to air our grievances in public.'

'But I'm not asking for a public airing,' Evelyn had replied. 'I only want us to talk among ourselves, talk honestly, resolve the differences between the boys and bring Philippa back home.'

'I know exactly what you want, but as I said before, we're very private people, and we prefer not to say things that later we might regret. We go about our business and in time the problems will right themselves. The Finemores have always believed that the essence of good family relations is to forgive and forget.'

She also said she had the utmost confidence in her husband and had no intention of interfering in his business affairs. And with that, had risen from the table where they'd been eating lunch, paid the bill, shepherded Evelyn from the restaurant down the street and into Madelaine's for Evelyn's opinion on the dress she was having made for the Jamiesons' masked ball.

With Selwyn busy, Gray frenzied and Melanie resolutely blinkered, it had been left to Evelyn to restore peace in the family, and the best way to do this, she had decided, was with a direct approach to Philippa. Philippa must return home, she must pull the boys into line, she must return the family to normal.

Evelyn made another left turn and found herself on Philippa's block. She knew exactly the line to take: she would appeal to Philippa's seniority, her life-long devotion to family, her skill in matters of relationships. At the same time, she would be sure to make Philippa feel needed.

She parked the car, noticed she was low on petrol – Philippa should foot the bill, after all, it was her fault that Evelyn had been wandering through these ridiculous streets for close on twenty minutes – checked her lipstick and hair in the rear vision mirror and got out. She had dressed carefully in beige skirt and rust-coloured jacket; stylish, she thought, in the Finemore way, and entirely suitable for her appointment with Brother Trevor later on – not that he was concerned about such paltry matters, but years of private sessions with him had taught her to be prepared. The middling brown hair was longer than usual and Evelyn had caught up the sides with hand-painted combs. The beautician's new course of skin care seemed to be working; her freckles were well-camouflaged and the blood vessels across her cheeks were not getting any worse. Of course the eyes were too small and the nostrils too flared and the lips too thin and the jaw receding, but she made the most of herself. And there was always her figure, perfect, irrespective of what she ate. 'It's in the genes,' Melanie had said enviously, as she struggled to discard a few more pounds of George's genetic legacy. And Evelyn was sure she was right; both of her utterly ordinary parents possessed lithe, athletic figures in which resided the only elegance in their utterly ordinary lives.

Philippa's Victorian cottage was at the end of a row of six. Small, so small, and indistinguishable from the rest, Evelyn wondered how much she had paid for such idiocy. Not that she couldn't afford it, but that wasn't the point, being well off, as she and Gray tried to impress on the children, was no excuse for throwing money away. She opened the gate and walked the couple of metres to the front door. Even before she rang the bell she heard Peach bark, and a moment later Philippa was in the doorway, kissing Evelyn's cheek and inviting her in.

Philippa looked better than she had for years. The olive skin, once so sallow, was infused with pink, the cropped hair curled prettily about her face, and the lines around the mouth and down the cheeks, so marked at the time of George's death, had almost disappeared. Despite her Finemore training and the purpose of her visit, Evelyn couldn't stop herself:

'You're looking extremely well, Philippa.'

'Feeling well too.' And led the way down the narrow hallway to the lounge. 'Coffee? Wine? I've prepared a light lunch, cheese, salad, nothing substantial, but enough to keep us going for a while.'

Evelyn mentioned her three o'clock appointment, that she would need to leave by half past two.

Philippa nodded and held up a bottle of wine.

'Not for me, coffee will be fine.'

While Philippa prepared lunch, Evelyn looked around. How Philippa could prefer this matchbox of a place to the grand old home was beyond her. Despite the renovations, the house was cramped and the front rooms dark, and the decor so – so *meagre*. Worst of all, the house was an irritating reminder of Evelyn's own past: the same era, the same cell-like rooms, the same peppery smell.

Not that her childhood had been unhappy or her parents anything less than kind. Rather, that period of her life was over, finished, superceded. And while she maintained regular contact with her mother and father, their being on the south coast of New South Wales, still living in the same house where Evelyn had grown up, meant she saw little of them. Which was, as far as she was concerned, entirely satisfactory. Long before meeting Gray, Evelyn had planned her escape. As a girl, she had watched the businessmen, politicians and academics, who, with their families, moved between holiday homes at the coast and permanent homes in the city, and learned that no one who was born on the south coast and lived there permanently could ever be taken seriously.

Evelyn loved her parents but wanted more from life. Her father had been a science teacher; at the end of his career as at the beginning he worked in the classroom, never wanting promotion out of what he did so well. Evelyn's mother had been happy as a teacher's wife; her husband's was a respectable job, and to be respectable was, in her opinion, the most important of qualities. They had raised three children; Evelyn's brother, a doctor, now worked in central Australia, and her sister was a social worker in Sydney's west. Evelyn, the youngest, was to have been a teacher, but against her parents' advice, gave up her studies when she married Gray. Never had she regretted it. She loved Gray and the children, and she loved running the house; she worked energetically for the Blind Society and the Children's Hospital, and she loved that too. She had everything she had ever dreamed of. More.

Now, as she walked through Philippa's house, she was annoyed that a Finemore would actually choose to live this way, annoyed and, she realized, insulted; Philippa's choices were an insult to her own. The passage from lower middle class, south coast respectability to Finemore family stability had not been easy, but always the goals had made the struggle worthwhile. Some lifestyles are clearly preferable to others, and only a fool would choose the servants' quarters when the mansion was available.

Foolishness or perhaps deliberate provocation? For the first time it occurred to her that Philippa might be playing some sort of malicious game, although why she would do such a thing defied reason; the family had always been good to her, and she'd never wanted for anything. Of course, George had played around a bit, but he'd always put his family first, had always been the model of discretion. No, malice seemed as unlikely an explanation for Philippa's behaviour as stupidity. Perhaps it was more simple, perhaps Melanie was right and Philippa was mentally unbalanced, for no one in their right mind would choose this pokey little place over the old Finemore home.

She peered into Philippa's study. Almost identical to the bedroom Evelyn had shared with her sister, small, dark, never enough space for two growing girls. She opened one of the folders on the desk, leafed through sheets of poetry written in an even cursive script, looked closer, and then, concerned she might be prying, shut the folder and left the room. She walked back along the passage to the bedroom with its double bed and single bedside table, all so spartan, and from there to the bathroom, with its adamant denial of children in the absent bath, and the toilet wedged between shower and basin.

Perhaps incipient madness had nothing to do with it, perhaps something had happened to Philippa that made her desert her old life. Perhaps she was worried about being a burden on the family, about having less to do now the grandchildren were older; perhaps George's death had reminded her of her own mortality and this had thrown her into some sort of crisis. Whatever had happened, Evelyn's role was clear: she must discover what was bothering Philippa, put it to rights and move her back to the family as quickly as possible.

She returned to the lounge room. Peach was asleep in a patch of sun, and nearby, spread across a low table, were a crusty loaf, cheese, a variety of dips and some pickled onions which Philippa said she had bought especially for Evelyn knowing how much she liked them. Evelyn felt herself bristle; she had learned long ago that pickled onions were definitely not Finemore food, and had, so she thought, successfully hidden her enjoyment of them. Philippa's gesture was not appreciated, and Evelyn chose to ignore it. The pickled onions too.

Philippa had opened a bottle of wine and Evelyn decided to join her, it could only relax her for the task ahead.

'Well, what do you think?' Philippa asked with a sweep of her hand.

Evelyn chose her words carefully. 'It's sweet, rather small of course. Such a change for you.'

'It certainly is, but that's what I like about it. All of it so new – a bit like being in a strange country.' She laughed, sipped her wine. 'Often these days, I find myself feeling just like a tourist; I walk a lot, exactly as one does when on holiday, take in so many sights, so many impressions. And I never tire, never feel worn down by familiarity; in fact, I can walk the same stretch over and over again and still be aware of its newness, still be surprised by it.'

Evelyn smiled at her mother-in-law. Poor, poor Philippa, so that was it! Her old life and the old house without George had defeated her, and when she could cope no longer, she'd felt compelled to move to a foreign area, one far removed from the pain and the memories and her inability to manage. If only they had realized they would have arranged a proper trip ages ago; Philippa could have had a few months away, a period in which to build a bridge between her old life with George and the same life without him, and on her return she would have felt strong enough to tackle life alone. If only they'd known, this escape across the city might have been averted.

'—all so new,' Philippa was saying, 'and yet providing a certain recognition, a sense of belonging.'

Exactly, thought Evelyn, her life was in pieces with George's death, and she couldn't see how she was to fit in.

'A sense of belonging unlike anything I've felt before,' Philippa continued. 'Of community.'

'Now, now, Philippa, you've always had community, you've always been at the centre of so many lives, and not just the family, but friends as well.'

'That's not quite what I mean. Let me give you an example. There's an Italian coffee shop up the street, I have coffee there quite often—'

'By yourself?'

Philippa smiled. 'By myself. I take a newspaper or book, I'm not the only one. Anyway, this morning, as I was passing, I stopped in for coffee and the young man there, Francesco, asked if I wanted "the usual". I've met this man a dozen times and already he knows how I like my coffee; I lived with George for more than forty years, and still he'd add too much milk.'

'But that was just George. I've always known how you have your coffee, so do Gray and Melanie.' And Jeremy probably did too, but Evelyn would prefer not to mention him.

'Yes, of course you do dear, but that's not the point. Francesco knows how I take my coffee; Lucia, his partner, knows the cakes I prefer; I walk past the newsagent and the proprietor smiles at me, so, too, the people in the hardware. The butcher knows the cuts I like, Janet in the bookshop knows what I read.' Philippa shrugged, 'I'm very happy.'

'I'm sure you are. But these people are strangers. We're your family, we're not the same as butchers and booksellers; we love you and need you and understand what you're going through. We know that when you share your life with the one person for forty years there's bound to be a period of adjustment when he's no longer around. Philippa, dear, we understand what a difficult time you're having, and—'

'But I'm not, or at least, not any more. As I said before, I'm very happy. I'm full of energy, feel very much alive.'

'But your family needs you, we love you.' Somehow the words sounded very lame.

Philippa smiled, an expression without humour. 'Yes, I know, but you don't recognize me.'

'I think you're being too harsh. We've always appreciated you, always loved you. Of course, if there's something else you're wanting, then all you have to do is ask. You know we'd do anything for you. We all need you so much and everyone's so upset.'

'But Evelyn dear, I'm here. I haven't left the country, I see you all several times a week, and if you need me at any other time, I'm at the end of the telephone.' She leaned forward, face creased with concern. 'Don't you understand? You're all very precious to me. As for the children, I'd be utterly distraught without them.'

Evelyn shook her head, it wasn't fair, she was doing her best, but Philippa was being deliberately difficult.

'Philippa, we want what's best for you, and to be blunt, what's best for you is not living miles away from the rest of us. Here you are, all by yourself, and in an area that by the looks of it is none too safe. And how do you plan to spend your time? You've given up your charity work, you have no friends nearby, and you can't expect us to drive for miles just so you can see your grandchildren. We want to look after you, and we can't do it properly while you're involved with this nonsense. Of course we understand, but you have to help us help you.'

Philippa's gaze was steady, her face serious, apparently thinking. She refilled her glass, Evelyn had hardly touched hers.

'I know you mean well, Evelyn, but the fact of the matter is I don't want to return home, I don't want to go back, and neither do I need looking after. I've plenty to do and much more planned, and I'm happy. Just because I've moved house—'

'It's not just the house, there was the trip to Japan, you've dropped your charities, and you're seeing none of your old friends.'

'Just because I've made a few changes, doesn't mean I've deserted the family. Far from it. And besides, how could I? How could you think I'd want to? You mention my grandchildren, well, since I moved over here, I've seen more of them than ever before, and because I've so much more energy, so much more to offer, our time together has been of a much better quality. As for anything else, an unforeseen happening or something extra you want me to do, I'm always available. But I'm not going back; I'm sixty-two, I have a right to this.'

'I hardly recognize you, Philippa. You've always been so unselfish, always put your family first.'

Philippa appeared to have stopped listening, she was offering Peach morsels of food, murmuring fond words of encouragement. To the dog, not Evelyn. And Evelyn realized her approach was all wrong; this was not the time for recriminations, although no one could deny they weren't warranted, a change of direction, a little sympathy, would be more appropriate.

'We want you to be happy, Philippa, believe me we do, and we're pleased for your new interests, after all, you've got a lot of life left in you. And despite what you think, we've always been supportive of you, and will continue to be as long as your interests aren't to the detriment of the family.'

'And they're not. All I've done is increase the dimensions of my life. I don't love you any less, nor am I any less concerned about you, I'm simply trying to incorporate more in my life. And any honest person would have to admit that mine was a life desperately in need of expansion.'

'I really don't think that's fair, yours was a perfectly good life, a marvellous life. Plenty of people would have been happy to trade places.' She popped a pickled onion in her mouth without thinking, then quickly followed with some camembert as if the latter could erase the former's vulgarity. 'Besides, people are talking.'

Philippa laughed. 'That's never bothered me. People talked for years about George and Lorraine Pascoe and I never minded.'

Evelyn was annoyed, certain topics were best left unsaid, and a long-time mistress of your husband's was one. Although it suddenly occurred to her why Philippa may have wanted to escape her old life. Perhaps she was embarrassed to face her old friends, that, despite her bravado, she really did mind about Lorraine Pascoe. Evelyn certainly would, Evelyn would have found the role of grieving widow impossible if there had been a long-time mistress on the scene. Thank heavens good steady Gray had not taken after his father. And again she found herself feeling sorry for Philippa. She took a sip of wine, leaned forward, an expression of sympathy grafted across her features.

'Is there something wrong, something you'd like to talk about? Some difficulty perhaps?'

Philippa shook her head.

'You can confide in me,' Evelyn persisted. 'I'm not as easily shocked as you might think. Why don't you tell me what's bothering you?'

There was nothing, Philippa said, and then added with a laugh, except perhaps too many options. She wanted to travel, South America was a possibility, and she was interested in the University of the Third Age, but was yet to decide on her subjects, perhaps she'd even try some part-time work. 'I really don't know what I'll end up doing, but for the moment, it's quite exhilarating to know that almost anything's possible.'

'You know that's not what I meant.'

Philippa looked genuinely surprised.

'Have you thought about seeing someone?'

'Someone?'

'A professional, someone who can help you. I know Gina Ballantyne found a very good therapist for her daughter when she was going through a rough patch.'

Philippa smiled. 'Are you suggesting I'm going through an adolescent phase? Is that how it appears to you?'

'I didn't mean it like that. But something has to explain your behaviour.'

'And so it does. I want a change, it's as simple as that.'

Evelyn saw she was getting nowhere, and with just under half an hour before she would need to leave, decided to change the topic and clear the air. For there would be a return visit, possibly several, and she did not want to antagonize her mother-in-law at this early stage. So she chatted on about nothing in particular, who had announced their engagement, whose divorce was through, who was pregnant and whose tubes had been tied, and at half past two rose to leave.

At the door Philippa turned to her. 'You'll remember what I said Evelyn, I'm here whenever the family needs me. Just ring and I'll make time. I've even bought an answering machine, one of those sophisticated models with a remote retrieval system, so no matter where I am, I can keep in touch.'

They touched cheeks and Evelyn hurried to the car before she exploded. An answering machine! What would Philippa think of next?

The trip across the city was maddeningly slow and by the time she pulled up outside Brother Trevor's, frustration over Philippa's intransigence had been inflamed by ineffective road laws, inefficient road repair teams, inflated petrol prices and incompetent drivers. Three hours ago her mission had been clear, her goals readily achievable, now she was returning without a single point won. It was all very well for Philippa to insist on her availability, her willingness to help, but none of the family was the least bit interested in Philippa's help as long as she persisted in her present nonsense. Mother could only do her job, they all said, if she were back where she belonged.

Which was the way of the Finemores. Conciliation and compromise had never been their approach. Why deprive both parties of what each really wanted? Either you converted the opposition to your way of thinking, or you didn't bother about convincing them, you just made sure you won. So, as far as the Finemore children were concerned, Philippa had to return home, and that was that. As for the problems between Gray and Selwyn, both men would, for the time being, go about their business, Gray at Selwyn's heels and Selwyn his gaze fixed firmly ahead, both of them refusing to recognize any view other than their own. And the tension would increase, affecting not only the dynamics at work, but family relations as well. Which had already begun; at the past two or three family dinners, despite the usual talk of parties and children and takeovers and bankruptcies, there had been a competitive edge to the silences, the jokes had been shot with malice, and the compliments very heavy-handed indeed.

All this Evelyn had known, all of it had fuelled her visit to Philippa, all of it made Philippa's refusal to see reason so unfair. Evelyn's only relief in the whole fiasco was in not having told Gray of her visit; she had planned to surprise him with results: the triumphant announcement that his mother was returning home.

Well, there would be none of that now, or at least not yet. She got out of the car, Brother Trevor's gate was, as usual, open, she passed through and walked up the path. Brother Trevor was already at his front door, and at the sight of him her spirits rose; the visit with Philippa might have been a failure, but her appointments with Brother Trevor never were.

Evelyn's first dalliance with religion had occurred soon after her marriage when she offered her services to the ladies' auxiliary at the local Anglican church. It had seemed such a Finemore thing to do, but it was also rather unsatisfying. When the church was deconsecrated and sold to an advertising agency, Evelyn took the opportunity to discontinue her association with God. Until three years ago, and then it was Jesus, not God, who caught in her heart, Jesus on the lips of Brother Trevor. Of course Gray and the others had no idea. In Finemore circles, religion was something akin to those white kid gloves packed in tissue at the back of a drawer, ignored until an auspicious occasion required their appearance. As for rousing singing and ecstatic revelations these were, from the Finemore point of view, in very poor taste. But Evelyn didn't care. Reverend Trevor Potter, 'Call me Brother,' had indeed called her and moved her and implanted within the brooding coolness of her body a shudder, a flame, a passion of sorts, that she understood to be belief.

'You have to believe,' Brother Trevor said, 'and our Lord will come to you. I will show him the way.' And Brother Trevor *had* shown the way, every Thursday at three o'clock for nearly two years, while Gray thought Evelyn was attending cake decoration classes.

Brother Trevor walked down the path to meet her, and they entered the house together. The air was steeped in the smells of baking; Marion Potter, a flour-streaked apron around her girth, popped her head through the kitchen doorway to say hello, offered a not-entirely-coherent apology for her appearance, and, with a wave of a wire-mesh tray, disappeared. Evelyn followed Brother Trevor into the study, waited until he shut the door, and then sat in her usual chair. Sat and sighed and ran a hand through her hair.

So good to be here, she says, and Brother Trevor, always so sensitive to her mood, suggests they start immediately.

He pulls up a chair, sits in front of her, takes her hands, and begins the thanksgiving prayer. She closes her eyes, sinks into the soothing incantation, focuses on the touch of his skin, how it seems to travel from her hands up her arms, down through her chest to lodge just beneath her breasts where it pumps adrenalin into her blood. It is a quiet and private pleasure that hurts no one.

With the prayer finished and his thumbs stroking, so tenderly stroking, the backs of her hands, he asks about her week. Terrible, she says, and rotates her hands just a fraction so as to feel the tips of his fingers on the soft flesh of her palms. A stronger spurt of adrenalin shoots through her body and pools low in her abdomen. Terrible, she says again. It's the family, nothing's changed. Gray hasn't been home for dinner all week, and Selwyn's being deliberately obstructionist. Brother Trevor rubs a sympathetic finger across her palm, her thighs involuntarily tense; seeing the movement, he lays a soothing hand on one of her legs, and his touch shoots up the limb to meet the adrenalin sizzling down.

Not that Brother Trevor would suspect she is anything other than composed; she sits straight and still, her face arranged for prayer. She closes her eyes while Brother Trevor recites a prayer for the family, his hand still on her thigh, her body flooding with his energy. And then she tells him of her visit to Philippa. He takes his hand from her thigh and rearranges his cassock. How she loves his cassock for their private sessions, such an arresting ecclesiastical touch that she suspects he does especially for her. He shuffles in his seat, pulls his chair closer so their knees almost touch, and replaces his hand on her thigh.

Their knees touch. Is that his skin she feels through the material of the gown? Might he be without trousers? And the first spasm occurs, a sparkling prod that she has come to identify as part of her Thursday feeling. She tells him about Philippa, how angry she is at her mother-in-law. Brother Trevor is agreeing with everything she says, he is nodding his head, and now his whole body, nodding back and forward, forward and back, and the thrill of his knees nudging her own.

'I went there with the best of intentions. George's death was a terrible blow for her, I know that.'

The deep prodding is now a throbbing; she knows this is the difficult stage, the hardest to control. She clenches her torso, moves her attention from her body to the chair, and the throbbing immediately subsides.

'So I don't want to be unfairly critical,' she continues, 'but it's been well over six months, and still Philippa's avoiding her responsibilities. She seems so wrapped up in herself, can't see that Gray and Selwyn are in trouble. And if they're in trouble then the whole family's in trouble.'

Brother Trevor grunts and continues his rocking.

'Gray loves the business, always has, his commitment to it is 100%. But,' she smiles at Brother Trevor, 'I couldn't say this to anyone but you, Gray seems to lack a certain something.'

A little groan escapes from Brother Trevor. He clears his throat. 'Perhaps Gray's just finding his feet, after all, it's still early days.'

At which point Brother Trevor finds his feet and suggests they move to the prie-dieu. Not a moment too soon, Evelyn is thinking as she crosses the room. They kneel in unison facing each other, their arms resting along the ledge, hands firmly clasped.

'You may be right about Gray,' Evelyn says, leaning against the partition. 'Although I think the main problem is that he cares too much. So different to Selwyn.'

'Selwyn has never disguised his ambition.'

Brother Trevor also leans against the partition, Evelyn feels his weight through the wood, feels it drain her strength, feels the insistent pounding at the centre of her body. She swallows; it is still too soon. And swallows again.

'It's more than that, Selwyn doesn't have the Finemore commitment to liquor. His heart's not in it. Selwyn's too much of a pragmatist.'

'Always has been,' Brother Trevor says, giving her hands a sudden squeeze, 'always been his way.'

Evelyn dares not move. 'Selwyn wants a period of rapid expansion, he wants to double the number of retail outlets and open a dozen new designer pubs. Can you imagine the cost!' She is speaking very carefully, any untoward movement could bring the session to a premature end. 'Gray says such expenditure would be suicide in this climate.'

'So why does Selwyn want it?' Brother Trevor leans sideways against the screen, and then returns to an upright position; his eyelids flutter.

'Something about increasing the public image of the company. "Exposure," he says, "is everything." '

Brother Trevor is swaying now, his grip on Evelyn's hands is very firm, he begins the prayer of joy. Evelyn joins in. There is a knock at the door and Marion Potter is asking if her husband is ready for tea.

'Not yet, dear.' Brother Trevor consults the wall clock. 'I'll be finished in about ten minutes.' Marion's steps fade down the hallway; he turns to Evelyn, 'But I'm ready to wind up, are you?'

Evelyn nods, not daring to speak. Brother Trevor returns to the prayer of joy, and now Evelyn, too, is swaying and praying, her breath quickening, breast beating, body rising and rising poised at the precipice, and Jesus comes, she feels him, she feels him. 'Feel the love of Jesus!' Cries Brother Trevor. 'I feel! I feel!' she says. Feels the thrill the joy the fluids of her faith rushing together and breaking, wave after glorious wave.

Only faith can feel this good.

She offers up thanks: for Brother Trevor, for her belief, and for the surprisingly powerful, and yet still largely private, miracle of her faith. And wonders what Brother Trevor thinks of her. Early in their association, having been quite overwhelmed by his sessions, Evelyn decided to discontinue them; Brother Trevor had worked hard to dissuade her, had been delighted when she succumbed. So she supposed he must like her, must like his time with her. He said it was part of his ministry, and of course it was; but while she always felt so much better for his ministrations, she remained perplexed over the particular manifestations of her faith. And would not want anyone to know, most of all Brother Trevor, upon whom it was so dependent.

Minutes later, both were sitting in their chairs smiling fondly at each other.

'I don't know how I'd manage without our sessions,' Evelyn said.

'Just doing my job.'

'I feel so lucky to have you.'

'Thank you, my dear.'

He stood up and took her hands. She looked up at him expectantly; but no, he said, she must go, his next client was due in half an hour. She, too, stood up.

'Thank you Brother Trevor, I feel so much better.'

'Until next Thursday then?'

'Thursday.'

He walked her to the front door. 'Marion,' he called to his wife, 'Evelyn's just leaving. Do you want to say goodbye?'

Marion came to the door, her youthful features pressed into a warm smile. Evelyn and the other women of the congregation so admired her; not yet twenty-five, it had been she who had comforted Brother Trevor when his wife Sarah had died from cancer – a double blow, as all were quick to recognize, for Sarah was the second wife to have left him under tragic circumstances. Marion had been his saviour during that awful time, not only had she nursed Sarah, she had moved into the Potter home to be more available in the last difficult months. Now she was leaning forward and giving Evelyn a hug. 'Perhaps you'll stay for a cup of tea next Thursday.'

Evelyn accepted the invitation, walked down the path to her car and drove home. The children were not yet back from gym; the house was quiet and peaceful. The Finemore problems were still there, her anger, too, but Evelyn felt so much better, so much more in control. Which was how it always was with Brother

Trevor, who somehow softened the difficulties, made them more manageable. She went upstairs to change her clothes and freshen her makeup, then to the kitchen, where she buttered some buns, made a large jug of cordial and waited for the children to come home.

FOUR

Lorraine Pascoe, long-time intimate of George Finemore, and former employee at Finemore's Fine Wines and Spirits, was standing at the stove in head-scarf and underwear frying fish. She did not need to work, she was thinking, George had taken care of that, rather it was her preference to work. 'I prefer to work,' she said out loud. Not that that had been a consideration when, a week before and just eight months after George's death, she had been fired from Finemore's, or, as Gray Finemore and Selwyn Pryor would have it, 'reluctantly let go' as a result of 'recent company restructuring.'

She reached across the bubbling oil to open a window – perhaps now she'd get round to replacing the exhaust fan – and gently turned the fish. It was to be expected, she supposed, that the boys would get rid of her, for hadn't she chafed at their ambitions for years? Indeed, her removal was probably the only action, either before or since George's death, over which Gray and Selwyn had agreed. But nonetheless, she had hoped, in the uncertain terrain of George's passing, they would have had the sense to keep her on. Not out of any moral scruples, the boys were devoid of those, rather their inflated ambitions should have convinced them that continued prosperity at Finemore's required the presence of the person who knew the company best. And with

George now gone, that person was Lorraine Pascoe. She knew Finemore's and she knew liquor; she was competent, astute, energetic, and had the loyalty and respect of the staff – qualities not readily demonstrable in the boys.

Although they would describe it differently. Lorraine Pascoe was a 'scheming female' who had 'inveigled' her way into George's confidence and had, in the process, trammelled the Finemore sons. On a daily basis, they had been forced to witness George and Lorraine in earnest and spirited conversation; they had listened while plans were made, promotions discussed, figures analysed, schemes evaluated, and they did not like it at all. If not for Lorraine, George would have consulted them, if not for Lorraine, George would have recognized what Gray and Selwyn had to offer.

Lorraine removed the fish from the pan and added some sliced eggplant to the hot oil. The boys had convinced themselves that sex was the sole reason for Lorraine's favoured status, and sex, as they were quick to point out, defied fair competition. They saw little point then, in extending themselves until the situation changed; they kept short hours, achieved little, and claimed their subordinates' successes as their own. Not that George was aware of any of this. Weak links in an organization, particularly when these occur in that spongy layer just beneath the uppermost level, are inordinately common and easily camouflaged. It's a stratum with little to do; the highest level makes the decisions and the people lower down do the work; in the case of Finemore's, George and Lorraine made the decisions and the Finemore staff were, almost without exception, extremely competent. Lorraine had more than once remarked to her sister (never to George who could be cutting in his own assessments of Gray and Selwyn but would hear no criticism from anyone else) how fortunate it was for the boys that, in addition to being employee and friend of George, she was also lover, for how could Gray and Selwyn have explained their poor performance if she were not.

Unlike George, Lorraine had always lumped the two boys together; Selwyn with his supple charm and Gray his narcotic self-righteousness were both lacking in integrity and quite as bad as each other. George, however, had admired in Selwyn his personable manner which, he said, augured well for a career in sales and marketing. 'And he's smart,' George invariably added, 'A university professor has got to be smart.' It had shocked Lorraine that George failed to see through Selwyn, failed to understand that the convivial drinker and lively raconteur was no more than a carefully packaged commodity aimed at eliciting his father-in-law's favour.

At which he had been quite successful. Selwyn managed to camouflage his lackadaisical performance with zesty ideas; risky ideas, as far as Lorraine was concerned, with practical shortcomings, but ideas that all too often appealed to George. The *Drink and Dream* series was one of the early brainwaves, in which cheap liqueurs were packaged in icons of wealth: a glass Rolls Royce, a Porsche, a yacht. More recently, Selwyn had developed *The Aussie Collection* to capitalize on the tourism boom. This included *The Red Centre*, a claret that gave 'the glow of sunset'; *Sydney Harbour Bitter* for a 'deep thirst', and *Drysabone Lager*, a low alcohol beer guaranteed 'to keep the man drinking through the long hot Aussie summer'. The worst of Selwyn's schemes had been, in Lorraine's view, unequivocally obscene: a variety of spirits sold in molded glass body parts designed 'to satisfy all tastes'. It was the only time Lorraine and George had a serious business disagreement. She had stood in his office, a glass penis filled with cream liqueur in one hand and a cherry brandy female torso in the other, trying to make him see reason. What she called obscene, he said was bawdy, what she described as pornographic he insisted was 'a bit of fun.' The only point on which he gave any concession was her appeal to consider the good name of Finemore's, so the products were marketed under a different label, although everyone knew where they came from.

Each of Selwyn's schemes was launched in a blaze of expensive publicity that might have been justified for products with some longevity, but none of Selwyn's schemes ever lasted for more than a year. And between schemes, when he might have applied himself to the routine workings of Finemore's, Selwyn always had something better to do. 'The Academy,' he would say when a subordinate made a request of him, 'I'm providing some lectures for a colleague, can't be bothered now.' And the subordinate, who as often as not had not attended university much less 'The Academy', would take the problem to Lorraine. Selwyn, it seemed, fancied himself as a harbinger of the new; he was a man drawn to the splash and sparkle of fast money. Time and time again Lorraine had pointed out to George, such an astute businessman in all other respects, that good business did not require quick manoeuvres, and while George would agree, while he would admit to some of Selwyn's shortcomings, he nonetheless maintained that Selwyn would prove an asset to Finemore's.

As for Gray, he was George's son, and blood was thicker than water. Or so George believed. Gray would 'come good,' George used to say, 'he's just a bit slow off the mark.' And while it was true, he was a bit slow, George never realized Gray liked it that way. Gray interpreted slow as thoughtful, careful as considered. When projects were proposed or problems arose, the snailshell of Gray's imagination would drag through plans, analyses and options, after which he would subject his colleagues to a seemingly endless trail of advice and opinion. Gray believed that on his birth he had taken up an option on perfection; he was that common individual, a man truly satisfied with himself.

Lorraine had never had any children of her own, yet well knew the allegiances of family. As the oldest of four girls, she had gone out to work early, studied accountancy at night, and contributed to the family upkeep; following her father's death, she had been the sole support for her mother and sisters. Time passed quickly under these circumstances and soon the youngest child had left home and Lorraine was thirty-three and newly employed at Finemore's Fine Wines and Spirits. Her first position had been as company secretary, and, until the boys fired her, they would always refer to her as a secretary, as if there were no lower being. When she had been at Finemore's for about two years, Harry Harrison retired and Lorraine took over as finance manager. That had marked the beginning of the problems with Gray, who, having just joined Finemore's, considered the role of finance manager to be rightfully his. But George was firm: if Gray wanted to learn about Finemore's there was little sense in his starting at the top.

So Lorraine settled into the office next to George, while Gray was despatched to stores.

In time, Gray worked his way into the executive offices of Finemore's Fine Wines, but always there was Lorraine guarding the managing director's door, and when Selwyn Pryor arrived, Gray found himself having to be doubly vigilant. Lorraine had used seduction with George, and Selwyn was not above subterfuge, but whatever the means, as far as Gray was concerned, both of them were intent on wresting his rightful inheritance.

The years passed; Selwyn became head of marketing and Gray managed the purchasing division. As for Lorraine and George, they continued to run the company together. Annual turnover increased at a healthy 15% per annum, a little more in the good years, slightly less in the sluggish. The move into retail occurred about four years before George's death. For some time, Lorraine and George had realized that if Finemore's was to maintain its level of profitability, they would need to diversify. While other companies moved off-shore, George and Lorraine turned to the local market for expansion opportunities, specifically, the local retail market, which they had long recognized as underdeveloped. The advantages to Finemore's were obvious: as a major wholesaler, Finemore's had a knowledge of the retail market that most retailers didn't have; all merchandise could be ordered from the parent company only as required thus minimizing the need for the retailer to keep large stocks, and with interest rates low and discretionary spending high, trade in luxury consumerables was assured.

Selwyn was thrilled; at last, he was heard to say, he would control an entirely autonomous branch of Finemore's; and Gray was appeased: at last, his very own piece of the company. So when Lorraine Pascoe was appointed head of the new retail division, the boys were understandably enraged. For close on a week they took it in turns to visit George's office, each railing against Lorraine's appointment and insisting it be retracted, each admonishing George to keep his private life separate from the business. George regarded the former advice as ill-considered and the latter as impertinent; the entire incident, he told Lorraine, showed that the boys had a lot more to learn before they could be entrusted with greater responsibility – and not just about business, he added, but about life in general.

From that time until George's death the boys avoided Lorraine. They let it be known it was loyalty to the Finemore family that motivated them, but few people were convinced. Selwyn turned his attention to the designer pubs he had finally convinced George to open and Gray took on the presidency of his wine and food society. At the office, they refused to speak with Lorraine and would communicate only through secretaries. At first, Lorraine decided to ignore their silliness, but when they persisted, she ceased to communicate with them altogether. Which was no loss to her: she didn't need them to do her job, but they needed her. So their jobs suffered, but so concerned were they with their vendetta they seemed not to care.

When George died, Lorraine knew her position at Finemore's was no longer secure, and yet she thought the boys would have had sense enough to keep her on. What she had not counted on was their arrogance, which is, after all, what protects the mediocre from their mediocrity. Selwyn and Gray fired Lorraine because they were convinced they could do the job better, because she should never have been given so much power in the first place, because they hated her and because she deserved to be punished.

Easy to understand why she was now without a job, Lorraine was thinking, as she lifted out the last slices of eggplant and placed them on brown paper to drain, but a mistake nonetheless. The final straw had come when she refused to give her signature to a loan application. It was Selwyn who had approached her with a plan for three additional designer pubs, a plan which she suspected Gray knew nothing about for his signature could have been used just as well as hers. But whether Gray had been consulted or not, did not alter the fact that Selwyn's proposal was ill-considered. In the eighteen months prior to George's death, Finemore's had opened two designer pubs; since then, the economic climate had changed, as had discretionary spending. Lorraine mentioned the steep rise in interest rates which made borrowing unwise; she reminded Selwyn of the weak dollar and the effect this had on companies such as Finemore's so reliant on imports, and she was about to explain how the leisure sector would be hit by the economic downturn when Selwyn stormed out of the room: he didn't need a tart to tell him about business, he said, and within a week the 'restructuring' had occurred and Lorraine had been given three months pay in lieu of notice.

She covered the food and left the kitchen. In the bedroom she dressed and did her hair, then sat on the edge of the bed wondering what a fifty-five year old woman with an assured income and a desire to work should do. But her mind was a pudding, no sense to be made, and she gave up. She slipped her feet into some comfortable shoes and wandered into the lounge room, an attractive, strong-bodied woman, long hair caught up in a chignon, dark hair, dark skin, dark eyes; Philippa's colouring, she had once remarked to George, although not Philippa's shape. But there was a certain similarity; indeed, when she and Philippa had gone to Japan, strangers had asked if they were sisters. They'd had such an enjoyable time together, although, Lorraine now realized, it had been a mistake to take leave so soon after George's death. The boys had used her absence to go through every single document, scrutinize every account, not together, each had left his own separate traces in the form of small changes that were well in place on her return. And yet mistake or not, the time spent with Philippa in Japan had been her greatest pleasure since George's death.

She wondered if the boys had told Philippa about her sacking. Probably not. She rang directory information for Philippa's new number, poured herself a glass of an excellent semillon - she'd have the rest with the fish that evening - and dialled Philippa's number. Suddenly Philippa seemed exactly the right person to speak to.

FIVE

'I've started a business.'

The children continued to yell, Melanie and Evelyn continued to direct table manners, Selwyn and Gray continued their discussion on the performance of the conservative parties, only Jeremy stopped eating and looked expectantly at his mother.

Who decided to try again.

'I've put my money into a new venture.' This time her voice was a little louder, but still there was no response. She tried once more. 'I've invested your father's money,' and now there was no mistaking Philippa had something to say.

The conservative parties were abandoned, table manners were ignored, and soup-spoons shunting between mouths and bowls of gazpacho came to a rude halt.

'I've started a new Finemore enterprise,' Philippa said quietly.

A relay of expressions – confusion, disbelief, horror – dashed about the Pryor dining-table. No one seemed to know what to say. It was the children who finally broke the tension, with a twittering and a squawking and a hearty exchange of kicks beneath the table.

Gray glared them into silence. 'What exactly do you mean, Mother?'

'Exactly what I said, Gray. I've started – I suppose you'd call it a type of business.'

'And what exactly do you mean by "a type of business"?' Selwyn's blue blisters looked ominous.

Philippa glanced at Jeremy and with a sliver of a smile answered, 'I've established a charitable trust, The Finemore Foundation.'

Gray tugged at his moustache, Selwyn jiggled his change, Melanie studied her gazpacho, Evelyn looked to Gray to do something and Jeremy returned to his soup. While the children shuffled and squirmed and stifled their giggles and perfected their under-table violence.

Melanie stood up. 'Into the other room, children.'

There was a wail of complaint. They wanted their dinner. They were starving. Why should they have to suffer because the grown-ups were cross? Melanie bought compliance with crisps and chocolates and bundled them into the family room. As for the television, she told them they could watch what they liked; desperate times warranted desperate measures, and the expression on Selwyn's face suggested these were indeed desperate times. With the children settled, she returned to the table and her soup.

Philippa looked at faces sombre above bloody pools of gazpacho. None of them would meet her gaze, each wore an expression of tragedy. 'It won't make any difference to the family holdings,' she said, as if that would ease the shock.

'And what would you know about family holdings?' Selwyn's blisters released their toxins. He shook off Melanie's restraining hand. 'You've gone too far this time, Philippa.'

'And with our money, too.' Gray was uncharacteristically blunt.

'No, Gray, *my* money.' Philippa was equally direct. 'Your father left it all to me.'

'Only in the first instance.'

'That's not correct, Selwyn, there were no conditions in George's will.'

'But it was always understood that everything would come to us, the children.' Melanie watched her mother closely, and when there was no response, added, 'After your death.'

Philippa swallowed, heard her own voice as if from a distance. 'George, by virtue of his will, entrusted me with his estate, in "the first instance" as you so delicately put it, Selwyn, and the second as well. I can dispose of it as I see fit.'

'Mother,' Melanie shook her head sadly, 'what on earth has got into you?'

'No, Melanie, what has got into you? Your father left a considerable fortune, and the Finemore Foundation will ensure we share it.'

'But he made the money for us, he never intended it for strangers.'

'If that was his intention, and I'm not so sure it was, then I hold a different view.'

'You know nothing about money, nothing about investments, how do you propose to operate this charity?'

'It's a foundation, Selwyn, and I've received the best of advice.'

'I'll bet,' Selwyn said, looking at Jeremy.

The conversation was going nowhere. Evelyn suggested Gray open the wine and Selwyn attend to the children, and with Melanie in the kitchen supervising Marcella's cooking of the snow peas ('She cooked the colour out of them last time,' Melanie explained), Evelyn turned to Philippa.

'So, tell me about it.'

Philippa leaned across and patted her daughter-in-law's hand. She was convinced all of them would see the benefits of the Foundation once they heard more about it, and was pleased for Evelyn to lead the way. She decided to begin with the financial side, this being the aspect that was causing the greatest concern, and explained that the Finemore Foundation was a charitable trust, established with an initial endowment of 1.6 million derived from the sale of the family home. An additional 8%, drawn from the income of the properties would be added to the capital annually. 'A small enough amount as you can see.'

'And the remaining income from the properties?' Evelyn asked.

'I'll use for my own living expenses, and, of course, it's there for you children as well. There's plenty to go around.'

Evelyn was about to inquire after the terms of the trust when

Selwyn, who had decided to let the children scream, wreck the entire house if they wanted, returned to the table.

'Who are the trustees?'

Philippa delayed answering until the others were seated, delayed even longer as she looked at each in turn, searching their faces for a skerrick of kindness or social concern, anything that might reveal to them the benefits of the Foundation. She looked from one to another and back again, and all she found in the frozen mouths and frantic eyes was a clutch of self-serving sentiments. No milk of human kindness here, she thought. And when finally she spoke she would have preferred to cry.

'Rather than trustees, we have directors, six at present, with provision for two more should we need them.'

And paused to swallow the pain.

But Selwyn had waited long enough. 'Who - are - they?' Each word a threat, a stab, a growl of hatred.

So she told them. She told them that, in addition to herself and Jeremy, there was a senior officer from Inner City Welfare, a woman called Hilary Johnson; Mike Maroni, an accountant; Leo Geller, a businessman, and - she paused just a moment - Lorraine Pascoe.

All Finemore finesse was forgotten in the abuse that followed. To set up a trust with their money, because it was their money despite what Philippa had said, was bad enough, but to involve Lorraine Pascoe was downright treachery. As for the other directors, they could be people Philippa had picked up on St Kilda pier. And Jeremy was involved too, although there was no surprise in that, his blatant disloyalty to the family had been demonstrated years ago in his choice of lifestyle.

'George should have put everything into family trusts.'

The others had gone, Marcella had been allowed to go to bed, and Selwyn and Melanie were tidying up. And talking. Not their usual post-dinner-party chatter about the amount of salt in the gazpacho or whether Marcella had finally mastered snow peas; not their usual laughter over Gray's pomposity and Evelyn's appalling dress sense; not even a pervert joke at Jeremy's expense, none of their usual pleasure tonight, Philippa had made sure of that.

'I advised him to do so years ago. Private trusts,' Selwyn was quick to add, 'for the family, not one of these charitable things that are simply a front for throwing good money away.'

'Darling, darling, darling,' Melanie's hands were on her husband's shoulders, 'you must calm down, after all, we know very little at this stage. It's possible this foundation thing will cease with Mother's death, or perhaps there's a plan to pay us back. Best of all, it may have advanced no further than the ideas' stage; we simply do not know.'

Selwyn slammed a crystal cruet-stand on to the granite bench. 'Whatever she's done, your mother's bloody impossible! We'll never see any of George's money as long as she's in charge, and we can't even plan our attack because we don't know the bloody terms of this ridiculous nonsense.'

Which was entirely their own fault given that discussion of Philippa's Foundation had occupied the entire meal. There was the initial announcement during soup. While the main course was being served on Melanie's new dinner-ware from Rosenthal, they were informed that potential beneficiaries would be women and children. Half-eaten racks of lamb lay congealing in a mess of claggy vegetables as they were told that the Finemore Foundation would fund groups rather than individuals, although, Philippa had added, there would always be some exceptions. Over lemon sorbet and chocolate-dipped strawberries they heard more about the other directors; Hilary Johnson and Mike Maroni sounded respectable enough, but Leo Geller was nothing more than a bookseller, plying his trade from the shop beneath the Foundation's offices. 'A shopkeeper!' Gray had exclaimed, 'a shopkeeper managing our money!' As they drank their coffee and liqueurs Philippa told them about Leo Geller's long involvement with social justice issues. 'A shopkeeper *and* a communist,' was Selwyn's caustic comment. Two hours of Philippa's folly and no one had asked what the Foundation would mean for them, the Finemore children.

Was this reticence a Finemore nicety? Selwyn wondered, as he dried the crystal, or just Finemore lunacy, because outcome was the crucial factor. And not just in the long term, although that was important enough, but owing to his mutinous liquidity problem, in the short term as well. The facts were clear: Selwyn needed cash, he needed it now, and he had counted on Philippa to supply it. The stupid bitch.

'Selwyn, darling, I think you're over-reacting. You must be sensible; there's no point in worrying until we know what she's done. And even if it's as bad as you think, it's quite possible that what's been done can be undone.'

Melanie wiped the granite benches, scribbled a note to Marcella about cleaning the ovens in the morning, buffed the halogen stove and activated the dishwasher. Then she sat at her brand new breakfast table at the end of her brand new kitchen and with one eye on the glories of home and the other on Selwyn asked, 'Can it really make so much difference to us?'

Selwyn switched on the waste-disposal and pushed vegetable peelings through the hole followed by a lemon for the fresh smell, and as the blades cut into the tough peel, he leaned on the sink to feel the rough grinding against his own clenching, as if that could ease the strain. For the truth of the matter was, Philippa's actions could make all the difference in the world to them. For Selwyn had plans for Philippa's money, indeed, Selwyn had already put Philippa's money to good use. In principle, that is, but in principle, Philippa's money was solidly committed.

He left Melanie's question unanswered, patted her head, went into the bar and poured himself a cognac. He took his time, knowing time was pressing heavily, and tried to think. How final could the scheme be? Could such a complex arrangement as a public trust be conceived, planned and executed in just a matter of months? And could all this occur without the consent of other family members? Surely not. Melanie was probably right, he was over-reacting, but he was upset, seriously upset. It was the insult of the thing, the giving away of hard-earned money, that really grated; that, and his being particularly stretched at the moment, not over-committed, he'd done his figures too well for that, rather, money was tight, and he had looked to Philippa's money, specifically cash from the sale of the house, to tide him over.

He drained his glass without tasting the liquor, and that made him even more annoyed. He hated not being in control, hated the thump of anxiety as it coursed his veins, hated his mother-in-law for making him feel this way; he was jittery and angry and had to regain his composure. He poured another cognac and sipped slowly, deliberately slowly, while he ran through figures in his head. He supposed he could increase his borrowings through Finwest; it was the obvious solution, and in the long term it wouldn't matter. And hadn't he set up Finwest for eventualities just such as this? Such a brilliant idea, so timely too, and Gray had taken no convincing. Although the figures had said it all; with beer sales in the west doubling in the previous two years, a new company to streamline sales to the region was a logical move. Gray, fully occupied with his new connoisseur wine series, had looked over the figures, remarked that Selwyn's sales people were doing nothing to improve the national palate, had signed the necessary documents, and returned to his wine journals. Finwest Pty. Ltd. had been duly established, the accounts staff appraised, and the first invoices mailed. The final stage, the diversion of funds for Selwyn's private use, had been the simplest part of the plan – just a temporary arrangement until the expenses on the Pryors' new home levelled out.

Which was Philippa's fault again. If she had not sold the family home then it would not have been necessary to buy another. Gray had rambled on about needing a larger place, but in his customary manner, had failed to proceed past the talking stage; so it had been up to Selwyn to act. Besides, at two million, Hopetoun had been an excellent buy, one that would benefit all the Finemores. For while he and Melanie and the children would derive some advantage from the home, all family gatherings, large business entertainments, charity functions, indeed, anything to which the Finemores wanted to append their name would be held at Hopetoun. Which was why the interim arrangement through Finwest was entirely justified.

An excellent buy at just over two million. Then renovations

had been required, for what was the point of owning one of the city's finest homes if, in its ageing opulence, it appeared as if you couldn't afford it? Although he had not counted on the renovations being quite so expensive and there was still an enormous amount to do. Then there was the business school, *his* business school, his own special project, he had planned to draw on Philippa's money for that, but if the worst came to the worst Finwest could cover those expenses too.

'We won't be able to bail you out if something goes wrong,' Selwyn had said between the gazpacho and the rack of lamb.

And Philippa had turned on him with that smug expression that had become increasingly common since George's death. 'Selwyn dear, what an absurd suggestion. Have faith, for I intend to succeed.'

But how could she? Philippa had never worked a day in her life, she couldn't even balance her cheque book. Although she insisted that running a philanthropic trust was vastly different from running a bank account.

'Really, Mother, how would you know?' Perspiration had caught in Gray's moustache, and while his voice was calm, there was a tightening of the lips that the family knew to be anger.

'I've had advice,' Philippa said. 'Good advice.'

Obviously not from Jeremy, for he knew nothing about business. And while Selwyn had been keen to learn the source of Philippa's advice, he'd decided there were other more pressing matters for his attention. But now, after hours of talking, he realized he was ignorant of all but the basic facts.

Although he found himself feeling calmer. Melanie was probably right, there was little point in worrying until he had all the information. How he wished he could rid himself of this tendency to expect the worse, and yet it was such a deeply ingrained trait, he wondered if it were now not with him for life. As a child, he had been different; consumed by optimism, he had expected the best and generally received it. It was the academic life that had changed him, the academic life that had taught him caution and cunning. And why not? The worst always happened in universities, particularly in the watery climate of the seventies and early eighties. People in their ignorance would refer to the comfort of the ivory tower, little did they know that brotherly love stopped at the university car-park. The game was all to do with fixing the figures, having the best contacts, and knowing how to lobby. Which made the university no different from commerce or politics, except in one crucial respect: in the academy most of the players were ignorant of the rules, lolling around as they were in an anachronistic humanism; as for the rest, knowing the rules was pointless because they were mostly inept. In an environment like that it would be naïve not to expect the worse.

He rested his head in his hands, thoughts of the university only brought back the other problems, the money problems, for he had left the university for money, George Finemore's money, one day to become Selwyn Pryor's money. Selwyn had never planned to become an academic, but a judicious thesis topic and an opportune shift to the political right throughout the university system had provided the momentum for his trek upwards. Indeed, by the time he found himself the youngest professor of economics in the country, his own department, despite a fair complement of cretins, had already established itself as the premier right-wing think tank in the country.

But Selwyn had his sights on bigger things. The university brought him status, but he was after influence, he wanted power. He was offered pre-selection for a safe conservative seat, but this was not the power he had in mind, he wanted money. So Selwyn, who, with his malleable principles and rock-solid pragmatism would have made an excellent politician, left the university for the world of business. George Finemore's world. And had never regretted it. For Selwyn had plans, plans that would take him far away from the world of liquor. These days Selwyn wanted nothing less than posterity, he wanted the name of Selwyn Pryor deposited deep within the sturdy granite of history.

In the shock that had greeted Philippa's announcement, Selwyn had seen his plans lurch and stagger, and it had not been a pretty sight. For he had banked on George Finemore's estate for some charitable works of his own, useful charity with worthwhile dividends: a series of large donations to support what would eventually be the premier business school in the nation, the sort of gift that would result in a Selwyn Pryor Chair of Economics, perhaps even a Selwyn Pryor Building. No wonder he had imagined the worst when Philippa said she was planning to give it all away. But time and reasoning now suggested his had been an over-reaction; he would look into the situation in the morning and soon have affairs back in order.

Selwyn poured himself another cognac and one for Melanie and went to join her in the atrium. This space, together with the kitchen and ballroom, comprised the first stage of the Hopetoun renovations, and he was extremely pleased with it. Its impressive proportions, in particular, the ceiling of glass that soared skywards in a hexagonal pyramid, instilled in him the pride of possession. Melanie had excelled with the decorating; the window seats along each of the six sides patterned in a soft sea-green, the exotic plants, the ornate aquarium which occupied the centre of the room, all helped to create the understated luxury that was the backdrop to his ambitions. This, he reminded himself, was what he had worked for, this legitimated any struggles that might ensue with Philippa, or, for that matter, any interim financial arrangements that might be required.

They sat, Melanie and Selwyn Pryor, sipping cognac and staring into the shadowy sky. Selwyn was feeling so much better he even managed to find an element of pity for his mother-in-law.

'She's clearly not over your father's death.'

Melanie agreed. 'Although she seemed to be doing so well.'

Which was how it was with unstable people, Selwyn said. Melanie nodded, leaned more heavily against her husband.

'We'll put an end to this charity thing; the time has come for a firmer hand with Philippa.'

He would speak to Philippa alone, make her see reason, and if that failed, insist she turn over her affairs to him. Before long, Selwyn was sure, he would assume control of the family holdings without sustaining serious damage to the life he had planned.

'I can't imagine why no one asked the details of the confounded thing,' Gray said to Evelyn, as she drove home from the Pryors.

'I would have but Selwyn interrupted. It really infuriates me the way he acts like the head of the family.'

'Well he's not, and while I'm around he never will be.' Gray shuffled his bulk, loosened his belt. 'Did the lamb taste all right to you?'

'Apart from being overcooked and cold it was perfectly good. I know Philippa held up the proceedings, but with a kitchen like Melanie's, plus a live-in housekeeper, you'd think she'd manage a decent meal.'

'Always been a shocking cook.'

'Gray, what are you saying! I thought you liked her food, you always make such a fuss over it.'

'Of course I do, she's my sister.'

But tonight she had made him sick, or rather cold fatty lamb combined with the horror of his mother giving away his father's estate had made him sick. Philippa's plan was an outrage, an offence against her dead husband and a theft from her grandchildren; Philippa had forgotten who she was, and, in so doing, had betrayed them all. And not only in the long term, although those effects could be devastating, but in the short term as well. For a start, Gray's plans for Finemore's *Fin de Siècle* series would have to be postponed until this business was sorted out. Such a terrible shame, all the work of the past few months, and the excitement – the first time he had felt truly himself since his father's death – in selecting the wines for this, the first of his connoisseur lines.

The thought of the wines drew a sweet spurt of saliva; such beautiful wines and how long had he waited. George had never been interested in quality, had known nothing about wines except that locally-produced varieties were best as they were not at the whim of a floating dollar. George believed that the strength of a business like Finemore's lay with its staples and its capacity to cater to majority tastes.

'But the average Australian knows nothing about wine,' Gray

had said over and over again. 'The average Australian's only interested in his beer.'

'Exactly,' George had replied, 'so let's concentrate on beer.'

When Gray protested that if you give in to poor taste you'll never create a demand for anything better, George said he was not in the business of changing the world, all he wanted to do was make a profit. Selwyn held much the same view. Selwyn said that if the market were willing to pay for vulgarity then there was little point in encouraging discernment, and turned his attention to designer pubs. But with George now gone and Gray running the business there was nothing to stop him. Certainly not Selwyn, who seemed to have become more amenable over the past couple of months, and certainly not his mother – although Gray's natural caution advised him, albeit reluctantly, to suspend further developments until Philippa was back to normal. For he wanted his connoisseur lines to succeed. Gray wanted to be seen in the trade as a worthy successor to his father; George had been regarded as a pioneer, well, Gray wanted to be a pioneer too.

But time was running out. He had just turned forty, had worked at Finemore's for nearly twenty years, had suffered the ignominy of seeing his father run the company in partnership with his mistress, had watched Selwyn's rapid rise through the ranks, so a measure of impatience was only to be expected. He could have accepted delays to his *Fin de Siècle* series as a result of financial constraints, or changing trends in the industry, but this nonsense of his mother's was really too bad.

And so unexpected. He had always regarded Philippa as someone who believed in family, believed in doing the right thing, but her wallowing in widowhood nearly a year after his father's death suggested otherwise. And not just the wallowing, but how she had chosen to do it: selling the house, moving to a dreadful area, and now this foundation business. She seemed to be getting worse rather than better. When Evelyn had asked a couple of months earlier if he thought Philippa would ever return to normal, he had been confident she would. Now he wasn't so sure. Perhaps it was a problem of not knowing what to do with her time, perhaps, in the absence of George's guidance, she was unable to organize herself.

'Why don't you invite Mother to your cake decorating class,' he said, as Evelyn turned into their driveway. 'I'm sure she'd enjoy it.' And when Evelyn nodded and smiled he was immediately reassured; if anyone could fix his mother, it was Evelyn.

'It looks magnificent.'

Jeremy and Philippa were standing in the offices of the Finemore Foundation. It had been Jeremy's suggestion to stop in on the way home from the Pryors as an antidote to the evening. Philippa had gratefully agreed; the vitriol had shaken her, she wouldn't sleep for hours yet, needed to calm down and in some way restore to the family, to her children, those qualities she desperately wanted them to possess. The bookshop was still open when they arrived and Leo Geller waved as they passed his window on their way to the stairs at the side of the shop. Leo was open late most nights, Philippa explained, as she inserted the key into the lock, seemed serious readers were nocturnal, or at least that was Leo's theory.

And so into the area occupied by the Finemore Foundation. A muted air of pinks and blues greeted them, of warmth rather than the usual chill of freshly renovated space. There was an open reception area, which would double as a conference room, and three offices along one side. Jeremy glanced into one and laughed at the pink filing cabinet.

'It looks perfect,' he said. 'The previous occupants wouldn't recognize the place.'

The premises had been used as an illegal gambling house. On their first inspection, Lorraine Pascoe and Philippa had easily located the position of the six, round, playing tables by the changing pattern of light and shade across the carpet. The gamblers had been heavy smokers and clumsy drinkers; the place reeked of nicotine, the walls were stained a grim mustard, and the sixties tweed carpet had become a modernist spatter of oranges and browns. The toilet was unspeakable. But the place was the right size, centrally located, and Philippa had liked the idea of working above a bookshop.

On that first day, Philippa had gone below to introduce herself to Leo Geller, a small, rumpled figure in balding corduroy trousers, thinning grey hair, cheekbones, she remembered noticing cheekbones and how for a short man he was very gaunt, and, behind the glasses, the startlingly blue eyes. They had talked about the former tenants. Leo had been very happy with them; the place had been empty during the day, and at night the patrons slipped in and out so quietly he was hardly aware of them. So satisfied had he been with the old tenants, Philippa wondered how accepting he would be of the new. But numerous meetings later and with a five year lease duly signed, it was apparent that Leo found the new occupants entirely to his liking.

'There wouldn't be a Foundation without Leo and Lorraine,' Philippa now said.

'Is there much left to do?'

'An enormous amount. There are still legal aspects to be finalized, and there's work to be done on the investment portfolio. But we've prepared the publicity material and have started contacting community groups, and, as you can see, our offices are finished.' She rubbed at a mark on the wall. 'I can't remember being this excited since,' she paused, 'I suppose since I had you children.'

Jeremy smiled. 'And that's not exactly yesterday. Seems to me you've waited quite long enough.' He was standing near the reception desk and the familiar shape of Philippa's Shirley Hawthorn sculpture. His fingers travelled the smooth cool stone.

'I thought I'd have it here,' Philippa said. 'It's where I expect to be spending most of my time.'

'And Lorraine?' Jeremy asked. 'Will she be working for the Foundation?'

Philippa shook her head. Lorraine was receiving plenty of work through the liquor industry. 'But she's keen to help out, particularly with the business side.'

Which pleased Philippa, who was growing increasingly fond

of Lorraine Pascoe. She was such a generous woman, warm, intelligent, a woman to love, Philippa could see that. And yet she found it difficult to equate the Lorraine she knew with the George she had known, wanted to ask Lorraine about George, what he had been like with her, wanted to know if the man Lorraine had loved was the same man Philippa had married. But there are certain things one cannot ask, certain things one must accept as forever unknowable.

'So if Lorraine is not to be employed, who is?'

Philippa told him about Beth Saunders, the Foundation's executive officer and a friend of Leo's, who had worked with one of the unions until twelve months before when she'd stopped to have a baby. She was wanting to return to work, Leo had told her about the Foundation and had arranged a meeting with Philippa. 'And there's our secretary, Tracey - you've already spoken to her - and me. We'll keep it at that for the time being.'

Jeremy gave his mother a hug. 'I'm so proud of you,' he said, 'and the others will be too, they just need a little time.'

But Philippa was not so sure. It was the reaction at dinner, less the force of it than the values it revealed, that inclined her to think the family might never come round to her point of view.

'Were you surprised at their response?'

Jeremy nodded. 'Although I've always found them impossible to anticipate.' And had never been much interested in making the effort.

Philippa, however, knew her children well; her mistake had been in attributing to them a moral dimension that, if ever it had existed, had clearly atrophied. She blamed their conservatism, with its blinkered perceptions and simple obdurate answers, and their all-consuming self-concern. Her children had changed, and whilst the change had not escaped her, the extent of it had. But after two hours of abuse all had been made clear, two hours of abuse during which none of them had shown the least concern for anyone other than themselves. Neither had any of them asked why she had chosen to do something so radical - for she was quite prepared to admit that starting the Foundation *was* radical - just an explosion of self-righteous indignation from people convinced of their position.

Not that she had expected their solicitude, that was not their way, not the way of many children with their parents, but she had been accustomed to a certain regard as a side-effect of their 'doing the right thing'. But tonight any pretence of – and suddenly she found the right word – of respect, had been discarded, providing Philippa with an unexpurgated edition of her children.

She loved her children but there were times she did not respect them. (Having now discovered the word, she found it had many applications.) How fortunate it was that a mother's love was both strenuous and amnesiac. And tonight's episode? Common-sense would allocate it to that vast twilight of maternal forgetting. She watched Jeremy as he wandered through the office; he, too, had given his share of pain, but what Jeremy possessed and what seemed to be missing in her other children was an ability to look beyond himself, to understand and feel intensely about people and events, to become involved in lives other than his own. And passion, Jeremy had passion, and would take risks, had to take risks, because when you realize you're no more important than anyone else there can be no pandering to certainty. The others directed their lives much like a television serial: a script, a schedule, all parts accounted for, a closed social environment, resolution at the end of each day. Different with Jeremy, and, she now realized, different for her. How she would miss her younger son when he went to England, and how she feared he might decide to stay.

Her thoughts were interrupted by a muffled voice from below. Philippa looked at her watch. 'It must be Leo, I expect he's just closed the shop.' She turned to Jeremy. 'Finished up here?' He nodded. 'Let's go down then, and see what he wants.'

Coffee and strudel were what Leo had in mind. But not for Jeremy, whose digestive system was in serious revolt against dinner. Philippa, however, thought it an excellent idea. She kissed her son, said she would be at his place at ten the next morning to help him pack up – he was leaving for London in less than two weeks, she explained to Leo – and saw him into the night.

While Leo was in the espresso bar next door buying supper,

Philippa took the time to collect her thoughts and sever herself from her maternal woes. She pulled two chairs to the front of the counter, sank into one, heard herself sigh and could have cried, except she did not want to: the evening had been bad enough, useless to prolong the pain. She rose again and searched a small cupboard for port and tumblers, poured two hearty nips and was sipping hers when Leo returned.

'Good idea,' he said, indicating the port, and passed her an espresso. 'The strudel's finished, we'll have to manage without.'

The two sat and sipped and talked amid that hushed tranquility that comes only with books, and, in spite of herself, Philippa told him about the evening, her shock and shame and sadness. And guilt too, for parents must take some responsibility for the children they have produced.

Leo disagreed, it had been many years since Melanie and Gray had come under her direct influence. 'A time comes in every child's life when he or she must make a choice of what will be taken from the parents and what will not. Otherwise, you'd spend your entire life blaming your mother and father for all your faults.'

'Which is exactly what so many people do.'

'Yes, but shouldn't.

'That's all very well, Leo, but I can't help thinking I could have done better. Perhaps still can.'

'But *ought* you?'

They both smiled, Philippa because of the gentleness of the rebuke, and Leo because he did not want to offend. They continued to talk as they had on so many occasions, easily, and with a certain familiarity that suggested a relationship of long-standing. Not a marriage, too much intensity for that, but an intimacy of which they were both aware. And marvelled at, for there were many differences. Leo was a few years younger than Philippa, and from a European Jewish, working-class background. It was during their second meeting he had announced his Jewishness; it was the fulcrum of his life, he said, had formed him, shaped his perceptions, circumscribed every major decision. 'I tell you I am Jewish, because if you don't like it, you won't like me.' And for the first time she detected an accent, a softening of his usually precise English, as if to portray more profoundly the strength of this atavism. She had asked him about belief, about God; he said that God was irrelevant to his kind of Jewishness, that his parents had been atheists and he was too.

'Being Jewish,' he said, 'is not for me a matter of God or religious practice. Being Jewish is to appropriate a history, the richest history possible, of scholarship and loyalty and tenacity and persecution. Being Jewish,' he added with a broad gesture at his adopted country, 'gives me a past in a country where history has no credentials. It gives me an identity.'

For a long time she had been afraid to ask about his family, fearing he would say they had all been killed. Six million deaths of strangers are easier to tolerate than the one or two deaths of people you know. Indeed, you can live a life knowing about the six million and be entirely untouched by them; then you learn of someone who was killed by the Nazis, a particular person with a name and a face and a family, who then acts as a vector for all the others. She was afraid to ask Leo about his family for it would bring the atrocity of six million deaths close enough to force her to make the effort to understand. And she dared not know because she feared she would not understand, or feared she would understand and was terrified of living with that knowledge. As she tried to ask her questions of Leo, as she rehearsed this phrase and that, the complicity of language in subduing the untenable, in touching up reality, became ever more clear. 'Holocaust' reduced six million deaths to an ugly word, it was the language of those who did not want to understand. And it was not an isolated instance, there was 'genocide' and 'extermination' and a host of other words from the Latin and Greek, as if classical roots could render the repugnant dignified. And because she knew she had welcomed the insipid language of atrocity, because she was guilty as are all the ignorant, she found herself even less able to speak. But guilt can be another crutch, she reminded herself, and set about asking her questions.

Leo had been born in France before the war. He had spent most of the war years in a Burgundy village, passing as the son of a Catholic couple. His parents were among the thousands of 'immigrant' French Jews who, in 1943, were handed over to the Germans by the Vichy regime and 'repatriated' to the East. And East they went, along with friends and family who did not return. That not one, but both Gellers returned was in the nature of a miracle. They said it was better to speak of miracles, because to utter what really saved them was to dismantle the scaffolding of a life. As for post-war Europe, it was a monument to menace and hate, it reminded them not only of those who had died but also the burden of survival, and they wanted to be as far away as possible. After the armistice, after the long trek westward to reclaim their child, they caught a ship to Australia; there was no place, they said, farther away from Europe.

The Gellers settled in Melbourne. Annie and Bernard Geller worked first in factories, then a small milk bar, and later, not long after Leo's younger brother was born, a delicatessan, which later still became their own. They worked and worked to give their sons an education, not that education had ever saved an individual Jew from death, but learning had, they said, saved the race from extinction.

Leo's brother, several years of medical practice behind him, went to Israel. He wanted to live somewhere where his Jewishness was not a burden. His parents tried to persuade him that the essence of being Jewish was always to be conscious of it, but the young man was finished with fear. 'In a nation of Jews,' he said, 'the one thing you can take for granted is your Jewishness. Here,' he said, meaning Australia, 'I feel I have something to hide.' So he left. Not long afterwards, Leo's father died; the war killed him, Annie said, the war robbed him of his old age, and soon she was gone too.

Leo must have loved them very much, Philippa said. He had taken a long time to answer, and when finally he did, his tone was resigned. His parents had loved him so deeply, were so full of their own love, that there was little opportunity for them to receive love in return. They loved and loved and gave and gave, and the only possible means of showing his own love was to accept theirs. 'Most children owe their existence to their parents, but my parents lived only for their children, lived for us and through us. No matter how much you achieve, you can never feel it's enough to justify your own parents' lives.'

They were proud of him, proud of their clever son. He came top of his high school, enrolled at university, arts for him and law for them, good degrees and much involvement with the university socialists. On graduation he took up a position with the Trades Hall Council. His parents were proud, for to have a political conscience was to be a good citizen. Then he married, a nice girl, and there would be children and grandchildren.

So when he gave up his job and bought into a bookshop they were full of grief. And when the marriage ended, for no particular reason, except he should never have married in the first place, they wondered where they had gone wrong. He explained there was no mistake on their part, only his own. He tried to ease their disappointment, and in time they seemed to understand, or so he wanted to believe. For he was happy. He sold books, he read, he talked with customers, he was an advocate for workers' rights, he published articles on labour history, and built a reputation for his shop. By the time his parents died, he had established himself within the intellectual life of a city better known for its sporting fanaticism.

Now, with her own parenthood under threat, Philippa asked how he had coped when his parents died. He smiled, a sad little smile, and shrugged: it had taken so much effort not to feel guilty that the acute grief stage had passed quite quickly. But the sadness he still felt. 'Theirs was not much of a life. The war robbed them of their best years, and so did their children. When finally they could afford to have a life of their own, they died.'

'And love? What now of love?'

'I wish I could bring them back. I suppose that's love, yes?'

As she wanted to bring back her own children, to the exact point where they had gone astray. But when that actually was, she could not determine. She accepted another port and moved the conversation to gentler ground. They talked and sipped their drinks and she felt herself relax; and in the fresh air of companionship saw Leo's dark, thin-skinned hand and wanted to touch it.

When in walked a young woman.

'Are you open?' Amy Vaughan asked through a bush of black, brambly hair.

SIX

Amy Vaughan wanted the day to finish. It had started badly with a dawn awakening, had continued with the milk sour and her comfortable jeans soiled; there had been a lightning tram strike which she wholeheartedly supported, but not at ten o'clock on a morning when she was to meet her supervisor at eleven. Then, after hitching a ride to the university, she had arrived to find a note pinned to her supervisor's door postponing the meeting until the following week. She went to the library, the books she wanted were out on loan; she went to the bookstore, her order had not arrived; she went to the cafeteria, all the iced doughnuts had been sold, and she went home, which on a day stout with disaster, seemed the only sensible thing to do.

But the day was set firmly on its course. Caught within a jumble of junk mail was a letter addressed in a round, pink, primary school hand that Amy recognized as her sister's. Not immediately recognized, for Wendy Swan, neé Vaughan, had written to her sister only twice before, the first time to announce her engagement and a year later to invite Amy to the wedding, but guessed soon enough because of the 'Miss Amy Vaughan' rather than the 'Ms Amy Vaughan' or plain 'Amy Vaughan' commonly used by Amy's friends and creditors. And the pink childish writing.

Time for the first pregnancy, Amy decided, as she withdrew

several sheets of floral notepaper from the envelope. For Wendy had always performed to expectation, and had been married for over a year, and was very much the type to advertise these insignia of a successful life - fiancé, husband, child - particularly to an older sister with conspicuously dowdy prospects.

And it was a pregnancy, although that was not Wendy's primary reason for writing. Estelle Vaughan, the girls' mother, long departed and, as far as Amy was concerned, best forgotten, had returned home. Wendy had thought it best to write to Amy before telephoning because she knew how 'mind-blowing' the news would be, knew Amy would need time for it 'to sink in', time to adjust.

Amy's whole body clenched. What patronizing twaddle! And from Wendy of all people, who was the last person to be deciding what was best for Amy. Wendy still lived in the town of their birth, had acquired her friends in kindergarten, had married the boy from down the street, while Amy had left home at sixteen, moved to the city, lived among strangers, worked, put herself through university, and done it all without reliance on anyone or anything. Including the perverse promises of family.

Amy felt the blood rush to her temples, the start of a throbbing head, and knew she must stay calm. She went into the kitchen, drank a glass of water and another, perched herself at the bench to think. 'The perverse promises of family' was how she saw it, but to Wendy, now intent on a family of her own, the promises were more than likely steeped in glitter. For it appeared that Wendy had actually searched for Estelle Vaughan; on a surge of atavism brought on, no doubt, by the discovery of her own pregnancy, she had traced Estelle to a coastal town and an unhappy alliance, and brought her home to be grandmother *in situ*. Initially the pregnancy had 'felt wrong' Wendy wrote, but now, having found their mother, the pregnancy 'felt right'. Estelle had been 'absolutely wonderful, as if she'd never been away' (for more than fifteen years, Amy would like to remind her), was 'dying to be a granny' and eager 'to make up for lost time'. Which brought Wendy to the real point of her letter: Estelle wanted to see Amy and Wendy hoped Amy would 'let bygones be bygones' and 'do the right thing'.

The tram strike, the cancelled appointment, the absent doughnuts were nothing compared with this. And of the double blight, the intrusion of Wendy and the return of the prodigal mother, it was difficult to know which was worse. Wendy Vaughan had always rankled; from the time she appeared, just fifteen months after Amy, Wendy had been convinced that, in every respect that mattered, she was a better person than her sister. And she had not been alone in this, Aunt Rose and Uncle Ken who had taken them in after Estelle's departure, fully agreed. Wendy was pretty where Amy was plain; Wendy was agreeable where Amy was sullen; Wendy had stayed home to care for the elderly guardians, Amy had deserted them for the city; Wendy had married nice boy Ian, Amy had always been wild. The comparisons were numerous and never in Amy's favour. Only once had Amy broken her silence: she was much cleverer than Wendy, she had shouted over tea one evening in early adolescence, and was punished for being proud – a characteristic that neither God nor her guardians appreciated.

For the first time in a long while Amy felt the familiar grind of a joyless childhood. Enough! She told herself, enough. She did not have to stand for this, not now, not after a decade of carefully dismembering those early years and casting the scraps aside. Sometimes a little forgetting is necessary, some deliberate fabrication as well. Not that she had consciously deceived herself, rather her approach had been to drop something off here, pick up something else there, and keep an accurate list of all her movements. As for the storeroom of discarded experiences, it was a necessary by-product of a not-altogether-easy life. And now Wendy waltzes in, trespasses where she doesn't belong, dislodges some of the more rusted items, and expects Amy to apply a little grease here a little polish there and deliver herself as good as new to the bosom of the family.

Well she was not going to oblige. She made herself a cup of coffee and, in place of the fresh milk she had forgotten to buy, added a dollop of cream. She went outside to the balcony, sat between her two plants, the peace rose that was thriving in the salt air and the fuchsia that was fretting, and tried to ignore the robust intrusion of her sister, who was, she was now convinced, a far greater irritant than the mother. She sat on her tiny balcony and willed the sea to work its magic.

It was a perfect afternoon; the late sun stretched across broad streamers of cloud, autumn winds lifted the waves in gusts of green – not the steel-grey of winter nor the common blue of summer, but the muted sage of her preference. There was a solitary swimmer; further out, almost in the centre of the bay were the bright triangles of a bunch of windsails and, over near the pier, the trawlers were leaving for the evening catch. The day grew hushed, frustrations fluttered in the salty air and were gone. All except Wendy. The letter flapped in the wind, its lurid, pink words mocking; Wendy, with a whole new plot in front of her, was rewriting their past, and Amy wanted no part of it.

Not that she put much value on this childhood of hers, on the contrary, it had been a rough passage. Up until the age of ten when Estelle had left, Amy had skirted the dangers with variable success. She trod carefully, studying her mother in order to determine what Estelle wanted from her. But Estelle Vaughan's clues, being neither reliable nor consistent, merely added to the obstacles littering Amy's way. It was worse after Estelle left. Aunt Rose and Uncle Ken had no children of their own and, as it happened, had never wanted any, but they were Christians and knew their duty. It was only after Amy had escaped their home and their deprivations that she realized the pleasure her Aunt and Uncle had derived from their martyrdom, and how indebted they were to Amy for such joy as had entered their mangy lives. Wendy in contrast, although a burden to her Aunt and Uncle, managed to find a little corner in their gelid hearts, but it was a tiny space indeed and one she guarded jealously.

Throughout the years of childhood, Amy picked her way through the rubble, hoping as she went that life would become easier. With the annual birthday she wished it, as the wishbone snapped she wished it, in her nightly prayers she wished it. Even after birthdays had lost their magic and she'd eliminated chicken from her diet and God was long dead, she still believed that the end of childhood would bring relief. But, as noxious as her childhood had been, it had, nonetheless, been hers, and she refused to relinquish it in order to feed the vapid fantasies of a sister with whom she had nothing in common and had never much liked.

As for the prodigal mother, when you've spent half a lifetime accommodating to her loss, it would be wasteful in the extreme to open your arms and take her back. That is, if you could open your arms to a mother. Or indeed anyone. For Amy's arms were clenched by her sides; Amy needed all her strength to ensure her own way was safe.

She removed a dead leaf from the fuchsia, ground it between her fingers, and sipped her coffee. At ten or twelve or even fourteen it would have been different, for then her desire for a mother's love had been painfully vibrant; but when, some four years after Estelle's departure, the desire had become unbearable, she had forced herself to accept there was no mother, and the one that had been hers, had been a grievously poor specimen. She remembered feeding in the information like the terrible medicine it was, shoving it in with stories of orphans – Kipling, Austen, Eliot – stories of good and bad parents, pushing it in until the desire was smothered. If you cannot feel then there is no pain. The last violent heave occurred when she decided to shelve her soul, to remove the bruised and battered little nugget, wrap it up and toss it into the storeroom along with the rest of the detritus of a failed life. After that, the absent mother, the ever-present deprivations, her own apparent worthlessness, mattered less. Indeed, circumstances improved so much that Amy realized she should have put her soul in storage long before it had become so mangled. There was a short-lived lacuna, which she quickly filled with orphan books. 'You'll ruin your eyes,' Aunt Rose said, 'and with your looks you can't afford to.' The eyes, largish and brown, were her best feature, or, as Aunt Rose would have it, her only good feature. Her dark hair was too thick and curly and Aunt Rose insisted it be kept short, her squat body was inclined to fat. 'She'll have Estelle's bust-line, too, by the looks of it,' Aunt Rose said, when she dragged the eleven-year-old

Amy to the town emporium to purchase her first bra.

In these matters of body, Aunt Rose had been right. At age twenty-five, Amy looked down on a huge excrescence where crumbs fell and drinks dribbled and her centre of gravity was forever challenged. Her eyes were still her best feature, although she now required glasses for reading. The hair, however, had undergone a radical transformation; she now wore it long and wild, talismanic of her release from Aunt Rose and Uncle Ken.

As you grow you make a life. You know your handicaps - absent parents, mean-spirited guardians, a face too full, a figure too fat, and you know your strengths - perseverence, resilience, humour and brains, although, in truth, the brains came first and everything else followed. From the beginning she was very bright, from the beginning, her days were harassed by an energetic search for meaning, and from the beginning she learned the double-edged sword of the bright child. For Amy saw too much; even with eyes closed, her mind chattered and chimed with insights far too weighty for any child. She saw through people and read between their lines; where others saw only space, Amy saw pretence and perversity. Which is not to suggest she didn't make the best of things; she knew the penalties of being different, she saw what happened to the fat girl with the dirty ears and the boy with the stutter, and became adept at hiding what she knew, whilst relying on her books and daydreams - such sweet dreams and solemn books - for respite.

Books and dreams and, for her ninth grade year, Mrs Duncan, who appreciated exactly those qualities that the others, Aunt, Uncle and Wendy, found so unsatisfactory. In the first week of term, Mrs Duncan had discovered Amy in the fennel-choked hollow at the end of the oval reading *Villette,* when she should have been at sewing. Amy, furious at being caught and sticky with the self-consciousness of one who hated to be singled out, awaited punishment. But Mrs Duncan, far from reprimanding her, appeared to approve of her behaviour, certainly she approved of *Villette.* She directed Amy to other novels, and not just the Brontës. There was Thackeray's Becky Sharp, a very clever but not always intelligent orphan, and a swag of Dickens's orphans, who, being so good and godly, often were rewarded with parent-substitutes, and as the year passed the work of other authors, Edgeworth, Mrs Gaskell, Henry James.

The emptiness returned when, soon after her retirement, Mrs Duncan moved to live closer to her sister. One Saturday, not long before she left, Mrs Duncan invited Amy for afternoon tea. She wanted to talk about Amy's 'gift' which was, she said, something rare and special.

'No one else much likes it,' Amy said.

'But they will, just you wait and see.'

So Amy waited and studied and when she was sixteen won a full scholarship to the university. Aunt Rose and Uncle Ken were pleased to see the back of her – such a broad back, and always such an embarrassment. Wendy, too, wanted her gone. But now, ten years on, it seemed Wendy had changed her mind, now, a sister was part of her plans.

But not Amy's. She had made a life and it was without family, without any real intimacies, although her friends would judge it otherwise. Her undergraduate degree with honours in literature had earned her a post-graduate scholarship; her MA had added a Faculty of Arts prize which allowed her to give up part-time work. She had constructed herself carefully, directing passion to her studies, never friends; the former were satisfactory ('brilliant' was the term most often used by her teachers) and the latter were satisfied. As for her hopes and expectations, Amy made sure they did not rely on other people. It was a matter of rejection, and Amy, with a lifetime's share in her first sixteen years, was not interested in having any more. Bright, superficial and well-insulated was she, and while she might dream of a fellow traveller in the shadows of early morning, never would she allow herself to look for one in the punishing light of day.

The insulation had grown more sophisticated with the years, and surprisingly effective. Many were the times when a friend would inadvertently happen on a tear, a weak seam, and Amy would feel her deformed self crying out for a gentle caress. But no one seemed to notice, no one seemed to see she was different.

Until Ralph, who perceived something was awry. He diagnosed

repression and arranged for her to see a psychiatrist. He insisted on a male therapist because 'abnormal rupture from the mother and an even earlier departure of the father had cauterized Amy's ability to realize a mature relationship.' Ralph, who was doing his PhD in psychology, knew about such things. So she went to a psychiatrist and they stared at each other for two sessions. He sat at a huge bare desk, a brittle light behind him, and Amy, recognizing that something other than her mental health was at stake, maintained a steady gaze, even though the late afternoon sun gave her a headache. Towards the end of the second silent session he asked her why she didn't speak, and before she had time to answer, suggested that her inability to relate to him was symptomatic of the broader problem of interpersonal relationships that had prompted her to consult him in the first place.

'Not at all,' she had said. 'It's the light. I can't concentrate looking into the light.'

'I've already suggested you'd find it more comfortable on the couch.'

And while she wanted to say *he* would find it more comfortable if she were on the couch, she maintained her silence.

At the next session the psychiatrist had moved round to Amy's side of the desk. Two months later they had sex. A month after that Amy asked him if theirs was a mature relationship, and when he said it was, she assumed she was cured and discontinued her sessions. As for Ralph, she decided he was pure gristle from the neck up, and discontinued his sessions as well.

But not sex, which had nothing to do with intimacy. Sex she found quite appealing, no place for self-consciousness in all the panting and pushing and sweating and grunting that orchestrated sexual pleasure, no place for thought. Sex provided respite, less a physical relief than a psychological thing; sex put a blanket over her grinding, pitiless mind and closed her eyes; sex was more restful than any other pastime, including sleep, there being no dreams and no consciousness of the dreamer. Its disadvantage was it required other people, whereas sleep you could do alone. But Amy was a failure at sleeping. As soon as she lay down, as soon as she relaxed her guard, there was a stampede of thoughts that made a bloody mess of sleep, and she would drag herself through the hours searching anxiously for the light of dawn. There was her sleepless reading, diaries and letters rather than essays and novels, snippets of other lives that she hoped would separate her from her own, but despite the soundness of the theory it seldom worked.

And would not tonight, Amy was thinking, as she sat on the balcony gazing at a now-feverish sky, Wendy's letter still in her hand. She was wondering how to pass the evening, which friends might be home, or if there was a film worth seeing, when the telephone rang.

'Did you get my letter?' Wendy's voice was wet with excitement. 'She's just so wonderful, has been through so much.' And Wendy natters on in a gossamer melody that requires nothing more of Amy than an occasional murmur. Finally there is a pause: 'Well, when can we expect you?'

Soon, soon, says Amy, who would do anything to finish the conversation, never, never, she thinks as she hangs up. At nine o'clock the phone rings again; at the sound of the long distance pips, Amy unplugs the cord and leaves the flat. Into the city she walks, five kilometres down a broad avenue, keeping to the outside of the pavement, confident and alert as one would be after ten years of late-night jobs and sleepless nights, and as she walks she grows evermore morose. For the fact is, she is tempted by the returned mother and wishes she were not. How many times can a person leave, and what indeed is the extent of the injured party's forgiveness? What of her efforts over all these years? Had they been for nothing? Had her strength been mere pretence? Her self-sufficiency a flimsy disguise? She hurries through the streets feeling sick and frightened; if she should weaken, what will happen to her then?

With relief she sees the bookshop; books will placate, she thinks, books will bring the solace that will allow her to return home to bed.

'Are you open?' she says with forced cheer, and struggles for composure when the man says no. Although what else could she have expected on a day such as this?

'But you're here now,' he says, 'and we are too, so why don't you stay and look around.'

She did not trust herself to speak, just smiled and nodded and retreated to a section out of view of the man and his companion. Although, so intent were they on each other, she doubted they were even aware of her. Love, she thought, as she dropped to the floor in the classics section, even here in a bookshop, late at night, between two oldies. Bloody love, she thought, and bloody mother love: perfect, unconditional, and pure myth. She wanted none of it, not even the desire for it; she wanted no pain. Light-hearted friendships and short affairs - no pain there. No desires, no illusions, no god, no redemption, and, with the exception of books, which were, after all, entirely reliable, few needs. And yet Estelle Vaughan's return had brought a sinister rattle: the greatest illusion of all, which was love.

Such pathetic bleatings! she thought. Weak, slovenly, indulgent snivellings which could have no place in her life. If ten years ago, five years ago, at any time in memory she had capitulated to such nonsense where would she be now? She must stick to the facts and the facts were simple: Wendy had looked for her mother, Wendy had found her mother, Wendy had brought her mother home. It had nothing to do with Amy.

She breathed deeply, took strength from her reasoning, and came to the front of the shop. Panic was crouching in the wings, but she managed a cheery 'thank you' and made for the door. The woman stopped her.

'Have a port?' She said.

(Philippa watched the girl, watched her brush the hair from her face, saw the pale, taut skin, the eyes flicker from contact with her own. Saw how the demeanour sought to camouflage - relaxed, confident, feet splayed, hands in pockets - how the face spoke far more eloquently. So young she is, with the roundness of a child. Nearly midnight and the streets full of girls alone, but this one looks as if she might stumble and fall. So have a port, Philippa says.)

Amy feels trapped between what she should do, which is leave immediately, and what she wants to do. She looks at the brown, smiling face of the woman, her outstretched hand, looks at the gentle, gaunt face of the man, the shock of his blue eyes, and gives in. Time enough tomorrow to stitch up the wounds.

She sits on the floor, her back against a bookcase, and sips the port. She is aware of a strange sense of having separated from her body, of having slipped away to a corner of the shop; the voices continue, soft and distant, only with effort does she know what they are saying. For the first time that day her mind ceases its skirmishing; she scans the spines of books sees only colours, letters, shapes, never words, watches the woman and the man as they talk, sees that Philippa is small, sees how she uses gestures to claim more space, thinks she could have been a gypsy if not for the neat tailored clothes, but is probably just someone's mother, wonders if everyone is defined by the scaffolding of family, and if so, what would that make her, what would that make Amy Vaughan? Orphan? Neglected child? Or, as of today, failed daughter? And what of the man? A bony frame, rough greying hair, beard, and the cerulean eyes; is this the face of a father? Is the loose, fawn shirt, with the shiver of hair at the throat, reminiscent of fatherhood? And the baggy corduroy trousers with the dusty knees? In his case, Amy cannot be sure. But he is someone's son. You can escape parenthood, but always you have been someone's child – this, no matter how expertly you discard your past, how neatly you dress your wounds.

Amy looks up, the woman is talking to her, is asking if she works. A student, Amy answers, her doctorate.

'You're very young for that.'

'Not so young,' she says. And pushes the hair back from her face.

'And your area?'

'English, twentieth-century literature.'

'Is there much demand for PhD's in literature these days?' It was Leo who spoke.

Amy smiles, feels the life returning. 'Very little I'm afraid, and with current trends we can expect even less.' She pauses, sips, begins again. 'I would have been wiser to have chosen a combined course, something like literature and accounting, or literature and computer science.'

'Is it that bad?' Philippa asks.

Amy nods, and finding herself on familiar territory, proceeds to tell them about Ellis, a friend of hers, an enterprising fellow, who, realizing there was no future in literature and yet reluctant to give it away, had chosen a joint PhD with media studies. His thesis was a multi-media package on the futuristic novel. 'He combines 8mm film, video, synthesizer and performance, he's even hired a few of us to do advertisements.' Amy was laughing. 'Of course, as a serious scholar, I'm horrified, but I'll guarantee he won't join the ranks of the unemployed. Who knows, he might even be awarded the country's first lectureship in electronic English.'

They were all laughing now, and Leo was going to the espresso bar next door for more coffee and Philippa was refilling their port glasses. When Leo returned, he asked Amy why, with such dismal prospects for literature graduates, she had chosen her area.

For a moment she toyed with telling the truth, how books made sense of her life, how without them, explanations for Estelle's defection, for Aunt Rose and Uncle Ken's cruelty would be forever caught in the weft and warp of her own idiosyncracies. But these are not words for strangers, nor indeed words for anyone who is not oneself, so she told him she'd always enjoyed literature, found herself majoring in English, 'And the next thing I knew I was doing a PhD. It just happened.'

'These things rarely do,' was what she thought Leo said. Thought he had said, but could not be sure, and then the moment passed and Leo had launched into a polemic of how contemporary values had sacrificed literature, that if ever there was a need for literature it was now,

'As a mirror to our lives, a moral wellspring. Although,' he continued, 'the problem with literature is, of course, only a fragment of the larger issue of the disintegration of language and thought.'

He went to the Modern Classics section; there was a low

murmuring, a turning of pages, then Leo's voice.

'Orwell in 1946 on the English language. "It becomes ugly," he wrote, "and inaccurate because our thoughts are foolish, but the slovenliness of our language makes it easier for us to have foolish thoughts." Isn't that the truth?'

The three of them talked into the night; they talked about twentieth-century English literature and the extent to which it was bound by the legacy of the nineteenth; they discussed whether a translation should be seen as a separate work to the original language text and if not, whether the great Russians could properly be studied in English; they talked about poetry, or rather Amy and Philippa did because Leo did not read it - one of the great failings of his life, he confessed, and now he was too old. Utter nonsense, Philippa said, and promised to rectify the situation.

At half past one, they rose to leave. Out in the street, while Leo locked the shop, Philippa turned to Amy, asked if she would like to meet again. 'Dinner perhaps?' And before Amy knew it she had agreed to a meal the following Friday. Philippa wrote name, address and phone number on a page torn from her diary, handed it to Amy, and shortly afterwards she and Leo were gone.

SEVEN

Amy woke early and lay on her back savouring the mellow greyness of the late autumn morning, a brief moment before memory took its first breath and replaced her pleasure with Philippa Finemore's dinner - tonight, Friday - the meal she did not want. Indeed, within twenty-four hours of stumbling on Philippa Finemore in the bookshop, Amy had wished never to see her again. For during the last week, her life had taken a turn for the worse and new people could only bring new demands; burdened with worry, Amy was already on her knees and should be shedding baggage rather than adding to it.

It was Wendy's fault. And Estelle's. There had been phonecalls from Wendy once, sometimes twice a day, with Wendy acting as her mother's proxy. Estelle wanted to see Amy, wanted to get to know her; she knew she had made mistakes, but now wanted to make amends. And if Amy continued to deny her, Wendy said, then the burden of blame would shift from mother to daughter. And Amy wouldn't want that, would she? Of course she wouldn't, says Estelle in the background, although there was no telling with Amy, the mother adds, for she was always a peculiar child. At the beginning of the week the phonecalls had been conciliatory, by the middle, Wendy was making demands, and last night she had been unequivocally menacing: their mother had had two angina attacks in as many days; if Amy insisted on being so cruel then she must be prepared to live with the consequences.

With each phonecall, Amy had felt progressively weaker. She was finished with mothers, knew she was better off alone, but still found herself wanting to be cared for. How exhausting it was trying to remain steadfast to your principles while your desires were urging otherwise. As for Philippa Finemore, an attractive mother figure at any time, she had only made the situation worse; a good ten years older than Estelle, but short and dark like Amy, she might have been mistaken for Amy's mother. Which, given that mother figures were currently in excess, was not a helpful thought. Philippa had complicated the situation; somehow she had fed Amy's desire to see Estelle, who had been, by anyone's standards, a less-than-satisfactory parent.

But at least Amy could get rid of Philippa. And her confounded dinner. She would ring and say she was sick. Which is exactly what she should have done days ago, but with Wendy's nightly hymn to motherhood, and the mother herself humming in the background, what Amy should have done was no more than music on the wind. She would invent a stomach upset, which, with the mashing and grinding that had assailed her ever since Estelle's reappearance, was not entirely untrue.

With the problem of Philippa's dinner now solved, she went to the bathroom and showered long and hot – too hot, if the truth be known, but sometimes that is necessary, and from there to the bedroom where she dressed in jumper and jeans for a day at the library. She took up her brush and applied it to her head. The bristles hurt, she attacked harder, knowing physical pain would displace the emotion. It was a familiar device, learned as a child, when the longing for an arm about her shoulders or a shiver of warmth grew so great that she filled with a greyish churning. It was a sensation she came to dread; it would mock her for having failed to win affection, and criticize her for desiring it in the first place, and ridicule her for being upset over its absence. As a young child, in an attempt to understand the feeling, she had imagined that the big bad banksia men from *Snugglepot and Cuddlepie,* their long black tentacles waving, had invaded her. As she grew older, she identified a luke-warm expanding blandness, swirling and swelling and filling all the cavities of her body, until she grew so frightened, panic, she supposed, that she longed for some relief.

She could not remember when first she discovered pain, localized pain and carefully inflicted. It was not often required, and these days, with her life so neatly arranged, very rarely. Once, a few years ago, she had spent an entire evening with a drink opener, one of the old-fashioned type with a pointed head to puncture the lid of the can, had used it to carve an intricate basket-weave pattern on her thigh. The skill was to score the skin without drawing blood. Sitting on the bed, legs bare, with a jacket across her shoulders to blank out the cold, she had scratched and scraped at her left thigh, mesmerized by the white marks swelling into rich pink welts, feeling only the spike of the instrument, a concentrated sensation that could, and did, suppress the panic. Hours later, with the night in silence and the instrument returned to the kitchen drawer, she had sat listening to Jacqueline du Pré playing Bach, reassured that the responsible person saves herself in the best way she can.

With her scalp now burning, she put the brush away. The subcutaneous longing was, for the time being, pacified, and she turned her thoughts to breakfast. The phone rang. There was a moment of indecision, waiting, starting forward, wavering (how quickly can a life be unravelled, she thought; so long in the making, so swift in the breaking) and finally stopping until the ringing had finished. For unless she was prepared to sacrifice yet another day to a mother she did not need and a sister she did not want, she must ignore the turmoil within, push it aside, confine herself to a narrow and well-trodden path.

Besides, she had wasted enough time already. And was surely capable of withstanding a touch for which she was desperate.

She walked the short distance to her local café where she sat at her usual table, ate a breakfast of eggs, tomatoes, two slabs of buttery toast and three cups of strong tea. Ate without tasting, ate as one might scrub a floor or mow a lawn, not that Amy had ever mown a lawn, but it had always struck her as one of the more methodical and purposeful of activities, and while she ate looked through the paper, the usual political propaganda, the jittery economy, religious wars, medical triumphs measured in dollars, and wondered why she bothered, a book would be much more satisfying. Easier to handle too.

Fifty minutes later, distracted by a sore and distended stomach she left the café and made for the esplanade. It was almost deserted; the air was cool with low-slung, steely clouds and a wind from the south-west that whisked sand and dust in her face. She licked her lips and tasted salt. To her right, was the hiss and swoop of fast-moving traffic, and on the left, a crescent of choppy water all greys and greens and splashes of white. The tide was high and the beach a mere strip of cream with a few gambolling dogs with ambling owners who, at ten o'clock on a weekday morning, were either self-employed and very rich or unemployed and very poor; that she did not consider the possibility of there being others like herself walking off a fretful life was the first familiar act in an otherwise apocryphal day.

But not the last. For she felt control returning. She walked the length of the esplanade, an increasingly peaceful stroll despite her labouring digestion and the impending phonecall to Philippa. The closest she came to comfort was here, alone, in this sliver of the world, winter lurking in the wind, no people about but strangers, and she lingered a moment longer, breathing deeply, as if she could store up tranquillity for later use. Then back to the flat for her books and on to the tramstop.

It was an old tram she caught, that shook and shimmied and savoured its draughts, and seated its passengers in two long parallel lines - an absurd waste of the limited space, but a goldmine for anthropological musings. The tram trundled through a crowded shopping centre, past the spot where a few months earlier a man had lain down in the middle of the road outside the social security office. Lain down between the tram tracks, his face against the filthy bitumen. Pedestrians had stared and hurried on, drivers had swerved, sounding horns at the inconvenience, and of all the onlookers, only Amy had seen the man's anguish. And what had her percipience achieved? Certainly nothing to benefit the poor fellow. Now, as the tram rolled over where his body had been, she thought that those with vision simply do not have energy enough to act on everything they see. And, indeed, should not. Where would Amy be now if someone had adopted her struggles? Resourceless certainly, perhaps dead, maybe a born-again Christian. Although the very thought of Amy on her knees for an almighty hand and outstretched arm was laughable.

The tram lurches, screeches to a halt. A car is making an illegal U-turn across the tracks. The conductor leans out the door, shakes a fist. 'Ya bloody fool!' He yells. But the car is a Rolls Royce, and the conductor's passion only luke-warm.

The passengers shuffle in their seats, reclaim lost space, gather tumbled parcels, crane necks to see, and settle back as the tram starts moving again. The conductor does a length of the compartment. 'Bloody fool,' he mutters, 'thinks he owns the world,' and goes back to sucking his tongue. A fascinating tongue, Amy is thinking, with its tip curled under and its broad expanse of pink pimply skin sloppy and cracked like the surface of old milk.

A man boards. He has a day's beard and several days' body odour. His clothes are pressed and clean, his gold bracelet sparkles. Despite there being several vacant seats, he chooses one next to Amy, sits far too close, occupies the length of her left side, takes up the tram's rhythm, sways heavily against her. One stop, two stops and Amy has had enough. She stands abruptly, slamming her foot down on his. She does not apologize, merely shrugs as if to say 'What else would you expect?' and takes a another seat, where she remains for the duration of the journey, staring him into discomfort.

Once at the university, she goes directly to the library eager to turn her mind to something useful. She smiles at one of the librarians, avoids a tutor from whom she borrowed a book weeks before, and goes up to the second floor, to the classics section which is rarely crowded. She sets out her work on her usual desk, swaps the metal-framed chair for one of the comfortable padded ones, and settles down to read. Such relief on opening Virginia Woolf, what better occupation than this? But just a couple of pages later, and despite her resolve, she knows there will be little work that day. For Mrs Dalloway's party acts as a trigger to Philippa

Finemore's dinner and the phonecall that must be made, and Philippa's phonecall points to Wendy's evening call with its demands and accusations, and Wendy's call is a mere splinter from Estelle.

Philippa, Wendy and Estelle. And it is Estelle who remains.

Several times over the past week, Amy has found herself in imagined conversation with her mother, she's even written to her, although has had sense enough not to send the letters. She's been distracted but has appeared involved, has met her supervisor and been particularly insightful, has had coffee with friends and been entertaining, has shopped and washed and cleaned and generally led a life. All this, despite the lurking Estelle, the prodigal mother, the mythical mother, the perfect relationship, a cradle of promises, a crater of disappointments. And if it were different, Amy has been thinking, if the myths and foolhardy promises were replaced only by what was humanly possible, then mothers like Estelle could leave home with impunity, and motherless daughters like Amy would not be made to feel as if they lacked something. As it is, Estelle is everywhere; even the work that has always provided a sanctuary is besieged by her. Amy packs up her books and leaves the library, declining an invitation for coffee from Ellis who, laden with his multi-media doctorate, has just arrived. Ellis pecks her cheek and heads for the stairs, leaving Amy to ponder a depleted array of options for the day. A light rain begins to fall; she shelters her books under her coat and raises her face to the crisp, sharp drops. Her skin is hot against the chill and she wonders how quickly she might become drenched.

Suddenly she knows what to do. She pushes against the lunch-time crowds, and crosses to the conservatorium. Inside the blue-stone building, she wanders the corridors, sifting through the muted notes, peering through the small glass peep-holes in the classroom doors in search of a cello. And when one is found, slipping in quietly to sit at the back of the room. Closer to the low platform is a small audience, mainly students with lunches in laps, listening to the music, a trio, in fact, playing Brahm's tribute to the clarinet. Although Amy hears only the cello. And cushioned thus, she listens and watches the cellist, a woman, hugging the long arm of the instrument, cheek grazing the wood, left hand beating like butterfly wings up and down the strings. Watches the woman's body leaning into the great body of the instrument, her legs grasping the cello's ribs, her eyes gazing down the ebony arm, her lips mouthing the notes in the sweet low refrain, eyebrows raised and a gentle shaking of the head. And in the sonority of the long notes, the filaments of the bow almost touch her thigh in a sure caress. The music fills the still room; in the distance a clock sounds the half hour, a door bangs, and from the corridor comes a flute of laughter, but Amy hears only the cello. Until the left hand folds its wings, flutters down the strings, down and down in a lissome theme that passes through the room and is gone.

Amy leaves quickly. The main theme lingers as she walks to the tramstop; she decides that in place of Philippa Finemore's dinner she'll treat herself to an evening of Jacqueline du Pré, and feels very calm indeed. The rain has eased, although the sky is thick and ropey; with most of the afternoon still before her and not a tram in sight, she decides to walk through the park and catch the tram a few stops further on. She crosses the road and enters the park, hears the wheezing traffic recede to a steady sighing.

So, here it is, the moment: a deserted park teetering on the brink of winter, the echo of a brooding cello, people in the background busy in their fast cars, and a swag of well-trodden dreams filed at the edge of memory.

The path is spongy with sodden leaves; Amy treads carefully over the mud-splashed yellows, the browns and reds, the odd mistake of green. When she was young she had hated the autumn fall; to grow and be fresh and beautiful merely to wither and die seemed so unfair; and she was sure it must hurt. Later, when she learned this was the fate of all living things, she stopped believing in God. Oddly, with God removed, nature burst into life and became a new focus of reverence. She breathes deeply, drawing the dampness into her lungs, almost tastes the pulpy leaves. And the smell of water-logged grass, a very particular odour this, prompting a search for long pink slippery pipes of earthworm. The park benches, splashed with bird-droppings and graffiti, are deserted. Such squalid seats these, with boards missing and nails exposed, seats for squalid moments. Here's the bench on which Amy once carved her name; 'Amy V' she wrote before her fingers seized up. It was a period of her life when time was torture and not even her books brought relief, when the wire in her head had pulled so taut that the slightest tremor set it screaming. Her name written long ago on a park bench, just once, and not even finished.

The park is different for her now; once the setting for desperation, it has become a place for solitude, or relaxation, or safe passage through a moment dipped in doubt. An atmosphere so veiled – smudged sounds, trees blurred in the glaucous light of a day hurtling towards winter, the soup of smells – that your own mind can sing. She strolls onward, picking out patterns in the exposed branches, admiring as she does each winter the beauty of trees stripped of leaves. She has never been interested in finding realistic shapes in the branches, it is the designs that appeal, the accidental criss-crossings that might assume any number of images. Hard not to smile at a particularly intricate web. So she smiles.

And touches as well. Amy is not a person to touch. When you touch you are touched in return and it takes a great deal of strength not to respond to a touch for which you crave. Not even animals with their furry warmth can be touched, it is simply not worth the risk. But plants are safe, or so she has convinced herself, and the feel of a tree trunk altogether satisfying. Stiff and stretched in map-like shapes is engraved a world; she closes her eyes and slides her fingers into the bark, feeling, or perhaps only imagining she feels, the scurrying insects that hurry to safety. The flower beds are fallow, awaiting the winter planting, birds pick amongst the loam in search of the juicy pink pipes.

And here's another person. Amy, a smile still on her face and her hand exploring a tree trunk, watches a young woman enter the park from the main road to the right. A woman alone, taller than Amy and slimmer, but much the same age. From a distance of one hundred metres her face is clear, an alert, watchful face, not happy, perhaps waiting. She sees Amy and sees Amy looking her way.

Amy leaves the tree and continues slowly down the path. She

is thinking the woman might be wanting company; perhaps she's a visitor to the city, lonely, disoriented, in need of a guide. She might be Canadian, or German, maybe American; whatever her origins, Amy would be happy to show her around. The woman appears nervous, keeps looking her way, so Amy decides to look approachable, which is different from being encouraging, and continues walking. Now the woman crosses the path just up ahead, walks up the hill, sits on the damp grass. She fidgets, hands fight each other, fingers pinch the tight skin of her forearms; she looks at Amy but cannot hold her gaze. Amy feels sorry for her, she seems so nervous, so alone, but is also excited at the prospect of unexpected company.

The woman with her stuttering gaze is up on the hill, perhaps twenty metres from the path. Amy is almost parallel to her, she turns to smile, sees the awful anguish on the young face. No tourist this, Amy thinks, no visitor here, and in the same instant, the woman rises, rushes down the hill across the path just a metre or two in front of Amy, dashes to the edge of the park, now to the road, on to the road past screeching cars and miraculously to the other side where she disappears down a narrow street. Drivers forced to stop, blast their horns and move off again in a burst of irritation. And Amy replaces the image of the visitor with whom she might have passed a couple of hours, with the junkie who had expected to meet her supplier and had not.

At the end of the park, where the path meets the main road, Amy stops and looks back to where the girl disappeared. She has returned, is huddled at the corner of the street, gaze directed to the park, an expression of abject misery on her young face.

Several hours later, Amy stood at the door to Philippa Finemore's house, one hand on the door knocker, the other clutching a bag of food from her local delicatessan. If not for the girl she wouldn't be here at all, but that desperate face would not let her be. On arriving home, Amy had tried everything; had taken up a novel, then poetry, had turned to an unfinished letter, stared at the evening sea, and still she saw that clenched grimace of survival.

After fifteen minutes of du Pré and twenty minutes of Annie Lennox, Amy finally conceded she could not spend the evening alone, and with nothing else on offer but Philippa's dinner, the choice was made.

She knocked and heard a strong, middle-pitched bark. That's good, she thought, a dog would be a distraction, would help pass the evening. For now that she was standing on Philippa Finemore's doorstep, now that it was too late to change her mind, she knew it had been a madness to come. She hated meeting new people, yet was about to be confined in an unknown space with unknown others (she assumed she would not be the only guest) for an evening of inane conversation and the embarrassed silences of people who have nothing in common. She should have made more of an effort to rid herself of the junkie, after all, this was not the first junkie she had seen, nor indeed the first desperate one. What had marked this girl as different was the shock of her when Amy had been expecting someone else; and her running into the traffic. Amy had seen a dead junkie but not one in the process of being killed. Had seen no one in the process of being killed, and did not want to. Even now, the girl's face was before her, and the pleading gesture of despair.

Enough, enough. And Amy knocked again. A moment later Philippa was standing in the doorway. Over the din of the dog, Philippa invited her in.

'This is Peach,' Philippa said, patting the dog. 'And don't mind her barking, it's nothing more than a clever disguise, she's actually very nervous of strangers.'

Peach shied away when Amy held out her hand. Maybe not such a good distraction after all, Amy was thinking, and followed Philippa down the hall.

In the lounge room, she handed Philippa the bag of food that now seemed as appropriate a gift as a pair of socks. She tried to be blasé, said she'd discovered a new delicatessan, had overbought. 'Besides,' she added with the humour that was *her* disguise for nervousness, 'you might have been one of those Finemores that own the liquor shops, and I couldn't have given you wine then.'

'Of course you could, and I am.'

Amy looked at her in confusion.

'Of course you could have brought wine,' Philippa said, 'and yes, I am one of those Finemores.'

Amy turned away, walked to the other end of the room, and wished she was anywhere but here. Could the situation be any worse? The day had been bad, the week had been a disaster, and now this. For prominent amongst Amy's fistful of weaknesses was a fear of wealth. The situation had long been glaringly clear: she had brains, the rich had money and there was no question who ruled the world; she understood about their money, they certainly did not understand her mind and still they would rule the world; she had a rich sensibility, they had rich bank accounts and were judged as better than she. Within wealth's orbit, a mote of dust she was and would always be. If ever Amy won the lottery – and she never would, because fear of winning prevented her from buying a ticket – her embarrassment at having so much would make her divest as quickly as possible. And not for the joy of giving, but for the relief of not having that savage advantage. Never would she wear the jackboots of greed, never would she forgive those who did. So what was to be done, now, tonight, locked in a smallish, strange room with one of wealth's mentors, and her intellect suddenly hobbled by fear?

Yet Philippa did not look so very rich. Standing there at the kitchen bench, she seemed ordinary enough in her check wool skirt and bottle green jumper, dark skin clear of makeup, a scrape of pinkish lipstick, greying hair cut for ease rather than fashion; and the house, although comfortable, was not excessive. Nothing here to suggest wealth. Although one could never tell, particularly with mother figures, who invariably had a surprise or two in the shadow of their smile. Amy, never one for surprises, determined to be very alert. And leave as soon as possible.

The doorbell rang. Philippa and the dog disappeared up the hallway and returned with Leo Geller from the bookshop and a woman Philippa introduced as Lorraine Pascoe. Amy, now programmed to pass through the evening in her minimum-of-damage mode, was on her feet waiting. After the greetings, Leo followed

Philippa into the kitchen where he gave her a book, in lieu of flowers, he said. Amy, who had long believed that looking at someone's books was akin to peering into their underwear drawer, eyed the book in furtive snatches, while trying to charm the dog.

'I'm starving,' said Lorraine Pascoe, and lunged for the food. She loaded eggplant dip on to a crusty heel of bread and took a bite. 'This is delicious, Philippa, where'd you buy it?'

'Amy's responsible,' Philippa said. On cue, Amy looked up from the dog and smiled.

She had not had a moment since breakfast, Lorraine said. The day had been a hectic dashing from one appointment to the next, talking always talking, hardly time for coffee, much less food.

Philippa asked about the job.

'A short consultancy at International Liquor, to tidy the edges of a new product.' Lorraine shrugged, 'Poor George would turn in his grave if he knew, but I'm happy for the work and it keeps my hand in.' She piled some egg salad on to a crust. 'This really is very good.'

Philippa told Amy about Lorraine's long association at Finemore's Fine Wines and Spirits. 'Unfortunately my son and son-in-law, who now run the business, don't feel they need her.'

'Although it strikes me your boys are simply part of an expanding breed. The sons at International are just like them, and so were the ones at Just Wine. No one can tell them anything; a taste of power and they think they know it all.' Lorraine paused, the food suddenly forgotten. 'They seem to regard money and ownership as nothing more than a licence for power, and a sufficient reason for authority.'

Philippa and Leo agreed, although Philippa, with her own boys in mind, said she hoped that some of these young men would acquire more acceptable values as they matured. As for Amy, she was astonished that rich people might think this way, and listened some more.

'Although it's more than just authority,' Leo said. 'Wealth seems to command a certain respect; wealth wears a certain righteousness, a resonance of goodness. Which is not surprising, I suppose, in a society where economics has become the bedrock of culture and ownership seems to have replaced the need for character.'

Lorraine protested, Leo was being over-simplistic. 'Wealth and goodness have an uneasy association, one that's clearly revealed in the widespread suspicion that people with a lot of money have come to it in less than honest ways.'

'No, no, no,' said Leo. 'The *fact* of the money is much more powerful than the suspicion, and it is the fact of the money that defines status. No one much cares these days where the money's come from or how long the person has had it.'

Which was all quite true, Philippa said, who had met an assortment of rich men over the years who were known to have done some shady business. 'Stretched the limits of the law.' 'Tax avoidance.' 'Clever manoeuvring.' 'Slippery deals.' The euphemisms were rich in themselves, she said. She tried to explain how it was, that it was not the fact of the dishonesty that mattered to most people, but whether you managed to get away with it. 'I often heard people talk about this or that fellow who had made a lot of money. "So and so's done extremely well," they'd say. "Such a capable young man." Even when there were doubts over the young man's methods, still the admiration and praise would persist. It was only when formal charges were laid that the praise would be withdrawn. Not to be replaced with criticism mind you, more likely a silence, or the sort of hushed exchanges that accompany a death in the family. The charges generally occurred after huge money losses, but while the money was there—'

'Or thought to be there,' Lorraine corrected.

'—or thought to be there, the person was insulated. Even when charges were laid, there were still men ready to champion the person's cause. Right up until the time he was proven guilty.'

Leo helped himself to the wine. '*If* he was proven guilty. Such faith in our legal system is touching.'

'I often thought there was a certain grudging admiration if one of these fellows managed to get off.'

'George never felt like that!'

Lorraine's voice was loud, forceful, it was clear she was

defending her lover rather than her former employer. The first time she had done so, Philippa was thinking. Not that George was omitted from their conversations, rather, when Lorraine mentioned him it was in his work capacity, while Philippa confined her remarks to the family man. Lorraine's comment signalled a new direction and Philippa was happy for it.

Lorraine, however, was less sure. She was unable to meet Philippa's gaze, indeed, had joined Amy in focussing on the dog. But Peach, refusing to be just anyone's poodle, picked herself up and left the room.

'You're right,' Philippa said, 'George wasn't like that,' and to provide further reassurance, added, 'with either of us.'

Lorraine smiled, nodded gently, and Philippa, taking the lead on a topic that had, until now, been carefully avoided, said there were matters she would like to discuss with Lorraine, not now, but later, just the two of them, things she would like to know. And Lorraine said, there were things she wanted to discuss too. They arranged to meet the following Sunday: 'Early in the day,' Philippa suggested, 'there's a lot to say after all these years.' She gave an affectionate squeeze to Lorraine's hand and suggested she try the tahina.

They nibbled and sipped and returned to their money talk; whether it was possible to have power without being corrupt, whether it was possible to have money without an abuse of power, and with the dog gone and the conversation surprisingly interesting, Amy found herself joining in. The university, she said, what's happening in universities is all about money and power. 'While chairs in the humanities are being lost, new business schools, sponsored by huge corporations are being established. And that's not all. At my own university, two chairs were lost last year, one in classics and the other in Italian. During the same period, the Vice Chancellor was provided with a new residence costing in excess of a million dollars. A million dollars would have covered the cost of the two chairs with some left over, but apparently, those who make the decisions deemed the house would do more for the profile of the university than Italian language or Greek civilization.'

'Although none of this is new,' Leo said. 'The humanities have been under threat for years.'

'What's new is that as departments disappear there's hardly a whimper, almost as if the academy is condoning what's happening. Priorities have changed, perhaps even the very function of the university. These days, given that the major growth areas in universities are business studies and computer science, it would appear people really do believe an MBA is more valuable than history or literature.' Amy shrugged. 'Such is the glittering narcosis of the modern interior.'

'But tell me, when did history and literature ever generate money?'

'And when did an MBA teach one how to live the proper life?' Amy returned.

'Right now, I'd say. Although what constitutes the proper life has changed.'

'You really believe that people think economics provides a better guide for living than literature?'

'Without a doubt.'

'That the J-curve is more informative than Proust?'

'Proust *and* the Bible *and* Dostoyevsky *and* Eliot.'

'It's a descent into barbarism.' It was Philippa who spoke.

'Yes,' said Amy, 'with an underground of homeless intellectuals.'

'Intellectuals are always homeless, it's a necessary prerequisite. Look at the Jews.'

And mothers, Philippa wanted to add. But didn't. Instead she suggested they move to the table before the roast was reduced to charcoal. The conversation shifted to a discussion of nationalism and the concept of the Nation State, which was, Leo said, probably the most toxic of all human groupings. Although only a larger version of the family, said Philippa. At which point it occurred to Amy that what was happening here was not a simple airing of opinions or a swapping of facts, there was a dynamic, a momentum, a continuity, a growth, and at each new junction the number of directions increased. Rather than the usual talking for resolution, a talking that led to silence, this talk produced more talk. And the landscape they drew from was so diverse, the reference points as well. They stopped here, paused there, drew on history, philosophy, literature to explore an issue or make a point, and Amy found herself thinking, not just remembering, formulating ideas rather than a simple ordering of sources.

Over cheese and coffee the conversation turned to the practice of philanthropy.

'You've gone into a dying business,' Leo said to Philippa. 'Most people make money in order to make more money, not to give it away, and when gifts are made, too often they're for the benefit of the giver, have nothing to do with kindness towards one's fellows.' He removed his glasses, turned to Philippa. 'Take your son-in-law and this business school of his, is he sharing his good fortune with the rest of the world? Is this generosity without prejudice? Or is he acting only to stake a claim on the future? Selwyn and so many of our modern benefactors. Indeed, one has to wonder if these bricks and mortar bequests are anything other than attempts at immortality, a sort of power in perpetuity.'

Philippa turned to Amy, explained that her son-in-law was on the planning committee for the new business school at Amy's university. 'I assume he's contributing money as well as expertise, Selwyn's just the type to ensure that any contribution he made would bring tangible rewards.'

'Which is exactly my point. Selwyn and others like him will live on through their public endowments.' Leo laughed. 'Of course, we ordinary folk would think that one life was more than enough for most of these fellows.'

'Selwyn aside though, surely some good comes out of these endowments. Look at the buildings that have resulted, the scholarships and art collections.'

'I'm not so sure.' Amy leaned forward, cut a slice of cheese and proceeded to dissect it as she talked. 'It's what we were saying earlier about money as a primary means of ranking people. The possession of money accords you legitimacy for no other reason than you or your spouse or your father or your grandfather made a lot of money. You could be dissolute, which many children of the rich are, you could be shallow, which seems a necessary prerequisite for living a privileged life, you could be a very nasty piece of work, but if you have money you'll find yourself admired, appreciated, even revered. As for principles or integrity, as for caring about other human beings which is what genuine charity is all about, such attributes seem entirely dispensable.'

'But does it matter that the spirit of giving might be a bit luke-warm?' Lorraine asked. 'Surely the most important thing is that the money goes where it's needed.'

Amy disagreed. The world was not better off, she said, for a gift that emerged from graft and greed, a gift offered out of vanity and pride. 'Far from generosity, such gifts are born of meanness.'

'You talk as if there's life in the bricks and mortar,' Lorraine said.

And so there was, Amy said, for the values underscoring a gift live on. 'If charity is a form of self-aggrandisement, and if giving accords the giver social approbation, then it's arrogance and vanity that are being reinforced, not compassion and benevolence. The very idea of charity has changed. Can you really call the endowment of a business school charity? Or the donation of money for a sporting pavilion? The rich will give millions for such causes, but when it comes to real charity, when it comes to recognizing that those who have less have a right to a better life, there's never enough to give.'

'Do you think we'd be better off with a system of tithes?' Lorraine asked with a smile.

Amy ignored the humour. 'Given the rise of the welfare state, it's not feasible, but I think there was a lot to recommend it. At least the tithe recognized that charity was a matter of right – for both the giver and the receiver. These days it has taken on punishing overtones, but only for the receiver. These days, charity tends to sharpen the differences between those that have and those who don't. You ask if the spirit of giving really matters, well it does if it helps cement inequality, if it reinforces values that will keep a segment of the population oppressed and, at the same time, rewards the oppressors.'

Philippa was watching closely while Amy was speaking. What a strange young woman she was, so reserved one minute, impassioned the next. And of the two strains, it was the passion that spoke of the person while the reserve reflected the life. There was something about the girl that opposed her mighty independence and devil-may-care attitude, a soft, yet eloquent plea, that during the passionate moments reached a crescendo, and then Philippa wanted to take her into her arms and hold her there. The oddest desire and it made her skin prickle. Or perhaps that was Leo's hand on her arm.

'Is Amy right?' He was asking. 'Are your wealthy friends morally derelict?'

Philippa sighed, cut some cheese, made a sandwich with two dried apricots, nibbled, collected herself and finally spoke.

'A good many are.' And proceeded to tell them about a luncheon which illustrated Amy's point perfectly. It had been a day she would never forget, years ago, during the International Year of the Disabled, an annual charity event in support of a society for handicapped people. All the right people attended, all the right people dressed in their usual finery creating that rush of energy that tends to accompany people engaged in good works.

Lorraine laughed. 'It's the same bustle I associate with business people who are less than effective, but by virtue of their position must be seen to look busy.'

'It's in the unions, too,' said Leo.

'And the corridors of academe,' added Amy.

'It's a wonder anything gets done,' Philippa said, and returned to her story.

The press had been there, and the cameras, which made not a shred of difference to what occurred, for the society columnists, with one or two exceptions, considered themselves as much a part of the society crowd as those they wrote about. Which was a shame, Philippa said, not that it was the media's responsibility to make people think, but this particular stratum of society did less thinking than most. 'It's their pace of life, these people never stop. They go from one occasion to the next, noting what everyone's wearing, contributing to the latest round of gossip, then a quick trip home to freshen up and change before moving on to the next event. They know stillness and silence only when asleep.'

The luncheon had got off to a rousing start; the noise was tremendous even while the ladies were having drinks and savouries, and it took a considerable time for the announcement to be heard: there were to be some 'special guests'. There was much wondering as to whom they might be, after all, anyone who was in any way special was already there. There was mention of the Duchess of Kent who was in Australia at the time, and the wife of a former American president; Nureyev was in town, so, too, Joan Sutherland. Much muttering and wondering when the special guests arrived: four disabled people, three in wheelchairs and one on crutches, clients of the society for which they were raising money.

'It was a disaster. The ladies tried to put as much distance as possible between them and the disabled people; it was not right, they were saying, and so tasteless. When the first shock passed, pity was expressed for the poor handicapped people for whom such an occasion would be so foreign; we can manage, the ladies said, but it's not fair on them. And when they moved into lunch and found that the four special guests would be eating with them, actually sitting at the same tables, any hope of redeeming the luncheon was lost. People hardly touched their food, conversation was sluggish, spirits were limp, but worst of all, the disabled people knew what was happening; they did what was expected of them and left as soon as possible. After they had gone, the ladies erupted, they were furious, insulted, they behaved as if someone had played not quite fairly.'

'All of which suggests that so-called good works are quite separate from a genuine concern for those in need,' said Amy.

'And why anonymous giving is such a rarity these days,' Leo said. Suddenly he turned to Amy, 'Does the idea of philanthropy have anything to do with your thesis?'

Amy shook her head, not at all, or certainly not directly, and reached across to fill her glass. As she had intended, the conversation moved on to other matters.

It was late when they rose to leave, and later still when it was discovered that Lorraine passed almost directly by Amy's door. Sitting in Lorraine's car, Amy looked back and saw Philippa and Leo walk inside the house together. Lorraine, too, had seen, and smiled. Only when Amy was alone in her flat did it occur to her they might be lovers, and she imagined them doing all those things she had done with her tribe of partners. Sex considered at a distance assumes barbaric dimensions, becomes nothing more than a grunting, clawing, scratching, heaving, brainless activity. As quickly as she had put Philippa and Leo naked together she separated them, ashamed she could have so reduced such an enjoyable evening. And not wanting to spoil it further, willed herself to sleep.

Over the next couple of months, Amy saw Philippa increasingly often, saw Leo, too, but it was Philippa who was the main attraction. Amy developed the habit of dropping by the cottage after finishing at the university. In the first weeks of their acquaintance, she would accept only a drink or a coffee, but soon she was staying for a meal and long hours of conversation. Once they had talked so late, Philippa insisted she take a taxi home. Amy laughed, and spent the next two hours explaining what it was like to live alone in the city, trying to make clear her lack of night fears. At the end of it, Philippa still insisted that Amy take a taxi. 'You don't have to live like that any more,' she said pressing the money into Amy's hand. 'But neither can I risk acquiring unnecessary fears,' had been the reply.

What exactly it was that attracted each to the other was never articulated. Each seemed to know, almost from the beginning, what the other needed. So it was that Amy never asked for Philippa's interest, nor her affection, Philippa simply provided these. And neither did Philippa need to shape Amy's perceptions of who she was, Amy responded to a richness in Philippa that Philippa had longed to know still existed.

Often they would eat out. The local restaurateurs assumed they were mother and daughter and neither Philippa nor Amy sought to correct them; it gave a certain credibility to a friendship they did not themselves fully understand. It was a matter of trust; each behaved towards the other with a freedom lacking in their other relationships; the trust allowed for honesty, allowed for personal revelations that were often less than complimentary. For each knew the other would not condemn – which is quite different from being critical. So Amy was able to reveal her method of leading a life, her juggling of deceptions in order to remain protected, her terrible fear of rejection, the loneliness, the panic; and Philippa talked about her sense of failure, her immense sadness over Melanie and Gray; she talked too, about Leo, and her shock at such strong attraction when she thought that sort of thing was over. It was a peculiar and wondrous friendship that each guarded carefully, for neither could know where it might lead.

EIGHT

What to do with a day such as this? Take herself to bed if she were tired, or sex if Selwyn weren't part of the problem, or catharsis if there were anyone worth talking to. But with none of these options viable and time to fill, Melanie decided on the garden. She checked that the children were busy and the casserole was cooking, and went outside.

The cool of the winter evening prickled her skin, gravel bristled under foot; Melanie crossed the driveway and entered the shrubbery. Overhead, the branches were almost bare, the path was fleshy with gleaming wet leaves, and all was smothered in a strange granular light that deepened the greens and glazed the browns. Melanie had planned the gardens at Hopetoun according to a classical design, with neat box hedges modelled on those at Versailles, and a white garden designed to surpass Sissinghurst's. There was a rose walk with more than twenty varieties and an arbour that would eventually be a brilliant canopy of wisteria and climbing roses. Linking the arbour to the house was the bulb garden, a spring mosaic of freesias and hyacinths and daffodils and lilies – a dozen varieties at the very least – and tulips and nerines. A perfect garden that, because of this morning's edict from Selwyn, would not be shown, or at least not properly, not publicly. Which was just the first of the day's debacles.

And who was to blame? Gray and his shocking business sense? Philippa? Or that dreadful man from the bookshop who was such a bad influence on her mother? Or was it Selwyn? And reluctantly, but with relief because her anger needed a target, she fixed on Selwyn: his problems were at the root of it all. It was Selwyn's financial difficulties that had, over breakfast, prompted his prohibitions on showing Hopetoun; Selwyn's depleted liquid assets that had driven her to Philippa's office; Selwyn's mismanagement that had placed Melanie in the invidious position of asking favours of her mother; Selwyn's misguided priorities that had put Melanie fair and square in the path of that awful little bookshop man. And while Selwyn might complain about Gray, how he was a hopeless businessman and was ruining Finemore's, the Pryor problems were not Gray's fault, they were Selwyn's.

She shivered, but whether from cold or Selwyn's bungling she did not know. What was, however, perfectly clear was her sense of uneasiness. It was as if Selwyn had betrayed her, or rather betrayed his own solid image of himself; Selwyn, so recently a substantial Victorian building with elegant neoclassical colonnade, had become a cement-rendered bungalow, and she did not like it at all.

She returned to the house, her beautiful, newly renovated, but not-to-be-admired house, and entered the marble foyer. She was walking the perimeter of the shining white space, each piece of marble selected by her and laid according to her instructions, when suddenly it occurred to her that Selwyn might not have told her the whole truth, that this morning's warnings might only be the preface to a full-scale calamity. He had said they would have to be careful, just for a few months, no unnecessary expenses, and no house-warming just yet. But as bad as this was, could it be worse? Was he holding something back? Had Gray ruined the business? Would they have to sell Hopetoun? Could they be poor? The possibilities stirred deeply within her, she felt giddy and slightly nauseated. Then, just as quickly, the discomfort passed: hers had been a life touched only with kid gloves, being poor was simply not an option.

She wandered through the grandly restored rooms and the full force of Selwyn's restrictions hit her: the house was aching to be seen. The renovations had been finished less than a month ago, and with the exception of a few decorative pieces – an Empire clock on order, a gilt mirror on its way from Florence – the house was ready to be admired. Months ago, after compiling the guest list for the house-warming, she had met with Raymond Pasquale to discuss the menu for the party. He had looked over the house, a sensitive man strolling through the half-finished rooms 'to get the feel of the place and connect with its intrinsic character.' Being much struck by the vivid colours and the boldness of the design, he had suggested an oriental menu. Jonathon the florist, following Raymond's cue and guided by the flowers that would be available in winter, had recommended a colour scheme of red and gold.

What on earth would she say to Raymond? What was she to say to Jonathon?

'That the party has been postponed,' Selwyn had said that morning. 'Can it be so very difficult?'

More than difficult, it was impossible, but Selwyn refused to understand. Early consultations with Raymond and Jonathon had ensured that the Pryor party was already common knowledge and common expectation. It was all very well for Selwyn to talk lightly of postponement, but those in the know would realize that something was wrong; after all, in the absence of illness or death, only scandal, financial or otherwise, was reason to postpone a party. And it was never 'postpone' everyone knew 'postpone' meant 'cancel'.

Selwyn had listened to her, a solemn indulgence across his face, and when she had finished, suggested she was over-reacting. She reminded him of the Walcott's cancelled party following Hamish's indictment, and the fiasco that occurred when Oliver Price Beatty & Rowe went into receivership and Jacinta and Brendan did not cancel but should have. Selwyn conceded her point, but still would not change his mind.

'Just until the summer,' he had said, 'that's all I'm asking, and by then—'

But he did not know what he was asking and people were not fools.

'Melanie, I wouldn't be making this request unless it were absolutely necessary. Interest rates are high, I'm committed to the business school—'

'So that's it!' She could have hit him. 'You'd sully the reputation of your family because of some stupid pet project of your own!'

He had accused her of being unfair, it was more than a pet project, as well she knew. 'What you don't understand, have never understood, is that the school will provide us and our children with a standing in this city. It's a monument to the Pryor name.'

'So, too, is Hopetoun.'

'Only in the short term. But the Pryor name will be associated with the business school long after we're dead and gone. It's our legacy to the future; Hopetoun will simply pass into other hands.

Not while I have a say in it, Melanie thought, as she continued through the magnificent rooms. Because Hopetoun was *her* legacy to the future. When they bought the house, she had dedicated herself to its restoration, and in less than a year had transformed it from a frowsy aristocrat with a desolate soul, to a glittering queen of the city. This she had done, and now Selwyn was demanding she hide her creation. *Her* creation, she reminded herself as she stood in the doorway of the drawing-room, stood admiring the period furniture upholstered in a range of oriental brocades, the pair of cabinets replete with glinting ormolu mounts and intricate ivory inlays, the rococo tables with their superb ornamentation, all illuminated by two magnificent chandeliers made especially for Hopetoun to an eighteenth-century design. The parquetry floor was covered in brilliant Chinese rugs profuse with wild and mysterious floral motifs, and exotic animals, lions and leopards and peacocks, rearing at the borders. And the walls, the walls displayed her pride and joy, a complete set of the unicorn tapestries. Earlier in the year, during a quick buying trip to Europe, she had stopped off at the Musée Cluny just to satisfy herself that her set was better than the original. And it was: more vibrant, more essentially opulent, and housed in surroundings far more congenial than the vast stone fortress of Cluny. She looked at her rugs, her chandeliers, her furniture, her tapestries: Selwyn was asking too much.

From the drawing-room she passed into the dining-room, a wine-red room with heavy velvet drapes, and sat at the head of the magnficient late eighteenth-century mahogony table. She looked at the four sideboards, superb replicas of those at Blenheim, the crystal in the cabinets, the converted gas lamps she had found quite by accident when taking the children to pony club. This was her dining-room, her creation. Already she had planned her first series of dinner parties, thirty guests on each of three consecutive Saturday nights, Selwyn at one end of the grand table and she at the other, while in between would be the cream of Melbourne society.

Throughout her thirty-seven years, Melanie had always made plans, and her plans had always involved fame. As a child, she had fancied herself as an actress on the London stage, had imagined herself accepting huge sheaves of flowers from a dozen different admirers, and being fêted and famous and always very gracious. In front of the bedroom mirror, she had practised her curtseys for Royal Command Performances, and blown elegant kisses to appreciative audiences. With the assistance of Philippa's *Complete Works of George Bernard Shaw* she had become one of the great ladies of the stage, had dragooned Gray and Jeremy to the minor parts, auditioned them, clothed them and directed them so as to enhance her own superior performance. She would stage whole plays for family and friends, and was thought to be really rather good.

As she grew, she acquired other ambitions, and while fame remained on her agenda, disciplined study did not. In the mid-school years, she exchanged her drama lessons for tennis, and the youth theatre for skiing. The attractions of tennis, skiing, dieting, shopping, gossiping, party-going meant a revision of priorities, so, on leaving school she decided on a career in public relations. But while she was good at public relations, she knew that no PR person ever earned more than a disappointingly brief shot of fame.

The only person she knew with a recognized public life was her father. George Finemore, while not famous in the sense of an actor or singer or royalty, had position, and every one acknowledged it. This, she decided, was fame Australian style, which suited her perfectly well, for being a big fish in a little pool was, so she told herself, preferable to life as a sardine. From early childhood until her marriage, she spent as much time as possible with her father, which, given his hectic schedule, was never enough. Most of all, she looked forward to those occasions when Philippa was visiting her sister in Sydney and the boys were occupied and she and her father would dine out, just the two of them. They would go to his favorite restaurant, which George said was the city's best; Roland would greet them at the door, show Mr Finemore and Miss Melanie to the best table, suggest the best food (George Finemore never bothered with the menu) and always they would finish with the famous chocolate soufflé, even though as a child she did not much like what seemed to be more air than chocolate, and as a young woman at war with a rebellious body would have preferred to avoid chocolate altogether. Dining out with George Finemore in a grand restaurant at ten years of age was a great happiness, and while it still brought pleasure at the age of twenty, Melanie decided she wanted more from life than reflected fame as the Finemore daughter.

On first impression, Selwyn Pryor did not accord with fame, he had no background to speak of and his present connections were indisputably flimsy, but closer scrutiny of Professor Selwyn Pryor showed him to be a person of promise. He was young, although not too young, and attractive with a muscular ambition. As for his being an academic, it added a dimension of culture that Melanie saw to be lacking in George and his circle. Melanie was twenty when she met him, and with the London stage decanted to memory, and public relations little more than a means of filling in time, she turned her attention to Selwyn Pryor and her social position. And had continued to do so for the next seventeen years. She had attached the Pryor name to the best charities, the best schools and the best holiday resorts; she had built the name from nothing. The business school was all very well as a means of lodging the Pryor name in the future of the city, but glory once you were dead lost much of its sparkle. Melanie wanted her glory now, and that meant Hopetoun.

Her footsteps sounded hollow in the huge ballroom. An empty

room designed only for pleasure has a sadness about it and this room, more than all the others, was crying out for people. And so was Melanie. This morning, before leaving for work, Selwyn had stood behind her, his hands on her shoulders, his thumbs rolling rhythmically over her neck.

'It won't be long,' he said. 'Just a short-term precaution while money is tight.' He straightened his tie and took up his briefcase. From the door he looked back. 'I suppose you realize none of this would be necessary if it weren't for your mother. It infuriates me, all that money—'

'All *our* money.'

'Yes, all our money.'

After he had gone and the children had left for school, Melanie made another coffee – the day's caffeine quota exhausted by nine o'clock – and retired to her sitting-room. It *was* their money, this whole Foundation lunacy was built on their money. And it was not as if Philippa were short of a penny, with the income from the properties, she would be waist-high in cash. Melanie had never gone cap in hand to anyone, but when it was her money, it was quite a different matter.

Only later did it occur to her she should have rung Philippa first, but never before in her thirty-seven years had she made an appointment to see her mother and had no intention of starting now. Besides, she wasn't to blame for the embarrassment at the Foundation, that awful little man wasn't *her* friend, he wasn't visiting her.

'Melanie and I have some family business,' Philippa said when the man barged in. 'I'll come down later when we've finished.'

Melanie saw those blue eyes glaring, felt the sludge of condescension slide all over her. Then he left and soon afterwards, so did she, having got what she wanted and more besides. Even now she could still feel his clinging gaze, the small dark man with the bright blue eyes, the man who was a shopkeeper, a nobody, a fungus on the Finemore fortune, who dared look at her with scorn.

She moved through the ballroom to the salon, and from there to the atrium and a seat beneath the darkening sky. She reminded herself that she had got what she wanted, and would have her party. As for that awful little man, she need never see him again. And the money? Well whose was it anyway?

'Your daughter wasn't too happy to see me.'

Philippa shrugged. 'It's more likely she wasn't happy to see me. Seems I do nothing these days to please her, most of the time she's not even interested.'

'She's interested enough when it comes to your money.'

'It's family money, Leo. I know George left it to me, but the children do have a right to it.'

The waiter arrived with menus and a determination to be of assistance. He explained the specials, gave them his choices, told them what he would recommend if it were a Friday, was about to provide his recommendations for every night of the week, when Leo interrupted and sent him on his way. With the waiter gone, Leo directed his gaze to the menu and his thoughts to Philippa's family.

For they did not appreciate her. Melanie only contacted her mother when she wanted something: baby-sitting, home-made biscuits, and, today, money, and while Philippa might insist this was all children ever wanted from their parents, Leo remained unconvinced. From his perspective, Philippa was nothing more than a sump for Melanie's comfort. Melanie knew only how to take from her mother, or rather, only wanted to take from her; it astounded him that a woman as generous as Philippa could have a daughter so mean. Which was not to suggest that he thought the Finemores exceptional. Most families seemed to be machines of disparate parts, united only by a common function and a shared name. A casual survey of his friends had shown that the only good relationships between adult children and their parents occurred when they lived apart – different cities, different countries, or, better still, different continents, as if the familial function could only survive with restricted information about the cogs and fuels of each member's life. Although there were exceptions; of Philippa's three children, Jeremy could withstand the demands of proximity and yet he was now in London. But, in general, what parents really wanted to know about their children? – unless, of course, the children were replicating the parental life. And what children really wanted to know their parents? Yet the family unit persisted, on the well-oiled momentum of illusion, deceit and habit, an exquisitely efficient machine that forged ahead irrespective of the individual actions of its parts. Which suggested that Melanie could probably do as she liked.

Now, if Amy Vaughan were Philippa's daughter . . . Indeed, if all of us could choose our parents as we choose our friends and lovers.

He looked at Philippa as she studied the menu, and knew that such unlikely thoughts as these could only be evoked by his feelings for her. Philippa's family was exploiting her and Leo did not like it. He knew he had no claim over her, but almost in spite of himself was wanting her company, needing it, was beginning to regard Philippa Finemore as essential to his well-being; his life was spilling its boundaries and he was doing nothing to stem the flow. She made him feel – what? Engulfed? Dissolved? Vibrant? How to find a single perfect word? She touched him, not with a warm water blandness, but a graze that demanded attention. He had a sense of excess and yet, simultaneously, a restraint, a repose – not waiting, nor particularly watching, but actively existing, the fragments of a life coming together, and being aware of it as if for the first time (*Little Giddens* so often remembered). With other people, familiarity bred fatigue, but with Philippa, the reverse was happening: his pleasure increased the better he knew her. It surprised him, excited him too. How thrilling it was to feel something, the very existence of which he had doubted; and how agreeable was the absence of craving, of being so absorbed in what he had that even desire was nullified. She was an exceptional woman, or so it seemed to Leo, a lush brew of audacious intellect and zesty spirit; to reduce her to shortbread biscuits or baby-sitting on Saturday night or a hand-out every now and then as Melanie was content to do, was to deprive oneself of an uncommon experience.

He was not a religious man, yet recognized in Philippa something he might call a soul, an otherness of great depth, intangible, but certainly not unknowable. At a time when so many people were putting so much energy in suggesting complexity where none existed, Philippa was a welcome anachronism. She did not disguise bits of herself with bright and irresistible tinsels, she was a person without artifice, without narcissism, without an all-consuming ego, and it made her startlingly honest. She seemed to lack that porousness so common in other people which blended them with their surroundings and to one another. She was distinctive, not a physical thing, for as a small woman she was easily overlooked, but more a matter of character; she stood apart from her environment, pursuing the new and foreign where others embraced a culture of stupifying predictability. Philippa knew that to understand was a matter of vision, that burdened as we are by a ballast of conformity, we increasingly fail to notice the ordinary. She saw nuances and meanings in everyday moments and events that others, myopically scuttling around in their highly regulated lives, failed to notice.

How, with her background, she could have become the person she was, remained a mystery to Leo, particularly when she insisted she had not suffered in her life with George. It had been claustrophobic, she admitted that, but she lived it because it had to be lived, and when it no longer was an imperative she returned to the white hopes of her youth, pleased to find they were still as sharp and urgent as they had been forty years earlier. 'But can you put your life on hold for forty years?' Leo had asked. She thought for a while; no, she said at last, you can't. 'So, how did you survive?' Again there was a long pause, and then she told him about certain moments so intense they will sustain you through the deadening times. She told him about Dora, her mother-in-law who wrote poetry, and the excursions to St Kilda pier; she told him of the wonder of young children discovering the world, and the pleasure in a child's face when she wakes and sees you waiting by the bed. She told about older children juggling their independence who will nestle in your arms with the relief and trust of babies. She told him about a trip she had made soon after Melanie had left school when she had lived enough in three months to nourish her for the next several years. 'You can store up life,' she said, 'like a bear stores sustenance for the long hibernation.' She had related many such moments while Leo watched and listened, soaking up her life, soaking up Philippa Finemore.

Leo was wary of love, not the sentiment, but its preposterous associations. After all, one cannot possibly love one's breakfast cereal, a clever greeting card *and* Philippa Finemore. Our poor famished language, our poor collapsing brains which would make of love a parody of itself. So what then was this sentiment he harboured for her? He, Leo Geller, a divorced, childless, Jewish bookseller, what did he feel for Philippa Finemore, wealthy widow, mother, grandmother, philanthropist? What to call the joy on seeing her, when, with other women, anticipation had always been enough? And the fervour of their conversations, punctuated by those eloquent silences of hers when he would feast on her face, the dark eyes as they gathered their visions, the eyebrows arching with curiosity, the mouth puckered in thought, the lips smiling their understanding, engraving it all on his mind for when he was once again alone?

'What is it, Leo?' She was touching his arm, the menu had fallen to the table. 'Are you all right?'

He was, yes, he was, but was not accustomed to strong emotion and not sure what to do with it.

They consulted the menu, and Leo, who, often these days, found himself acting like an obsessed teenager, decided to order the same as Philippa. For there are many ways to share a life.

'You shouldn't judge me on how I am now,' she would warn, 'there were forty years of someone quite different.'

Not really, he would reply, by her own admission, that was not true.

'I played my part well, Leo, and I doubt that even you would have seen through it. But whether contrived or not, you can't ignore those forty years, they're continuous with the present, help form it.'

She still had a family, was still a mother, and the very fact of the forty years helped ameliorate the pain of not being what her children would have her be, of not having the children she had wanted to produce.

'Such are the grotesque claims of family.'

'No, Leo, it's not that simple. You always want your children's happiness. No matter what they do, you always want them to be happy.' She paused for a moment. 'It's the peculiar alchemy of motherhood.'

Ropey discussions they would have, sprawling, strenuous ideas, shaped and shaped again. How happy she made him, and yet happiness was not something he had ever sought. It had always seemed an end-state, a destination, which, for a man on the move, was never an attraction. But with Philippa, the essence of happiness was different, it was dynamic, changing, a luminous state, forever acquiring new tints.

It was still quite early when they left the restaurant. As they walked home, he linked his arm through hers as he usually did these days, felt her move in closer, touched lightly the bare skin on the innerside of her wrist. Felt too, the trembling high in his stomach, an emotional trespasser that had followed Philippa into his life. But not the only one. There were tinglings and thumpings and shiverings and quiverings and beatings, enough to suggest that the hordes of scientists who were earning their keep on the gambit that emotions were all a matter of biochemistry, were heading in the right direction.

'You're trembling,' she said when they reached her house. 'Or is it me?'

They stepped inside, shut the door, and in the narrow hallway she turned to him, her arms outspread, a vague smile on her beautiful lined face, and in the unlit passage they held each other.

Leo did not stay for coffee, he wanted to leave while her small soft frame was scored against his, the arms with the fine lacy texture, the tissue-fine skin of her neck, the downy suppleness of the cheeks, the crêpe-soft touch of the lips.

Can you store all this in memory? He wondered as she closed the door.

Selwyn stood at the bar pouring the evening drinks, a Scotch for him and a brandy and soda for Melanie. It was later than usual, which was not surprising given the eventful day. He had accomplished a lot in his forty-eight years, success in the academic sphere, a reputation for innovation in the commercial, but today's achievement surpassed them all. He knew Melanie was still brooding over their breakfast row, but he refused to allow her mood to contaminate his, particularly as his request for moderation had been perfectly reasonable.

Although now, twelve hours and a major triumph later, he was prepared to forgive. He added ice to the drinks, two blocks for him and one for her, and paused a moment, elbows resting on the marble, chin cupped in hands. An excellent day. Even Gray and his torrential inanities had failed to irritate. As for Melanie, she would come around, she always did. For she wanted his happiness even more than her own, and knew how strongly committed he was to the business school.

'The Selwyn Pryor Business School.' He uttered the words aloud for the first time. Or perhaps, 'The Selwyn Pryor School of Business' was better. Although there was an obvious temptation to abbreviate that to the Pryor SOB and that wouldn't do at all. No, his fellow directors had been right. And he said it again: 'The Selwyn Pryor Business School.' It was so much more than he had expected. Privately he had hoped for a Pryor Chair of Economics, at the very most a Pryor building, but that the entire school would be dedicated to him had been, before today's directors' meeting, merely the stuff of dreams.

He sipped his drink, swilled the ice-cold fire around his mouth and swallowed. Good Scotch should be taken without mixers, Selwyn had once heard someone important say, and ever since had been training himself to enjoy a sensation that always seemed too large for his mouth. The second taste was an improvement, the mucosa having been greatly anaesthetized, and he sipped again. He realized how extensive the lobbying on his behalf must have been, and made a mental note to invite Sir Charles Scurry, Ronald and Homer, the three he guessed had spear-headed his honour, for lunch. Separately of course, and very soon.

The Selwyn Pryor Business School, it was the start of something big, something great. The sclerosis of education, for which the absurd politics of the 1960s and the navel-gazing of the 1970s must take the blame, would gradually be healed. What Selwyn and his fellow directors had planned was education founded on sound values and good commercial principles; an educational facility set up as a limited shareholding company, a sensible user pays system, and a policy that recognized tertiary education was definitely not for all. For Selwyn knew he was not alone in recognizing that neatly stratified societies functioned best; some people were made for money and success, others were not, and there was little point in wasting good education on the losers. Order was what was required, ordered social arrangements in which everyone knew their place.

Indeed, a desire for order had been the attraction of economics in the first place. Unfortunately, economics, like all branches of applied mathematics, had suffered badly in recent years. Conciliation, conflict resolution and group problem solving might have a place in air-filled disciplines like psychology, but not economics. The Selwyn Pryor Business School would mark a return to conservative educational values, with a sensible organization where everyone had clearly defined goals and individualized strategies for achieving those goals. In planning the school, Selwyn and his co-directors had drawn on the best ideas from the United States and Europe, and combined these with the post-entrepreneurial spirit of efficiency and leanness that typified the contemporary Australian commercial scene. In fact, now that he thought about it, a more advantageous name might be The Selwyn Pryor Business School of Australia. He would suggest it to his fellow directors.

The effort that had gone into the planning of the school was well-reflected in the range of study programmes to be offered. There were group concessions for overseas students, tax deductibility for local students, special deals for large companies, different special deals for middle-sized companies, intensive study, full-time MBAs to be completed in sixteen weeks, part-time MBAs to be completed in time frames varying from eighteen months to five years, with an incentive-based fee scale to encourage students to opt for the shorter courses. The Selwyn Pryor Business School of Australia (yes, the national identification was perfect!) would be the centre of excellence for business-related studies in the southern hemisphere, the northern as well.

Selwyn had long been convinced that with the right marketing strategy they would attract enrolments from Europe, Japan and the United States. The courses on offer would equal the best available in those countries and, in addition, there was the congenial Australian climate. Already there were agreements with local tennis and golf clubs for temporary memberships for business school students, and negotiations were proceeding with a number of the city's men's clubs. Where else in the world could one take out a degree of the highest academic standard and, at the same time, polish up those extra skills essential to the well-rounded businessman? Which was not to suggest the courses were restricted only to males, not at all; the directors had prided themselves on being progressive, and all prospective students would be evaluated on their merits.

Selwyn was excited. Now that the designer pubs were running themselves and Finwest was easing his most pressing financial problems, he could give the business school his full attention. And while his efforts to date had brought him nothing but pleasure, the honour so recently bestowed would ensure even greater enjoyment. An unparalleled honour, and it was not simply the money he had pledged, although at 2.2 million that was considerable, he knew his academic credentials had also stood him in good stead.

'Selwyn understands the meaning of academic excellence,' Professor Homer Jenkins of the Department of Economics had said that evening in the discussion that had preceded the unveiling of the business school's name.

'And he knows that universities must serve the needs of the community,' said Ronald Debets of Neptune Rubber.

'Selwyn knows business *and* he knows the academy,' said Sir Charles Scurry, former Vice Chancellor and Chairman of Directors for the new business school, 'which is why he's been so valuable to this enterprise. Selwyn Pryor represents everything our new business school stands for, it's a name one associates with free enterprise, excellence in learning, and extraordinary generosity. As such, the name of Selwyn Pryor is an ideal choice for Australia's newest and finest educational institution.'

And while Selwyn had agreed with everything that had been said, he was nonetheless surprised; fame, it would seem, was not as elusive as he would have thought, although no less satisfying.

Time to share it, he now decided, and with a glass in each hand went to tell Melanie of his honour; despite the constraints it had put on their finances, he knew she would be thrilled.

NINE

'Perhaps the boys should just be done with it and divide the business.'

Brother Trevor rose from the prie-dieu and adjusted his robes.

'After all,' he continued, 'there's plenty for two companies, two very substantial companies.'

'Break up Finemore's?' Evelyn returned to her chair and performed some discreet adjusting of her own. 'It's almost unthinkable, but it may be the eventual outcome. For the sake of the family.'

Brother Trevor put a comforting arm about her shoulder. 'It helps to talk these things over.'

Evelyn nodded vigorously. Just twenty minutes ago, the family problems had been as formidable and intemperate as a thick fog; now, whilst no less aware of the gravity of the situation, she felt stronger, more able to see the situation clearly. And what she saw was the Finemore family sheltering in a den of deceit, pretending all was safe and sound, while the elements gathered outside - in the executive offices of Finemore's Fine Wines and Spirits to be precise. Brother Trevor might well be right, Finemore's might be the price of saving the family. 'Although,' and this had just occurred to her, 'it's difficult to imagine how the business could be split to the satisfaction of both the boys, and unless they believed the division to be fair, the family would still be in jeopardy. No,' she said, 'there has to be another way. Besides, it's almost impossible to think of the Finemore family separate from the Finemore business.'

'Let's join Marion. She has a talent for fixing family friction.'

Evelyn smoothed her hair and brushed down the fine wool skirt. She and Brother Trevor left the room together and joined Marion in the kitchen.

'The problems between Gray and Selwyn haven't improved.' Brother Trevor put a hand on his wife's plump shoulder. 'We thought you might have some ideas.'

Florid, frumpy Marion poured tea and dispensed pikelets, and with everyone provided for, listened while Evelyn recounted the latest dramas at Finemore's Fine Wines and Spirits.

'The boys don't talk to each other. They're supposed to be running a business together but they don't talk. In fact, whole weeks can go by without a word passing between them. They've never had all that much in common, but while they're still managing in family situations, they're not even trying to maintain appearances at Finemore's. I've no idea who's running the business.'

'What about the Pascoe woman?'

'Gone, long ago.'

'But if they're both doing their jobs, is there a problem?'

'That's just it, I don't think they can be doing their jobs.'

When Selwyn wasn't renovating his house, he was building his new business school. As for Gray, after trailing Selwyn for months, which had markedly affected his own productivity, he'd turned his attention to his connoisseur wines and had done little else since; and while Evelyn was pleased to see her husband so happy, such exclusive dedication to anything had its costs. One series, the *Fin de Siècle* series, had already been launched, and the second would be available in time for Christmas. 'And he's keen to establish his own wine and food society as well. But that won't run Finemore's.'

Brother Trevor held out his cup for more tea. Waited while Marion poured for him, added sugar and stirred, took another pikelet and turned to Evelyn. 'I'd like to know more about this wine and food society.'

As would Evelyn. Although it was not a new idea, Gray had always fancied himself as host to wine and food sophisticates, had for years dabbled with his fantasy, made lists of possible members, had once or twice even inspected potential premises. The idea had gathered momentum in recent months because of developments at one of Selwyn's designer pubs. Gray had noticed decreasing stocks of some of his best wines and had followed up the orders to this particular establishment. He had then supplied the pub with an increasing variety of top-of-the-range wines and noticed a dramatic increase in sales - patrons too, but that was not his main interest. What he was considering now was the transformation of the pub into a properly constituted wine and food club.

'But aren't the designer pubs Selwyn's jurisdiction?'

'Strictly speaking, yes, but he seems to have lost interest.'

'So Selwyn must be running the main part of Finemore's.'

'That's just the problem. As far as I can determine, no one's running Finemore's. I ask Gray who's looking after the wholesale area, which accounts for around 80% of revenue, I ask and ask, and he prevaricates a bit or tells me I shouldn't worry about such things or simply says that the wholesale business runs itself. And yet it's clearly not running itself. The half yearly profits were down for the first time in Finemore's history, and while Gray says it's to do with interest rates, I know for a fact the business has never had large borrowings. As far as I can work out, and believe me it's not easy getting the information, revenue from sales is down, and no one is doing a thing about it.'

'So what exactly is Selwyn doing?'

'Building a business school, renovating a house, spending money. As for his source of cash, if anyone has interest repayment problems I expect it's Selwyn. Unless, of course, he has an income that none of us knows about.'

Evelyn had never trusted Selwyn, he was a man without scruples and she wouldn't put it past him to engage in a little financial hanky panky - nothing that was actually illegal, he was too smart for that, but a little stretching of proprieties in his own interests. Perhaps some secret investments or some fancy playing on the stock market; more than once she'd heard him mention junk bonds, perhaps he was a player. But whatever he was doing, it was yielding cash, and plenty of it.

'You don't think he could be siphoning funds from Finemore's?' Marion asked.

Evelyn looked at her with surprise, fraud and the Finemores didn't bear thinking about. 'I don't see how he could, don't see how he could hide it. He'd have to get past the internal accounting systems, external audits, biannual profit and loss statements, I just don't think it's possible. More to the point, I don't think he'd stoop quite that low.'

'Borrowing then, perhaps he's borrowing from the company.'

Evelyn shook her head: for the same reasons, it would be impossible to hide.

Before Marion could ask another question, Brother Trevor turned the conversation back to Gray's plan for a wine and food club.

'I hope he doesn't go ahead with it,' Evelyn said, 'it would only move him further away from the essential Finemore operations.'

'Unless he were able to share the responsibility of a club, perhaps run it as a joint venture. That would leave him plenty of time for Finemore's, and still provide him with the enjoyment of his own club.'

For Brother Trevor had some plans of his own. The congregation had doubled in the past eighteen months, and he and Marion were living better than ever before. But if the church were to continue its growth, an infusion of entrepreneurial spirit was required. He had watched with interest the expansion of the new Christian churches and the concurrent diminishing of the traditional denominations, and it was obvious what the people wanted. They wanted entertainment, they wanted to be lifted out of the everyday in their connection with God, and they wanted to enjoy themselves. So, if you could make a holiday or a rock concert into a religious experience the worshippers would be there in droves, or dining out or an interest in wine.

He could see it already, The Wine and Food Society of God; his flock would grow, the revenue for his church would grow and everyone would be happy. Little did Trevor Potter realize the diversity of his calling all those years ago when he trained for the Anglican church, but, in recent years, the message had been clear: unless he were amenable to change he, like so many of his peers, would be preaching to a dwindling congregation of ageing members. As it was, Brother Trevor's flock was thriving, and the fastest growing segment was not the very young nor the very old, but the affluent thirty to forty-five year olds looking for new experiences. A high-class Christian wine and food club was bound to appeal.

'I think it's time I met Gray,' Brother Trevor now said to Evelyn. 'I've never told you before, but I have a very great interest in fine wines and good food myself; your husband and I have a lot in common.'

Evelyn blushed, picked at a pikelet, started to speak, once, twice, three times, and gave up.

'Now, now Evelyn, you worry unnecessarily. A little lie in the service of the Lord would, I think, be permissible in this case. Invite Marion and me to dinner, explain that Marion is a member of your cake decorating class and because of my interest in wine and food I wanted to meet Gray, whose reputation is well known to me.'

'I'd wanted to keep you special,' Evelyn's voice was sad, 'separate from the rest of my life.'

'But if I can help you and Gray with your problems—'

'As you have already,' Evelyn added quickly.

'If I can help in other ways, it's my duty to do so.' He turned to his wife. 'What does our calendar look like?'

Marion consulted her diary and gave Evelyn five different dates over the next month. After that there was nothing more to say. The three of them rose from the table, Brother Trevor linked arms with both women and together they sidled down the narrow passageway. At the door, Marion stood on tip-toe to place a kiss on one of Evelyn's cheeks, and Brother Trevor applied a priestly pat to the other.

'Let me know as soon as possible which date suits,' little Marion says, 'there's such a demand on Trevor's time.'

And Evelyn leaves them standing close in the doorway, takes a last longing look before starting the Mercedes and heading for home.

It was only as the waiter poured the coffee, that Evelyn Finemore allowed herself to relax. And why not? The meal had been excellent, the conversation couldn't have been better, and everyone had played their part to perfection. Marion had provided a humorous description of their cake decorating class, and Brother Trevor, or rather, Trevor, had been witty, urbane, in short, his perfect self. Gray was clearly very impressed; a man of good taste, he had said, over Trevor's selection of a Levine Slopes semillion to accompany their seafood entrée; a man after his own heart, he had said, at Trevor's choice for the dessert wine. And Trevor had described Gray's choice of a 1977 Canning Creek Shiraz Grenache for the main course as visionary.

It had been Marion's suggestion they eat out. 'The restaurant environment will show them how much they have in common. It'll open them up, bring them together.'

And so it had, not the least because Trevor's choice of restaurant had matched Gray's. 'Must be a discerning sort of fellow,' Gray said to Evelyn when she relayed Trevor's suggestion. 'You did say he was a clergyman?' Evelyn nodded. 'What denomination?'

'Ours. Anglican.'

'Must be feeling the pinch. People are deserting the church in droves.'

Evelyn spoke with care. 'Not his church apparently. Marion tells me their numbers are increasing. A youngish crowd, people in their thirties and forties who are wanting a spiritual dimension to their lives.'

'He must have come up with a formula that's escaped most of his colleagues.'

Evelyn nodded vigorously, 'I think he has.'

'And Marion, his wife, been at your class long?'

'Oh yes, she was there from the beginning. Almost.'

That was a week ago, and now they were drinking coffee and

sipping a 1976 port at a well-placed table at *Le Beau Monde*. Both men were very jovial, very sympatico. When one leaned forward, so did the other, if one laughed the other followed. And when Marion and Evelyn went to powder their noses between noisettes of lamb with brandy and rosemary and a bavarois with warm raspberry sauce, they returned to find their husbands had changed places, that Gray's large blondness was now seated alongside Brother Trevor's brown softness.

'Hope you ladies don't mind,' they said.

And of course they didn't. Or said they didn't, but as Evelyn watched Gray with Brother Trevor, the two men so close, talking, laughing, occasionally touching, she couldn't help but feel she had lost something.

From the beginning, conversation had focussed on the men's shared interest in wine and food. After the initial mention of mutual acquaintances to establish each other's credentials, they moved on to restaurants: how X was better than Y, and Z was dreadfully over-rated; and then to restaurant specialities: the poached rockling in champagne at Bruno's, the stuffed quail at Marijke's, the seafood ravioli at Mario's; and from there on to wine.

The men ranged the fertile slopes of the Australian wine growing districts and most of the French. They assessed the local industry as being in excellent shape. 'Full-bodied,' joked Trevor, 'And ripe,' added Gray, 'the reds especially.' 'Although there's been a marked improvement in the whites over the last decade,' Trevor was quick to note, 'with more fruit and less front of palate sugar.' Gray agreed. 'All to our benefit,' said Trevor, and ordered a Sauterne.

Trevor told Gray about his wine and food society, and then asked about Gray's. 'You belong to the Royal, don't you?'

Gray nodded. An excellent organization, he said, although a little conservative for his taste. The wine list, while sound, lacked imagination, and the food tended toward the unadventurous.

'Mine's the same,' Trevor said, 'but given all these clubs grew out of the British tradition, it's not really surprising.'

'No, not surprising at all.'

'Although, I would have thought your being president would have allowed you to make some changes.'

'Not many, I'm afraid. There's tradition and there's the committee and both have the determination of Churchill. Between you and me, a lot of the old guard would have a stroke if the mixed grill were removed from the lunch menu.'

Everyone laughed.

'What you ought to do is start a club of your own,' Trevor said. 'Do it properly from the beginning, attract only those people whose expectations have not been shaped by the old ways. A club whose *raison d'être* really is food and wine. You could even open membership to women. Now wouldn't that be a pioneering idea?'

Marion smiled at her husband, while Evelyn, now realizing where the conversation was leading, tried to appear jolly, even though she was feeling, if not betrayed, certainly bereft.

'I recognize a pioneering spirit when I see one,' Trevor continued. 'I have to. After all, my work is with people. And I'll tell you something, Gray, my young people would really appreciate the sort of social scene a club like yours would offer. My young people aren't interested in singles bars, a good many of them aren't single anyway, and often a restaurant doesn't suit them. They're looking for a home away from home, a place where they can relax and enjoy the fruits of their labour.'

Gray asked how these young people earned their money.

'The professions mainly, but also business and a few academics.'

'Children?'

'Not many.'

'I've an idea,' Marion said suddenly, turning to her husband. 'Why don't you invite Gray and Evelyn for Sunday evening service.'

'Excellent suggestion, then you can see for yourself the kind of person who'd be attracted to a truly modern wine and food society.'

Evelyn looked to Brother Trevor. Please, not this, she was thinking, but he didn't see her, being wholly occupied as he was with Gray, who thought it a fine idea. Arrangements were made, a light meal at Marion and Trevor's beforehand and supper with the congregation afterwards.

And so the seeds were sown. Within a month, Finemore's Faithful Pty. Ltd., the company behind the first new wine and food society to be founded in the city for over a quarter of a century had been established. There were four major shareholders: Marion and Trevor on behalf of the church, and Evelyn and Gray on behalf of themselves – or rather, on behalf of Gray. For Evelyn, the club represented only loss and sadness and a pain she was resigned to suffer in silence.

TEN

Amy Vaughan stood on a stool in front of the bathroom mirror. She moved up and down, to left and right, she observed arms and legs and head and torso, particularly the torso that preposterous hulk, and knew the outfit wouldn't do. She looked neither serious enough nor conservative enough (nor slim enough nor elegant enough, but these were not, she had decided, the criteria uppermost in the selection committee's collective mind), and while hiding her hair in a plaited bun would help, and a discreet use of makeup, these would not compensate for all the rest. For no matter how elegant the hair or delicate the makeup, the black jumper with the beaded yolk together with the Indian print skirt produced entirely the wrong effect. What was required was an outfit in nonchalant beiges and pale greens, a skirt, but not this one, and a blouse and jacket; what was required were the tailored and predictable insignia of steady, serious, intellectual habits.

After years of applying for scholarships, Amy was adept at reading the subtext of application guidelines. Although the British Scholarship information devoted several pages to the scholastic brilliance that was the major requirement of the successful candidate, Amy had learned long ago that when scholarship applicants were awash with high distinctions, as those for the British Scholarship undoubtedly were, one student's high distinctions were much the same as the next's; other criteria, therefore, were used to select the winner. Besides, if it were a simple matter of scholastic brilliance, then Amy was well-served by her academic record, the half dozen letters of recommendation all testifying to her exceptional intellect, and the samples of work she had included as part of her application materials. It was a rounding out of her abilities that was required, and a highlighting of those qualities that would convince the committee of her suitability as an emissary for Australia. In short, given the prestige of this scholarship, she needed to demonstrate that despite her lame beginnings, her state school education and her early independence, she could deport herself as well as any conventionally raised, privately educated, well-to-do applicant.

The clothes mattered; specifically, the right clothes would provide the reassurance that was lacking in her biography. Philippa would know what to wear, but Amy did not want her help, not in this; the whole business of clothes was a fraught one that Amy knew showed her at her worst. Besides, she wanted to surprise Philippa with success. Or conceal her failure if need be.

She had reached the short-list of five, which, considering the lack of money, religion and good works in her background, was commendable. Church attendance and involvement with Community Aid Abroad would have been an advantage, although her association with the Salvation Army had clearly impressed them. What she had failed to explain, and fortunately neither had Major Bednall in her letter of support, was the reciprocal nature of this association. In the early years when money had been scarce, the Salvos had meant she didn't go hungry, and if she helped them out in return, that only seemed fair. They were hard years; she had hated college life and relinquished her scholarship after a semester, and while part-time work was available, it was impossible to earn enough to eat, pay the rent, and have sufficient time left to study for high distinctions. In those days the Salvos had been her salvation, and might still be.

The art of writing a good application is to make creative use of the truth and Amy prided herself in this regard. It was the interview stage which she found difficult: persuading the committee members she was exactly what they wanted, even when they were not yet sure what that might be. The committee of six comprised five men from conventional, privileged backgrounds and one woman, a lecturer in English literature and one of the very few working class winners of the award. Amy felt her own unorthodox circumstances together with her area of study would recommend her to the latter, but she'd need to harness all her resources to win the support of the others. For while the information material spoke of the committee's desire to award the scholarship to a student from an 'untraditional background', what they had in mind, Amy was sure, was the church-going, social-service-minded child of Vietnamese immigrants who had worked hard and made good. A street-wise child with no parents to speak of, who had worked hard to get this far and needed the scholarship to make good, would be, in the opinion of some of the committee members, too untraditional. Which was why the right clothes mattered.

Amy wanted this scholarship; it meant escape from Estelle and Wendy and an end to their grotesque demands, it meant the best teachers in the world and a good degree; but most of all, it meant she could quit Australia before it was too late to make something of her life. At twenty-five, after years of work and little to show for her pains, she found herself running out of breath. She observed her surroundings much like a ship-wrecked soul, who, having made it to dry land, finds nothing there to support life. As for the energy to leave, it takes the alien and threatening, like Estelle's reappearance, to drag you to your feet and set you going once more. Amy knew she was trying to escape a situation that was beyond her, knew also she was wanting to invigorate a life grown yellow with effort. But then she'd always been one to recognize her limitations. The scholarship would remove her from Australia, give her a British PhD and establish her in the academic career she had long desired. She climbed back on the stool and looked in the mirror: the clothes were definitely wrong.

She changed the jumper for a plain white shirt, but without a suitable jacket she looked like a tram conductor on a hot day – exactly the impression she must avoid. She removed the clothes, threw them in a heap on the bed and started pacing the tiny flat: from the bedroom into the living room through to the kitchen and turn, into the living room on to the bedroom reach the window and turn, and while she walks she pummels her outer thighs, punching hard with fast clenched fists, pacing and punching, until the pain inserts itself between her mind and its problems.

The sound of the telephone brought her to a halt. She looked at her watch – too early for Wendy and Estelle – and lifted the receiver. It was Philippa to suggest a film the following evening, an early session with a meal afterwards. Perhaps it was the familiar warmth in her voice, perhaps it was simply the extent of Amy's desperation, but she found herself telling Philippa about the interview.

'When is it?'

'Next Monday.'

'Are you nervous?'

'A little.'

'Have you rehearsed what you want to say?'

'Yes.'

'But you don't sound confident.'

'I'm not.'

'What are your chances?'

'I've reached the last five, so I guess I have a 20% chance.' She paused. 'No, less.'

'Why less?'

Amy didn't answer.

'What are you going to wear?'

'I've no idea.'

'You can't mean that.'

'I suppose not. I'm full of ideas, but can't decide, and have none of the clothes.'

Amy heard a rustling at the other end of the phone.

'Would you let me help?'

'How?'

'This evening, the shops are open late, we'll go shopping.'

'You and me?'

'Of course, we'll buy you an outfit.'

Within minutes of hanging up, Amy was dialling Philippa's office only to be told she had just left for an appointment and wouldn't be back that day. Amy then rang Leo, but he didn't expect to see her until much later for supper. Amy was frantic. She had been right not to involve Philippa; after five minutes of seeing her in her shopping mode, Philippa would desert her, never to be seen again. Shopping for clothes was a torture; Amy could never find anything suitable, was entirely without patience, and with shop assistants eager for a sale, lacked all imagination. In the interests of self-preservation, Amy had always shopped alone, preferring second-hand shops where no one bothered you for fear of getting a protracted tale of woe. What lunacy had she agreed to, and, she rifled through her purse, with a mere fifty-three dollars to her name? If it were anyone but Philippa Finemore she would simply not turn up, but it was Philippa, the only person she truly cared about.

Four hours later, Amy, a colourful beacon in the drowsy hours of early evening, arrived at the designated meeting place. She had dressed carefully, in a manner designed to sabotage Philippa's social service, but still preserve the friendship; her nylon tights were leopard-spotted, her socks bright yellow, her shoes a red patent leather like Dorothy's from the *Wizard of Oz*. The skirt, rescued not long ago from a mess of seaweed at the base of the pier, was black and billowing over her solid hips and thighs, and above it she wore her beaded jumper and a yellow-spotted handkerchief knotted at the throat. But the *pièce de résistance*, and the article selected to concentrate Philippa's embarrassment, was the hat, a recently acquired turquoise brocade with a wide wired brim, which, while never the height of fashion, would have been the prized possession of a provincial post-mistress in the fifties. If the leopard tights and yellow socks failed to stop the shopping expedition, the hat certainly would.

Amy found a space near the main entrance of the department store. She wondered at so many people going in and so few coming out, wondered too, at so many smiling faces. She leaned against the wall, wriggled from side to side across the small curved tiles in a furtive massage, withdrew *Nightwood* from her bag and began to read. Or rather, not to read, for only someone with the poorest judgement would read in such rabble, rather to hold the book and wait. Amy had never learned to wait unoccupied; it was a matter of appearances (and indicative of a self-consciousness she would prefer not to have), but to wait and actually look as if she were waiting had always unnerved her. The waiting person invites attention; wearing her aloneness like a suit of armour lined with horse-hair, the waiting person is one who is dissatisfied with the present. Of course, the incongruity of Djuna Barnes as a crutch against oddity did not escape Amy, although if odd Djuna were holding court in some celestial Bohemia, Amy felt sure she would recognize a sister soul and forgive her.

'What an amazing hat!' Philippa Finemore appeared from out of the crowd. 'Just like one the children's nanny used to wear. Must say it looks better on you,' took Amy's arm and guided her into the store.

Six months had passed since Amy had happened on Philippa and Leo in the bookshop, six months since Estelle's reappearance, and just under six months since Philippa had rung Amy to ask if she would give an opinion on some poetry that had been written by her mother-in-law. Amy had thought it an odd request, knowing that with Philippa's money and connections she could obtain a far weightier judgement than any Amy might give, and when, a couple of days later, seated with Philippa in her courtyard, she had been interrupted every time she began to read, it occurred to her the poems might have been incidental to the meeting. Over the next several hours, her suspicion had been confirmed; the poems had been ignored while she and Philippa sat beneath a distracted sky, drinking strong coffee, and conversing with that peculiar intimacy that isolates you from the passage of time, the need for food, a ringing telephone, even the consciousness that beyond your immediate confines are other people and other lives. Afterwards, such an event is sealed in memory, along with a range of sensations – the scent of daphne, the sound of a particular word or phrase, the clothes worn that day – any of which can trigger the pleasure of those hours.

Again and again that day, the conversation had returned to family. Amy had been intent on locating its foundations in deprivation, denial and deception.

'And not just the foundations, these are the legacy of family as well.'

'You're being too harsh,' Philippa had said. 'There's plenty of love and loyalty in families. Why else do they hold together?'

'Habit, convenience, and historically, industrialization, urbanization,' replied Amy. 'It's got nothing to do with the human psyche, which is only diminished by it. To live so closely with so few people sucks the curiosity out of you, starves your imagination. The family protects itself by constructing a shield against diversity, it authorizes again and again the correctness of just one position – that occupied by itself. When you live with your own sort, know only your own sort, then it's easy to think, mistakenly of course, that your own sort is the most legitimate and the very best. It's the way wars begin.'

Philippa had laughed, reminding Amy that wars were far older than the nuclear family.

'I'm not suggesting the nuclear family is the only cause of war, rather the nuclear family strengthens those conditions that promote intolerance towards others.'

The conversation had moved on to the effect of the family on the formation of the individual. Philippa was convinced the family made you. 'And not just your first family. As surely as I shaped my children, so, too, have they shaped me.' She shook her head slowly. 'That's why it's so difficult when your children go astray.'

Amy had been horrified, argued strongly for a position of self-determination, but Philippa refused to be persuaded.

'How then, do you accommodate for change?' Amy had asked. 'People do change, people do become other than what their familes are.'

And while Philippa had agreed that might be true, people nonetheless carried with them a residue of family. 'More than a residue, a thick blood-rich sediment.'

'No such primordial sludge for me.' Amy laughed. 'I'd be dead, or if not dead, terminally boring if I hadn't left my family far behind. Lock, stock and barrel. The whole catastrophe. Gone. It's just fortunate I thrive on change.'

'Perhaps circumstance has merely trained you to welcome it.'

'You may be right. Although in the long term the reasons don't really matter.'

Philippa sat forward, wanting to disagree.

'The reasons *don't* matter,' Amy had continued. 'They provide you with understanding, but once you have that, the reasons can do nothing more for you. Indeed, to hang on to them is to saddle yourself with unnecessary baggage that will eventually wear you down. We both know people who blame their personal failings on their parents, their father didn't love them enough or their mother loved them too much, and they cling to their reasons, hating the father or resenting the mother, rather than using the knowledge to rid themselves of their undesirable traits. So intent are they on preserving their reasons, that even after the parents are dead and buried, the children are still blaming them, albeit with a tidy infusion of guilt. As for the personal weaknesses, they'll carry them to the grave.'

'It sounds as if you're defending the family, or, at least, defending parents.'

'Of course I'm not, but I am being critical about the ways in which people run their lives. Families are full of pain. Pain should be exploited, you take what you can from it and then move on. If you persist in collecting it, there'll come a time when you can no longer move.' She laughed, a small matter-of-fact explosion. 'As for myself, I'll be on the move for the rest of my life.'

Philippa had talked about George's death, and the rupture it had caused. 'You try to adjust to death's permanency, and in that way attempt to reclaim the stability you once knew. But like life, death doesn't last. After a while death becomes simply "gone", a crater in your life that you learn to walk around.' She leaned to one side, picked an early stem of daphne, sniffed it, handed it to Amy.

The two sat for a time, each with her own thoughts, and then had talked some more. Clouds came and went in the autumn breeze, a no-longer-certain sun shone palely while the conversation continued, skimming the hours so gently, so utterly naturally, that when finally they stopped they were shocked to discover several hours had passed. 'Would you like some coffee before you begin?' Philippa had asked at two o'clock handing Amy the folder of poems, and at six, with the coffee pot long empty and the cheese and biscuits grown soggy and unappetizing, Amy rose to leave. As for Dora's poems, they had not been mentioned again.

'I give you my word,' Philippa now said as the two sat at a table in the department store cafeteria, 'that our shopping expedition will not suffer the same fate as Dora's poems. By the time the shops close tonight, we'll have bought you an outfit. I just need a little sustenance before we begin.'

'What exactly was the point of Dora's poems?'

Philippa smiled. 'A convenient device to see you again, without making you feel hounded.'

'Did I appear so fragile?'

Philippa looked at her and recalled the taut white face and flickering eyes set above the carefully casual posture that had been Amy the night she had walked into Leo's shop. It was an image caught at the centre of memory, the face and stance in such stark contrast with each other, but the face, without doubt the face, that spoke the truth.

'Not fragile, but easily put off,' she said, and touched Amy's hand. 'Now, what did you have in mind for an outfit?'

Immediately the flickering began, the eyes darting all over the place, anything to avoid Philippa's gaze, and rapid blinking as if that might wipe away the fears. The shoulders tense and the jaws clench and Amy slaps a smile to her face, stiff and transparent against the backdrop of anxiety. In a life-time of performance, even experts like Amy have less than perfect scenes; behind the swagger, the weathered surface, were fears, desires, frailties which had been petrified in childhood. That the clothes or the shopping or, indeed, the interview made Amy uneasy was obvious. Or the money. Although Philippa had anticipated that. From her pocket she withdrew an envelope, deliberately left unsealed so Amy could see the notes inside. She had written on the front,

'For Amy's Scholarship Clothes' and, taking the girl's hand, she now placed the envelope in it. Amy blushed, prepared to protest, but Philippa spoke first.

'The idea to go shopping was mine, indeed, from the look of you I'd guess this is not one of your favourite pastimes.'

Amy's eyes flickered more vigorously. 'Although it's not because of you,' she said quickly. 'The problem is clothes and shopping and having the wrong body, and—'

'I know, I know. Now, unless you really object, I think the best plan is to let me do the talking, we can choose together, and,' she closed Amy's hand over the envelope, 'you can pay.' She saw bewilderment, a hesitancy that scudded over Amy's face, then suspicion, and added, 'I know how important this scholarship is, and I'd like to help. I've no intention of intruding where I'm not wanted, neither do I have any plans to take over your life.' She smiled, 'It's simple, Amy, I'm here because I like you, love you, and can help with this small problem of clothes.'

'It's not small, it's enormous.' Amy looked as if she might cry and it was the mention of love that made the tears.

Philippa finished the last of her sandwich, took Amy's arm and the two rose from the table.

'Now, did you have something in mind?'

Amy cleared her throat, made mention of a jacket, or perhaps a blazer, in understated colours. Philippa asked about the scholarship, about the tone of her written application and then gave her opinion:

'I think you need something smart, but a bit different. You'll only confuse them if your application materials suggest a creative, innovative person, and you turn up looking like a Ralph Laurens prototype.'

'Who's Ralph Laurens?'

Philippa smiled. 'Never mind. But do you take my point?'

Amy shrugged, unwilling to concede anything at this stage, but neither did she protest when Philippa guided her past the navy blue blazers and pleated skirts on to other more lively clothes.

It is an odd experience taking someone shopping, or rather someone who is not your child or husband or mother. And when that someone is uncertain and self-depreciating and soaks up, albeit doubtfully, every compliment that comes her way, you feel an enormous responsibility. Because you're doing more than shopping, and you know it, and while it shouldn't be the case - appearances ought to be nothing more than appearances, and the essence of a person ought to be the same whether clothed in designer labels or threadbare rags - appearance does matter, and the distinction between mind and body is very tiny indeed. At times, Amy's nervousness was so great that it was all Philippa could do to stop herself from taking the child into her arms and holding her there. Amy might stride the streets with equanimity, she might deflect aggression and give a man as good as he gave, but when it came to dealing with herself, revealing herself, she was a novice. She found it impossible to talk to the shop assistants, and when they made their comments, simply ignored them. What was truly remarkable was the poise that enabled her to wear a blue brocade hat and red patent leather shoes disintegrated when something other than parody was required.

Which was not to say the shopping expedition wasn't a huge success. Back at the bookshop, Leo asked for a private showing. Amy recoiled at the suggestion, and only with Philippa's encouragement did she go into the back room and change, and only if Philippa accompanied her. She put on the clothes, handling each item like the rare and precious artefact it was, and once dressed, stood transfixed by her image in the mirror. The collarless jacket was black with a fine white stripe, the yellow silk shirt was long and loose, low at the neck and without fastenings, the skirt was tailored and black, and the shoes - 'Please don't make me wear heels,' she had pleaded - were flat and black with yellow splashes. The stockings, too, were yellow, but she decided not to put these on for fear of laddering them. Philippa took her arm and led her into the front of the shop.

Leo's admiration was abundant.

'Do you really mean it? You're not just trying to make me feel better?'

He assured her he spoke only the truth.

'Well, if both of you think I look all right, I suppose I'll do.'

Philippa stayed with Leo while Amy changed into her old clothes. They were discussing where they'd eat when Amy called Philippa into the back room. There was money in her hand. 'This was left over.'

'It's yours, Amy.' And when she protested, said again, 'It's yours. I gave you the money, what you chose to do with it was your business – ' Philippa smiled, 'with some executive advice from me.' The hand remained extended. 'Buy yourself a hankie. I've always used a new hankie for special events; even now I can look through my handkerchiefs and take an inventory of the important occasions of my life. Buy yourself a hankie.'

'I've never had one.'

'What? A hankie?'

Amy shrugged her shoulders. 'I never have.'

Philippa told her to wait, went into the front of the shop and returned with her bag. 'Here,' she said, a white handkerchief edged with lace in her hand, 'let me make you a gift.' The hankie was scented with Philippa's perfume. Amy looked at it, held it to her face, inhaled, and when she put it in the bag with her new clothes, Philippa saw it as a sign that the girl was learning to trust her.

Three days later, Philippa and Amy entered Cumberland House for the scholarship interview.

'Are you sure you wouldn't prefer me to wait in the car?'

Amy shook her head. 'Besides, they're probably running late and you can help calm my nerves.'

But they were on time, and within a few minutes Amy was called from the reception area. Philippa sat and waited, nervous for Amy but confident she would acquit herself well.

'Philippa Finemore!' Boomed a familiar voice. 'What on earth are you doing here?'

She looked up to see Colin Reading already on his way down to kiss her.

'Betty and I were saying just the other day that we must have you round for a meal.'

Philippa smiled: she knew how busy they were.

'But that's no excuse, particularly when it comes to old friends.'

He stood back and surveyed her. 'I must say Philippa, you're looking extremely well.'

To deflect another kiss and one of his strenuous embraces, Philippa asked about the family. After several minutes of Betty and the four children and the seven grandchildren and two more on the way, he straightened his tie and buttoned his jacket.

'Now, that's quite enough about me. I want to know what you're doing here.'

'I'm here with one of the finalists for the British Scholarship.'

'Which one?' And misinterpreting Philippa's hesitation, assured her that in no way would she be contravening confidentiality. 'I'm on the selection committee, you see, have been for years. One of my more enjoyable social responsibilities.'

Philippa smiled, how elastic was the concept of confidentiality, and, having decided she could do Amy no harm, gave her name to Colin.

'Oh yes, the young waif. Very bright, resolute too, and an admirable application, although I rather think she lacks the freshness we like to see in our candidates.' He hesitated and frowned, clearly a doubt had entered his mind. 'You weren't one of her referees, were you?' And before she could answer: 'No, of course not, I would have noticed if you were.'

Philippa chose her words carefully. 'Not a referee, more a guardian I suppose. I've taken a special interest in her.'

'She's a lucky girl.'

'I'd call her exceptional.'

'Really? Would you now? I'd like to hear what you've got to say.' And was about to sit down when a secretary appeared to tell him the committee was waiting. 'Amy Vaughan, very interesting, very interesting indeed. I look forward to seeing how she presents.'

Philippa stood up. 'You'll be impressed, Colin,' and gave his arm a squeeze.

'I'm sure I will.' He pressed his body against hers and followed the secretary through the door.

ELEVEN

'Has Amy heard about the scholarship?'

'Not yet, but then it's only been a week.'

'She bearing up all right?'

'About the scholarship, yes, but this business with her mother and sister is wearing her down. I don't know how much longer she can put them off.'

They were in their usual places, Philippa at one end of the couch, Leo in a nearby armchair and Peach on her rug near the fireplace. Peach was asleep, although alert in dreams; intermittently, her eyelids would flicker and her nose would twitch and there would be a flutter of gentle yelps, and Philippa would look fondly at the dog and make mention of instinctual yearnings.

'No such thing,' Leo the rationalist would reply.

To which Philippa would smile, and so would he, this being one of those disagreements that couples hold dear, a talisman of sorts that, if ever alluded to by one or other in public, produces an air of collusion and the satisfaction of knowing there is someone special in your life.

So here it is, late November, the daffodils finished, the freesias still in bloom, bred as they now are for a lengthy season achieved at the cost of that sweet heady fragrance hushed forever in memory, evenings still chilly despite the warmer days. It is midnight at Philippa's house, Peach is running in dreams, Philippa and Leo, a pot of tea still warm, port glasses already refilled, are talking about the events of the day and Amy Vaughan.

For nearly six months, ever since the start of winter, Leo has taken to dropping by on his way home from the shop. He closed around eleven, so it was late when he arrived, but both he and Philippa looked forward to this companionship at the end of the day. Even the awkwardness that occurred when it was time for him to leave had acquired its own special markings: the stopping at the end of the hall, the embrace, the kiss, the 'goodnight, sleep well', a second kiss - a mere shiver of skin - and the fresh air of night. Months ago, Philippa had decided she would like him to stay, had rehearsed a range of invitations, but somehow, when the time came, always found herself mute. And Leo, who had lain beside her a hundred times in the isolation of his own bed, knew how to make the request, but Philippa's reticence, her apparent satisfaction at the current state of affairs, had ensured his silence.

None of which, Leo's longings or Philippa's hesitations, was to suggest a discontent with each other. Philippa looked forward to his nightly visit, his 'May I come in?' and 'I hope I'm not too late?' And of course he could and never was. She might have been reading or watching television, tonight she had been studying a submission for a large grant that was to be discussed the following day, so Leo made the tea while she finished her work.

'Music?' he asked when she joined him a few minutes later.

She nodded, and nodded again at his choice of Ella Fitzgerald singing Cole Porter, and sipped her tea.

'Seems Amy's not the only one of my girls with problems. Melanie rang today.'

'More money?'

'I'm afraid so. It really does worry me, not that I begrudge her the money—'

'You should.'

'Now, now, Leo, we'll never agree on this so there's little point in goading me. The fact is I don't begrudge her the money, but it's the fifth request in as many months.'

'Perhaps it's her modest way of asking to be put on the payroll.'

The attempt at levity rankled; she and Leo, compatible in so many respects, occupied different universes when it came to the Finemore children. Fundamental to their disagreement was Leo's incomprehension of the thorny bonds of family.

'Bonds of habit, that's all they are.'

And while he was partly right, in this one thing Philippa would not change. She could peel away the gilt of a wealthy widow and give the riches away, she could anger her children, even disappoint them, but she would not turn her back on them and neither would she tolerate their turning away from her. A mother's concern, regularly replenished and purified, runs in the blood; a mother's concern flows steadily for as long as there is life.

'But they disappoint you so! Melanie and her artifice and Gray with his dullness. Really, Philippa, you'd have to agree only a person entirely bereft of imagination would own two Mercedes the same colour as your son does. Admit it, your children are a disappointment.'

Philippa nodded slowly, her mouth contracting to a rueful smile. 'Although it's irrelevant. It may be true but it's irrelevant.'

And so it was. Her children were grown and separate and making their own choices, as indeed was she. But they were still her children. Besides, when she looked at other families, it seemed that to like one's children was a luxury, one of those select extras. She knew she would suffer Gray and Melanie much more if she were dependent on them for companionship or to fill otherwise empty days, but this was not the case; hers was a busy life, what with the Foundation and Leo and Amy, Tuesdays with the Pryors, Thursdays at Gray and Evelyn's, at least part of each weekend taken up with the grandchildren, and while Jeremy was now in London and they used to see a lot of each other, she nonetheless found herself with little time to spare.

She was perfectly willing to concede that family was an irrational business, but the family persisted nonetheless, so clearly more than irrationality was required to run it into the ground. And the fact of the matter was, Philippa was concerned about Melanie. After the second request, which at twenty thousand dollars was not a particularly large amount (indeed none of the amounts had been greater than thirty thousand), Philippa had asked what the money was for. Initially, Melanie's lowered gaze, the emotion in lip and chin, suggested she was about to confide in her mother, then, in a surly tightening of the muscles, the moment passed.

'I'm not one of your charity cases, Mother,' she had said, 'and I won't be treated like one. So don't expect me to account for my use of family money.'

On subsequent occasions, Melanie had rung through her requests and Philippa had brought her a cheque the following Tuesday, a cheque that was to be given to Melanie and not mentioned to Selwyn. Which was the most worrying aspect of all. With the exception of her clothes and beauty treatments, Melanie did nothing without first consulting Selwyn. So what was she doing without his knowledge that cost around twenty thousand dollars a month? And surely with the millions he was sinking into his business school, a few thousand more for his wife was not too much to expect? Might she be in some sort of trouble? If it were anyone else one might think of a secret gambling habit, but not Melanie, neither was she the type to give money away, and there had certainly been no change in the Pryor lifestyle. On the contrary, since the completion of the Hopetoun renovations a few months before, there had been a string of parties, all of them consummate occasions with exotic delicacies and the finest of Finemore's wines. Melanie was living the life to which she had always aspired, what secret could she be protecting at a cost of twenty thousand a month?

It was after the third request that Philippa wondered if Melanie were having some outrageously expensive beauty treatment. Certainly, in her daughter's terms, she was looking better than ever, slim enough to be considered angular, and not a trace of a wrinkle. One might feasibly guess at cosmetic surgery if there had been days of illness or intermittent holidays, but there had not.

'I asked again what the money was for,' Philippa said to Leo, 'and she gave the oddest response: said she wouldn't be needing any more because everyone would be away for the summer. "Who would be away for the summer?" I wanted to ask, but didn't.'

Of some comfort was the fact that Melanie herself was not

concerned, indeed, during the past few months Melanie had seemed more content than she had for some time. And now that 'everyone' was to be away for the summer there appeared to be no change in her spirits. In fact, all Philippa's children were in high spirits, even Jeremy, who had found a satisfaction in London that had eluded him in Australia. And it was not just his job, although he seemed to be liking it well enough, nor his colleagues, who were, he said, particularly congenial, nor the concerts which were numerous and of excellent quality, there was, in addition, a new friend, a special man, according to Jeremy. Philippa, who missed her younger son greatly, was terrified he would stay away permanently. But wanted his happiness.

'How's Gray's wine and food club?' Leo asked.

'By all accounts it's a brilliant success. Evelyn seems a bit flat, but Gray can speak of nothing else - or at such length.'

All her children so happy and satisfied, and while the Finemore figures were down, neither of the boys was concerned - just a symptom of these difficult times, they said. Although it wouldn't do any harm to show the monthly statements to Lorraine: the boys told her not to worry, but at least Lorraine would explain what the figures meant.

When the doorbell rang.

It was a Wednesday night approaching midnight and Amy Vaughan did not want to be alone. She recognized the same taut despair of her childhood with its welts of disappointment. And throughout the evening, the recurring thought that once in a lifetime was enough: one mother, one loss, one huge measure of despair, one supreme act of courage. Not that anyone had ever promised justice in this life.

She had spent the past three hours wandering the familiar shadows of the university, its gardens and cloisters powdered by night, sitting first here, then there, returning again and again to the library door which was always and clearly locked. What sort of culture put its mind to bed at nine o'clock? She asked herself. And where else could one go when the hour was late, one was alone, female, and the solitude of a brisk, empty flat was more threat than comfort? And what a telling indictment that a university modelled on the age-old British tradition maintained civil service hours, while many American universities, recognizing that the mind was not to be confined to pragmatic scheduling, kept their libraries open nearly all night.

Poor Amy, since nine o'clock she has been trudging from main library to law library and across to the medical library merely to read again and again the same sorry message appended to various closed doors. Shuffling and shambling and labouring under an anxiety that drags her ever more tightly to its bosom. And she knows she must stem the havoc wreaked by returned mothers, knows that this wandering, this treading a rut, only engraves the anxiety still deeper. How naïve to have thought that having avoided a meeting with Estelle for six months, she would manage to avoid her forever.

Amy sits on a bench outside Humanities, breathes deeply and slowly, watches the rise and fall of her chest in the light from a lamp, feels the anxiety sink to her legs. She cannot move, or at least not for a while, and draws from her satchel a volume of Akhmatova borrowed from the library earlier in the evening, a deliberate selection in the hope that real, life-threatening problems, would stifle her own. And, indeed, for an hour, she enjoys the first relief since Estelle's ambush at four o'clock that afternoon in the university cafeteria where Amy was sitting with her supervisor, Professor Joanne Finkelstein.

'So there you are!' Estelle had shouted. 'Older, fatter—' a giggle, 'aren't we all? But still my little girl.' And fell upon Amy's neck with a torrent of kisses, while sister Wendy, hugely pregnant, stood back and admired the heart-warming scene.

The weakness, truly a feebleness, that had shrouded her ever since, had come upon her immediately. It had taken a mighty effort to suggest to Joanne they should continue their discussion at another time; had offered a bleak smile, a limp wave of a hand, and her supervisor was gone.

'Who was that?' Estelle had asked, pointing at the retreating figure. And without waiting for a reply, not that Amy had any intention of giving one, shook her head and tightened her wrinkles, saying it was a shame that some girls did so little for themselves, how 'that person' and she nodded at Joanne's back, would look a hundred per cent better with some colour in her greying hair and a bit of makeup. 'Why do you think they do it?' She had asked Wendy. 'Why do so many girls go out of their way to make themselves plain?'

'I guess they're women's libbers, Mum.'

Estelle nodded sadly, as one might on hearing of the death of a friend, and sat down at Amy's table. Wendy pulled up a chair and joined them.

Estelle peered at Amy's makeup-free face. 'You're not one of those libbers, are you?'

Amy touched her fine, clear skin, already on the defensive, clutched at herself and turned to Wendy.

'What are you doing here?' Each word a clean, deliberate stab.

'What do you mean, Amy? I've been telling you for months that Mum wanted to see you.'

'And for months I've been telling you I didn't want to see her.'

'That's a shocking thing to say!'

Wendy reached for her mother's hand, and the two sat in silent reproach of the wayward Amy. Who was struck by the extraordinary likeness between them. Amy had always leaned towards the nurture side of the nature-nurture argument, and yet with nurture eliminated almost from the beginning in the case of Estelle and her daughters, biology had enjoyed an unimpeded and apparently successful run. Wendy was a faded version of her mother; her mouse-brown hair had become a shrill copper in Estelle, her wisp of a figure with whopping stomach had been filled out and strengthened, her watery blue eyes had been intensified by what Amy guessed were tinted contact lenses, her thinnish, pinkish mouth had been expanded to a full-bodied crimson. Only the skin was different, Wendy's so smooth, while Estelle's, under its matting of powder and rouge, was scarred by cigarettes and sun. And the voice: Wendy's a light, high-pitched, nasal twang, and Estelle's, a hollow resonance varnished with nicotine.

Amy sneezed, blew her nose.

'Got a cold?' Estelle asked.

It was innocuous enough, so Amy nodded.

'Had it long?'

She nodded again, the cold had dragged on for over a week.

'Taken anything for it?'

'Just a cold capsule, nothing special.'

'Exactly!' Estelle's hollow rasp was triumphant. 'I could have guessed. All those tablets just make you worse, in fact, they cause the cold. A cold in a capsule, that's what I call them. Throw 'em out and you'll be good as new in no time.'

Amy was flabbergasted. The woman who had walked out of her life fifteen years before with neither explanation nor farewell, was instructing her on how to manage a cold. 'Throw out those tablets,' she is saying, 'try an inhalation if you have to do something, but throw out those tablets.'

The face, with its kaleidoscope of colours, leans forward large and lobate, and the hand, released from Wendy's grasp, leaps across the laminex. Amy puts her own hands in her lap; mustn't touch, she tells herself, as temptation trespasses high in her stomach, rises to her throat. She swallows, and swallows again; must resist this touch for which she is desperate.

Was once desperate, she corrects herself, but not any more, which is the essence of the injustice of Estelle's reappearance. Some situations should only be suffered once. Amy does not like this chattering woman, nor does she have anything in common with her, but she feels a certain curiosity, a morbid fascination. For doesn't everyone have a right to family? Doesn't everyone want a mother?

Yes and yes, but she would prefer it were otherwise. She wants this woman to leave before more damage accrues, before the protection of a lifetime is dismantled and the labile ego of the unloved child is laid bare. For Amy knows who she is. She might fool the world with her wit and wisdom, be the envy of her friends with her *laissez-faire* attitude, but this is simple cladding; below and beneath lurks the maimed Amy Vaughan, an ulcerous, festering mess, raw with watchfulness, and infected by waiting. Two distinct layers, and hardly a whole person. Yet she manages better than most, and only rarely does the pain seep out.

Although it had quite recently, with Philippa Finemore, who, unlike other people, had peered closely, recognized the cladding for what it was and applied a barrage of questions. The first law of survival for the person with a self to hide, is always to ensure you are the interrogator: keep the others talking and thereby preserve your own secrets. Which is not so difficult, given that most people like to talk about themselves and will seize every opportunity to do so. For years, Amy had asked her questions and adopted an encouraging listening posture while private lives spilled forth. But Philippa had choreographed a different role for her; question followed question and the very stuff of her was exposed. Amy hated it, would regret each outburst, and yet could never stop herself, for she wanted Philippa's interest, more than that, wanted her understanding. Which made the situation even worse, for in a life lived at a distance, to want anyone or anything is extremely dangerous. And now it was happening again, another older woman prodding those scarred depths, no questions this time, indeed, Estelle hardly paused for breath, and no confessions, rather it was Estelle's mere presence that was the problem, prompting as it did the promise of motherhood - myths of motherhood, Amy knew well enough, but alluring nonetheless - and the bitterness was very great indeed.

Oddly, it was more directed at herself, her own weakness, her own disgusting, unwelcome desire for love. How she longed to be done with it. Estelle was a simple, egocentric woman, all she cared about were her belated maternal desires and her belief that forgiveness was a simple matter of words. Estelle could not be expected to notice, much less anticipate, other desires that contradicted her own. But Amy knew, and should have known better than to suffer the presence of a woman for whom she should feel only cool indifference.

'—so hungry,' Estelle was saying. 'We came straight from shopping to see you, and haven't had a thing since breakfast.'

Amy rose without a word, walked to the counter to buy food. As she stood in the queue, she looked back to mother and daughter talking and laughing and nodding together; they had each other, why did they need her?

'Because I have two daughters,' Estelle said over her scone and coffee. 'Two daughters. And while in the past I mightn't have been the perfect mother, it's better late than never.'

'Better late than never' 'let bygones be bygones' 'forgive and forget' 'everyone makes mistakes' 'no use crying over spilt milk' 'families have to stick together', a stream of sanitized sayings, sometimes from Estelle, sometimes from Wendy, offered as balsam to the relationship they expected to have. As for explanations, as to whether Amy wanted this relationship, these were of no concern.

'A mother's love is strong,' says the pregnant Wendy, 'stronger than anything.' And pats her bulging stomach while smiling at Estelle.

Amy thinks she might scream. She runs to the bathroom; it has not yet been cleaned and the cubicles are spattered with the day's use; she goes to the alcove at the end of the row of stalls where the cleaner stores her things, and perches on an up-ended bucket. She could simply disappear, escape by another exit, but knows they will only ambush her again. For it is clear that what they are wanting is a happy family and everyone to be nice, and if they don't achieve it this time, they'll come back and back until they do. Which makes Amy think that if she appears to acquiesce this time they will leave her alone.

Not such a difficult role, even for one as famished as she, but still she is disturbed. She thought she was finished with mothers, thought she was immune to the promise of that sort of love. She knew it was possible that Philippa with her attentions and questions had awakened the desires, but Philippa was not Estelle and a child does not choose her family; an adult, however, must make her own way, and no one bleeds without first standing in the way of danger. Amy rose so abruptly that the bucket clanged to its side: if it was a daughter they needed in order to leave her alone, a sister too, then that's what they'd bloody well get.

The next three hours were interminable, and while Akhmatova

might have suffered for better reasons, greater reasons, Amy never wanted to sit through another trial like that again. When it was over, only snippets of conversation remained, but a more general sense of the time prevailed: futility, passivity, a kind of death, and a return to childhood when everyone is bigger and more powerful than you.

Estelle and Wendy were booked on the 7.20 train and they wanted Amy with them until then. At a quarter to seven, she walked them to the tramstop, waited for the tram that would take them to the station, suffered the hugs, their careless affection, said the words they wanted to hear, and when finally they were gone, hurried to the library knowing that work was the best palliative. But then it was closing time and work had to stop; doors shut on a growling despair, and hardly recognizing herself, she could not know what to do.

It was a fifteen minute walk from the university to Philippa's place. The streets were quiet, the air so cool; soon she was standing on Philippa's doorstep. Through the stained glass panels, she could see a light at the end of the hall, and rang the bell.

Leo poured Amy a brandy, who took the drink, swallowed and grimaced. 'I've never much liked brandy.'

'Consider it medicinal,' Leo said, and poured her another.

Philippa and Amy were sitting on the couch, Philippa's arm about the younger woman. Amy looked terrible, locked in a glazed staring, her dark eyes were huge against a pallid skin, her marvellous black bush of hair was limp and exhausted; she seemed smaller, younger. Philippa tightened her hold, stroked gently the girl's arm, her hair, and for five, ten minutes, no one spoke. It was a hushed and solemn atmosphere, of the type one associates with late night solitude, an atmosphere so quiet and attenuated that there's a tightness, a brittleness, which is nothing other than the knowledge that in the middle of a big city and a busy life such moments are temporary. So, when Amy sat forward and began to speak, no one was surprised, although the fierce embarrassment that propelled her was a shock. Never before had she behaved like this, she said, never before had she burst in on someone unannounced, and certainly not in the middle of the night, never had she been so inept in the conduct of her own affairs, never had she so indulged her failings. And would have continued, but for Leo and Philippa, who silenced her with reassuring words, and offers of food and drink, or anything else she might want.

'How about a new identity? A new name, a new face, a new city, it's just what I need.'

She told them about her day, about Estelle and Wendy and the torturous time with them, and the feelings and desires that made a mockery of everything she had struggled for these past fifteen years.

'And what makes it worse is that it's not me, Amy Vaughan, they want. I'm irrelevant. All they want is a daughter and a sister, a shelter for their illusions, the missing card in a pack of happy families.'

Which made her distress even more futile. Not only had Estelle inspired a welter of feelings that Amy had learned to do without, these same feelings were incidental to Estelle's quest, and impossible for her to satisfy.

'Pathetic, isn't it?' Amy sucked in her cheeks and tightened her lips against a despair that finally staggered out in the voiceless gasping of one unaccustomed to crying.

Leo wondered whether he should leave, but Philippa shook her head, nodded to a chair, where he sat and waited and watched the two women. In time the sobbing grew quieter and a minute or two later had ceased altogether. Amy turned away to wipe her face, sat back on the couch, looking first to Leo then to Philippa.

'Either of you interested in fostering a twenty-five-year-old remedial case?'

Leo smiled. 'Only if you're interested in taking on a remedial father figure.'

But for Philippa there could be no joking. She held Amy tighter, saw the dark eyes fill again, wiped the tears with her own handkerchief. How she loved this girl with her odd ways, her rough generosity. And her toughness, Amy was tougher than anyone Philippa had known. And passionate too, although she tried not to show it, passionate about her work, her writers, her independence, her lifestyle. She stroked Amy's cheek, smiled down at the girl; Amy looked up and smiled back.

Leo, with no part in this, went to the kitchen and made a fresh pot of tea. When he returned, Amy was composed, sitting quietly at one end of the couch with Philippa at the other. Leo poured the tea and the three sipped in silence and nibbled ginger biscuits.

'So what's to be done?' Leo said finally.

He and Philippa looked to Amy, who met their gaze, nodded almost imperceptibly for several seconds while she organized her thoughts. Her voice was steady when she spoke,

'This period of my life, Estelle's return, has been difficult, although not a total disaster; I've learned of weaknesses I didn't know were mine, and I suppose that's been useful. In the past, when things went awry, I always managed to stay afloat, I'd turn my mind to the problem and, sometimes better sometimes worse, resolve the situation. But these past six months with Estelle lurking in the background, I've been floundering, drowning, I seem to have lost my bearings, lost the ability to reason; I'm at the whim of these awful emotional eddies that pull and push and toss me about and refuse to go away. I go to my desk and, for a time, feel myself again, then there's another phonecall from Wendy, another change of the tide, and I become someone I hardly recognize.

'I have my faults, many many faults, I know the sort of character I've shaped for myself; and while a little more softness here, a little less deliberation there might have been better, the fact remains that the person I am has been, still is, effective enough. I've been accused of capitulating to a painful childhood, of avoiding emotions for fear of further hurt, and while that may be true, it's simply not relevant; to get along I need to *know* more, not feel more. I've also been accused of excessive self control. "You never lose yourself," friends have said, "never let yourself go." And neither I do, there's no peace for me in forgetfulness or oblivion.' She gave a hard little laugh. 'You can see why I've never been tempted by drugs, I've always been terrified of a truant mind, of the confusion in which I now find myself. For years I've rehearsed the facts of my life, believed I'd quelled the desire for family, for love, and now I find those bloody desires refuse to be tamed.'

Amy paused, her gaze now on Philippa, took a sip of tea. She had more to say, smiled, blushed, sipped again, stayed perched on the edge of the couch so as to keep Philippa in view.

'Although it's not quite as simple as that. These feelings that give me so much grief are not entirely unwelcome, because there's you, Philippa, who entered my life around the same time Estelle reappeared. You've not been easy for me, but at least I can trust you to know what you're doing, can trust you to take some responsibility for it. Besides, I ask for your engagement, at times in deeply embedded ways, I know that, but I do ask. It's different with Estelle. She has no idea what she's doing, she'll walk all over me and not even stumble. You show me ways of living a life, Philippa, and I'm strengthened by that; but Estelle empties my mind, depletes me of those very qualities that have sustained me all these years. She can only damage me.'

Amy finished her tea and continued. 'I had thought, wrongly I now realize, that if I complied for this one visit Estelle would leave me alone. But Estelle won't leave me alone because she's motivated entirely by self-interest; she doesn't know the effect she has on others, because she doesn't even bother to look; she should not, indeed cannot, be trusted.' Amy shrugged, 'She could be panting around the corner of my life for decades.'

'And you couldn't insist she stay away?'

'That's what I've been doing for the past six months and while I've managed to avoid her actual presence until today, ever since her return, I've been plagued by an awful conflict of wanting to see her and, at the same time, wanting her to disappear off the face of the earth. Estelle, or rather, the idea of a mother, has hijacked my thoughts, and I do not like it at all.'

'It's quite possible she'll leave you alone after Wendy's baby arrives. Becoming a grandmother can have the most extraordinary effect on a woman.' Philippa smiled, 'There's something very special about grandchildren.'

Leo raised his eyebrows, clearly he did not agree.

'You don't know, Leo, but I've seen it time and time again, and in people of whom you'd least expect it.'

'Well, I can assure you, Estelle is not one of them. She's never shown the least interest in babies and children, witness what she did with her own children, and far from looking forward to becoming resident grannie, she said today how eager she was to visit me on her own "after Wendy was settled with the baby." Wendy looked quite distressed at the prospect, but Estelle assured her it was in her own best interests, that after so many months together, Wendy would welcome the break. Grandchild or not, I think it's unlikely she'll leave me alone.'

Amy leaned back, stretched her legs, and the glazed look returned. Tears oozed out, rolled down her cheeks, silent tears that she brushed away, but still they came. Like blood from a deep cut. She sank deeper into the couch, was clearly exhausted. Philippa left the room to make up the spare bed, returned with toothbrush, towel and nightgown for Amy.

'You're sure you don't mind?'

But Philippa would have it no other way. 'Call me when you're ready and I'll come and tuck you in.'

A short time later, Amy was in bed. She called to them both, kissed first Leo then Philippa and thanked them. 'It will be better in the morning, clearer, we'll arrive at a solution over breakfast. See you both then.' And turned on her side and closed her eyes.

Philippa and Leo stood in the hallway facing each other; there were questions in their wavering smiles. Then, quickly, before she could change her mind, Philippa extinguished the lights, reached for Leo's hand, led him into her bedroom and shut the door.

'You're up early,' Philippa said, when she entered the living-room the next morning and found Amy already seated at the table with toast and coffee. She bent down and kissed the top of her head.

'I would have brought you breakfast in bed, but,' nodding at Philippa's skirt and jumper, her damp hair, 'I can see I'm too late. Besides, I know about your fruit and toast, but have no idea what Leo likes.'

'Neither do I.'

Amy was surprised.

'Herewith our first breakfast.' Philippa was laughing. 'Seems Estelle has rocked more than one boat.' She poured herself some coffee, prepared a bowl of fresh fruit and joined Amy at the table.

Soon after, Leo entered, also fully dressed, hair wet from the shower. His blue eyes were smudged from too little sleep and there was an uncertainty about him, a gentle hovering; Philippa had it too. Amy looked from one to the other.

'Are you all right?'

And it seemed they were, although a little unsteady. For to lie with someone in the comfort of night, to speak only in whispers, to explore only with hands, limbs grazing limbs, skin awakened by skin, to feel another body at the same time as your own, learn a face through touch, feel fingers on your mouth even while you are kissed, is a truly private experience and ill-at-ease with the morning. So you creep in the daylight and treat with care the person with whom you shared this intimacy. Both Leo and Philippa were nervous and were pleased for Amy's presence. And Peach as well, whom they addressed as if she were another person, feeding her fond remarks and pieces of toast. Although by the time they were drinking their second cup of coffee and Philippa had phoned the office to let them know she would be late, the uneasiness had largely dissipated.

So it was they moved on to Amy's problems. Which were problems no longer, Amy said, for during the night she'd had an extraordinary dream. She had dreamt she was in labour, about to give birth. She was in a house with sparse furnishings; there were many people, friends, she thought, although she recognized no one, and a lot of activity. She was forced to lie on a bench in a bare room waiting for the baby to come. It was an irritation, and she would have preferred to be with the others. She was aware she should have felt excitement, anticipation, at the very least should have been in pain, but felt only boredom and resentment of her enforced inactivity. Finally the baby arrived; how easy it was! Why did women complain of the pain? Why was such a fuss made of birth? The baby was encased in a camembert cheese; such rich protection, she thought, but did not find it odd. Estelle came into the room, took the camembert and broke it open to release the child, then, with the baby perched in the palm of her hand, walked into the next room. Through the open doorway, Amy could see her mother attending to the baby. She felt detached from the proceedings, and no sense of loss. She realized she did not know the baby's sex, was simply not interested, neither was she interested in lying on the plinth waiting for the afterbirth. Again, she acknowledged her boredom, her irritation, her resentment at having to wait while so much was happening outside. She stayed a while longer watching Estelle with the baby, and then suddenly got up, left the room by another door and left the house; if the afterbirth was as easy as the birth, then she would manage.

'You left your baby!' Philippa was aghast. 'Are you so defeated by her that you'd give up your own child?'

Amy looked surprised. This was not the response she had expected. In the dream, there had been no difficulty leaving the child, on the contrary, leaving both the baby and Estelle, and leaving them together, had been liberating.

'Perhaps the baby was not really her own child but was, instead, a symbolic self,' Leo said.

'And perhaps it was an aspect of myself I would happily relinquish, an infantile part that's no longer useful.'

'But the camembert, so rich and special, the baby was contained in the camembert, you gave away something precious.'

'And felt no distress. It wasn't precious to me, it wasn't rich or rare or special in any way. But it was to Estelle, she couldn't keep her hands off it. She saw something she wanted and took possession of it with neither request nor explanation. And I didn't feel a thing. Which suggests to me I don't need to suffer because of her; what she wants, what's important to her, is not what I want. The Amy she wants, the acquiescent daughter, I can be, but the essential me, not only does it not interest her, she doesn't even know it's there. I gave her what she wanted yesterday, now it's time to walk away. If I don't, she'll just take, mindlessly take, and come back for more; she'd take my very self if I let her. In the dream I walked away and felt liberated. I've managed all these years without her, and while I may have managed more reluctantly than I used to think, I made my choices long ago. And they were right.'

Philippa had been listening quietly. She could see how the distress of the previous evening, the confusion, resentment, the desires, all had abated. Amy was perfectly calm. A dream in which she had given up her child, or a part of herself – did it really matter? – had provided a solution to her problems. Philippa could understand Amy's analysis but it rested uneasily; she would have liked time to think, to have postponed decisions until later, but this was Amy's drama and it was clear she was ready to act.

'When do you expect to hear about the British Scholarship?' Philippa asked.

'Shortly, certainly by Christmas, and yes, it is the best means of escaping Estelle, I know that. But even if I do win, I'm still stuck here until August. These scholarships are awarded ages in advance.'

'You'd go earlier if you had the money?'

Amy nodded. 'Of course.'

TWELVE

Amy dodges her way down Great Russell Street, avoiding tourists huddled over maps, or standing happy and handsome for the camera, or simply idling in the manner of those who, dazed by travelling, must rely on the weather or appetite to start them moving again. Swerves around them, through the gateway, across the pigeon-infested courtyard, through the colonnade and into the British Museum. Her pace slows in the foyer as she wends her way through the rush of fussing tourists. A dozen languages resonate, groups gather, others disperse, ever-patient warders indicate toilets, cafés, the Elgin marbles, and Amy loiters in the mêlée, in order to magnify the pleasure just ahead, in the blue, muted ambience of the Reading Room.

How commonly it happens that one knows a place before actually seeing it; films, literature, dreams, the signposts of memory, have made it familiar. Three months before, when first she entered the great circular Reading Room, Amy felt as if she had stumbled upon a long lost friend. She had lingered just inside the doors, inhaling air muffled in history, the smell of books, of age, of readers past and present, and had known that here, finally, she had found a sanctuary, here was ground firm enough to support a life.

She would never forget that first day. She had found a seat on the outer edge of one of the radiating spokes of desks, and although she had set out her papers ready for work, her gaze, her very consciousness had been drawn upwards to the huge segmented dome. She studied the fine horizontal cracks that tracked over the surface, the gold-laced lantern at the apex, the tall curved windows, the aquamarine blue that seemed to cleanse and polish the dingy London light. And lower down, encircling the walls from the floor to the base of the dome, the books, thousands of them, mostly leather-bound volumes in greens and blues and maroons. The shelves had been constructed in three broad bands, like the storeys of a building, and spanning each of the upper two levels was a narrow gallery; occasionally a door-sized section of books – timber facsimiles, Amy later realized – would open to one of the galleries, and a person would emerge in a rush of cool air. How orderly the room would look from up there, Amy had thought, how utterly symmetrical. And smaller too, the observer being part of the huge space, rather than a speck at its base.

The room claimed her attention, the people too: the readers and starers, the sleepers and writers, Amy watched them all. In the early days, she had attempted to marry appearance with scholarship, to attach the grey man in brown tweeds to England of the nineteenth century, the fine-skinned woman in the exotic turban to revolutionary politics, the brittle-voiced American to modern popular culture. That she was invariably wrong was a relief: a society in which the products of mind were visible in the cut of a coat or the texture of skin would reduce intellectual work to the vagaries of fashion. A savage situation indeed. And gave up the attempt.

From the very beginning, she had been aware of a rare calm, a sense that finally her shadow was rid of danger, that she could read and write and breathe without a hand clenching her shoulder or a hostile figure threatening to pounce. It seemed that nothing could disturb this feeling, not the muffled noises from the cataloguing area, nor the occasional deep-throated screech of a chair pushing backwards, nor the slap of pages as a heavy text was closed, not even the people as they moved past her to the catalogues or the dictionaries or out through the doors for a break. We all have our temples, she had thought, our gods as well.

Three months on, the effect of the room is no less strong. As she walks the perimeter in search of a desk, she is aware of loosening muscles, a smile about her eyes, and despite pleasure's tendency to sink like sand into the routine of a life, she is as acutely aware of these reactions as when first they occurred. She believes her competence with pleasure, her ability to grasp it and hold it without letting it slip through her fingers, could be attributed to her own peculiar past, in particular, her experience with fear. She had learned to be vigilant, had learned to be forever on the alert, and while fear flaunts a strength that pleasure ordinarily eschews, pleasure, too, can acquire similar tenacity. It is a matter of training, of learning how to recognize pleasure, knowing how to maintain its vibrancy. In three months or three years or three decades the Reading Room would still be a haven for the likes of Amy. She shuddered, for she made a point of ignoring the library's future, the terrible betrayal. For soon, all the readers would be evicted and relocated to new premises atop an old potato depot at St. Pancras. And the Reading Room would be left to – To whom? And for what? A prospect too dreadful to contemplate.

It was already eleven o'clock and the room was filling fast. As a rule, on a Tuesday, Amy was among the ten o'clock arrivals, but this morning, she had first to deliver student papers to college, and once in the department, other tasks had presented themselves, transforming a five minute detour into a cramped, circuitous hour. Not that she resented the job; if not for the few hours of teaching, she would need to take even more from Philippa in these months before her scholarship began. She had Jeremy to thank for the work; he taught in the philosophy department, had heard about the position from friends in English and mentioned it to her; he'd also spoken on her behalf. She was very grateful to him, and for the job.

Her pace slowed as she approached the area where she usually sat. The regulars were already well-entrenched: the liverish man with his second world war, the shiny young American with her Greek, and the thin, white-skinned historian with Sarah, the first

Duchess of Marlborough. All strangers, and yet by working alongside them, passing their desks and observing their books, one learned about the central passion of their lives. This is the stuff of dreams: to know someone well enough so the imagination is piqued, but not so well that daydreams become ordinary. Many of the readers had figured in Amy's daydreams; she had given them husbands and wives, children, parents, houses, jobs, joys, miseries, and thereby passed many an evening alone in her flat. One in particular, the historian, the white-skinned woman hunched over her Duchess, had entered Amy's dreams and stayed. It was her approximation to Amy's vision of her own future that recommended this woman as an excellent subject for daydreams. She was about forty, perhaps a little older, a woman who wore no rings, no ornament of any kind. Her clothes were functional rather than fashionable, her hair more sensible than stylish; the impression she conveyed was of someone without emotional ties. For hours at a time, she would pour over her Duchess, glancing up only occasionally with the glazed vision of a reader too long at her work, to reveal a face shot with effort, and thoughts scudding behind the almost-black eyes. Her presence in the library was always a comfort to Amy, her participation in dreams a pleasure.

Amy found a desk in her usual row not far from the dictionaries; her companions either side were both older women already intent on their work. She unpacked her notes, collected her volumes from Kept Books, and settled down. The last few months in Australia had been devoted to selection of the novels that would form the data for her thesis, works by Virginia Woolf, Jean Rhys, Henry Handel Richardson and Djuna Barnes. Since her arrival in London, she had immersed herself in literary theory. It had not been a fruitful study. She had read theory and had drafted outlines for her dissertation, so many outlines in fact, that she was reminded of those guest lists she had made as a girl for the parties she never had, numerous lists over several years and not a single party. But hope being the nursemaid of youth, compiling the party lists had been a deeply satisfying pastime, and it was only after each was completed, that she knew it would come to nothing. So, too, with the dozen or more outlines for her thesis. 'Challenging the Orthodoxies: the New Woman of English Literature 1920-1940' should have been a radical, provocative and lively work, but so far, all her conceptions had been limp and prosaic. Wearied by these early attempts, and, if the truth be known, worried as well, she had decided to leave her outlines and plunge straight into the chapters, only to find that each sentence had to be wrenched from her word by graceless word, resulting in a prose so leaden and ungainly it was an agony to read. It was not that she did not admire the novels, but the more she studied them, the more she prodded and poked, the less able was she to write about them. The passion of the books was drowned by the drudgery of the dissertation, indeed the books and the dissertation were emerging as natural antagonists. Where the novels bristled with life, where they seemed to burst their covers in a rush of ideas, her own scholarship was cramped and crotchety, clinging to systems cards and a determination to contain the novels to the printed page.

Which was another reason for concern, for it had been the rigour of literary criticism that had attracted her in the first place; she had perceived it as a disciplined study, logical, focussed, and shaped by the limits of the material. Now, however, as the limits pressed in on her, she decided they had little to do with literature and everything to do with the rules for studying literature. Increasingly, she found herself avoiding the analytical texts in favour of the now-familiar novels, and the more time she spent with the novels, the less inclined was she to lift her own pen. It seemed an act of the greatest effrontery that she, Amy Vaughan, an insignifant modern hyphen, had decided these great works of literature required interpretation and she was the one to do it.

She wrote about her difficulties to Philippa. She was worried she had taken Philippa's money under false pretences, worried too, that the one reliable pathway in an otherwise uncertain life – that she would study, gain a PhD, teach, write, in short, she would dedicate herself to literature – had begun to sag. Philippa wrote back at length: Amy was being too harsh on herself, expected too much too soon; no one else attempted to write a thesis before they'd enrolled in the course, so why must she?

Philippa advised her to take her time and enjoy the work; the threatening figure standing at her shoulder was none other than herself and it was time to give the guard a vacation. 'There can be no effective action without a reliable defence,' Amy had protested. 'Life is not a game of chess,' Philippa had replied.

But Amy was impatient and uneasy and mightily wary. When a life is orderly and needs are few, problems are readily anticipated and surprises kept to a minimum. Winning the scholarship, Philippa's paying for her to leave Australia early, the part-time tutor's position, her flat at the top of a house, should have provided a welcome predictability, yet Amy was aware of a thickening fear, as if her successes merely opened the way for new failures. Doubt assailed her at every opportunity. The scholarship was all very well, but if the thesis were bad, what then? Or if she were awarded her PhD but the thesis wasn't suitable for a book? Or if she converted the thesis to a book, but was unable to think of a topic for a second book? What if she turned out to be simply ordinary? And how would she get through life if she were? So many questions to feed an already bloated anxiety.

'What's your hurry?' Philippa wrote. 'Do you have to be the youngest English professor in the land? Look at my son-in-law,' she had continued, 'a professor in his early thirties, and it's not done much for him.'

Fortunately her teaching was going well; the students seemed to enjoy her classes, her colleagues were quite lively, and Jeremy worked in the next building. The problem was that after years of being on the move, of striving to increase the distance between the neglected country child she had been and the resourceful, independent adult she intended always to be, to relax, slow down, tease the enjoyment from a particular situation or activity, was to court danger. And yet she suspected Philippa was right, that if ever there was a time when the usual dangers were dormant this was it.

She turned to her books, opened *Mrs Dalloway* to that peculiarly tense section when the clocks strike three and Richard Dalloway returns home with flowers for his wife, and he can't speak, can't tell Clarissa he loves her, but she, like all women who know too much, understands what the flowers mean, and is prepared to do without his words (although Peter would have said them, which was why he was not the man to marry); she accepts Richard's flowers along with his silence, thereby leaving his inadequacies unheeded and his pride preserved. At which point, Amy sighs and grimaces and takes up her pen, knowing she must again consult the feminist analyses of *Mrs Dalloway*. She rifles through her index cards, neatly colour-coded and cross-referenced, and *Mrs Dalloway* is pushed aside for commentaries on *Mrs Dalloway*, notes are made and margin marks appear and while her initial approach is reluctant, soon she accommodates to the task, is taken up by its momentum, so, when the historian walks by, clipping her chair as she passes, Amy is taken quite by surprise. She looks up, sees the historian pause, sees the shade of a smile cross the white, almost blue-white, angular face, then watches her walk towards the catalogues.

Thoughts as fine and fragile as a spider's web, and just as carefully constructed, are threatened. The historian has found a niche in Amy's daydreams, she is not a person Amy wants to know. A few minutes later, on her return from the catalogues, Amy receives another smile, a tell-tale twitch at the corner of a stranger's mouth that heralds the spoiling of dreams, of events being wrested from the dreamer's control. The panic is immediate, forcing Amy from her desk, out through the double doors, past the flurry of tourists, into the cool air of the colonnade.

This is where the smokers come, the talkers too; the thinkers remain inside, and yet it is to order her thoughts, to deflect this threat to her dreams, that sets Amy pacing. Dreams, hopes, it matters little what they are called, have always been a careful luxury in Amy's life. As a child she used them for revenge; she would have Aunt Rose and Uncle Ken reduced to paupers begging the hugely rich and much-loved Amy Vaughan for charity; sometimes, when real-life Aunt and Uncle had been particularly malicious, the dream Amy Vaughan would respond generously, other times she would not. There were daydreams of Estelle with a terrible illness, and Amy, now a famous doctor, the only person with the knowledge to cure her. And the boys at school, so cruel to the clever girls, also received their comeuppance in Amy's dreams. She had imagination enough to create volumes, and volumes enough to cushion the blows of an unhappy childhood.

When Amy first left home, there had been little time for dreaming, and even less energy, but in brief moments of respite she would create a warm room, a table laden with food, a person sitting opposite, sparkling conversation, scenes pilfered from Iris Murdoch and the early Doris Lessing, and always richly satisfying. Later, when scholarships made for an easier life, the dreams again increased; Professor Amy Vaughan, the famous scholar would be fêted around the world; everyone would want to meet her, everyone would want to hear her speak. In the landscapes of her imagination, Amy would travel from city to city, meeting to meeting, lecture to lecture; graciously, generously, she would allow people into her orbit, but never too long nor too close.

Until Philippa. Who made the dreams redundant. Who marched through all Amy's barriers and welcomed the person she found hiding behind. But now, with Philippa thousands of miles away and Amy far too self-conscious to write as often as she might like, time has again been allocated to dreams, although still in accordance with rules established years ago. For if you do not place limits on your daydreaming or if ever you forget that these are games of fancy and fantasy, the dreams will absorb you, become your master, rather than the other way round. In fact, it is these very rules that give the dreams their power: for a prescribed period of time, you can be whoever you want, doing whatever you please, because you know none of it is true, and in ten or twenty or thirty minutes the pleasure will be over and life will reclaim you once more. Of course, there's nothing preventing you from returning to a particularly appealing scene, tomorrow, next week, even next year, but by then you will have had ample time with battle-scarred reality to keep the dreams in perspective.

All this Amy has carefully known. Some people do drugs, others do alcohol, Amy does daydreams. And into them she brings people living and dead, people known and created; she brings authors and actors, foes and friends, Philippa and Estelle, and recently, she has brought in the white-faced historian. And why not? Hasn't Amy watched her often enough in the library, the pale and hardy face framed by a crop of strong greying hair, the sort of hair that stays in place even when the head is bent to a book? And the large, white hands turning pages, or writing, or clasping her forehead as she sits and thinks. And while she is undoubtedly older than Amy, it is not lined skin, nor drooping eyelids that reveal her age, rather the unflinching gaze, the stern mouth, the strength of the brow, the absorption in her work, all suggest she has been at this life a while.

An ideal candidate for dreams, Amy decided one evening, and in the intervening couple of months had been much occupied with her. Indeed, so much time has been spent with the historian of her creation, she would not know how to talk to the real one. And does not want to, reality being such a poor representation of dreams. Again, her thoughts turned to Philippa, always the exception, who had enriched her life more than any dream. Although such pleasure exacts a price, for to be satisfied with a snug cocoon after one has stretched one's wings is beyond the bounds of reason; which suggests that a butterfly should never become a caterpillar if the way is to be forward. Was it possible, Amy had asked herself over and over again since arriving in London, to be a complete person without Philippa Finemore?

Which was where the historian fitted in, but only as the stuff of dreams. Amy had contrived to pass her desk to discover her area of scholarship, and had created imaginary conversations that, if she were still in Australia, she would have had with Philippa. She missed Philippa, but it was the only aspect of Australia she missed. Even from the aeroplane, she had acknowledged her pleasure at leaving the place. She had watched Australia in miniature, the wide brown land most assuredly, carved with its serpentine creeks, and the darker splotches where the occasional rise, lit from the side by the morning sun, cast a shadow. She saw sheep grazing, clumps of them beneath struggling clusters of surly gums. No lushness, hardly any life except to the trained eye. And hers was not; never had she acquired that particular vision that could endow this huge land with variety and complexity and beauty, always would she see dullness, a land of surfaces, any possible history parched and breathless in the wrinkled waterholes. Even as a child she had known that the land exacerbated her difficulties, that the land, loved by so many, was not for her.

In particular, she hated its brownness, a deep, grabbing red-brown mostly, but yellowing in the miserable creeks, and fading to a brusque dirty straw on the grazing pastures. Poor bastards, she thought as she saw huddles of sheep from the aeroplane window, they too, nearly starve here. Such a brown land and so very flat. And no people. Not that she preferred the daintiness of the English countryside, not at all; she liked sparseness and solitude and loneliness but she liked these when they did not oppress or stifle or mock or dilute. A stone cottage in the wilds of Scotland was, in her imagination, the ideal place, harsh but not deadening, not like this land, with its great expanses of sameness and nothingness. Even the clusters of buildings, bent brown buildings, some here, others there, the careful patch of green lawn, a solitary swing and slide, did not suggest life.

Hours had passed while the plane sped onwards, and still the Australian landscape stretched endlessly below. This land does not speak to me, she had thought. She could admire its hostility, even its toughness, but she would never forgive its arrogant emptiness. And the cities were no better. Her own city, Melbourne, was huge and sprawling, one hundred kilometres from one side to the other and only four million inhabitants. Such a lot of space these city people have, and expect it too. Thirteen million people live in Manhattan, she had once read, and yet Manhattan is a mere fraction the size of Melbourne. Manhattan is full, Melbourne is empty. And how she hated the emptiness! If she had stayed she would have moved from the beach-side suburb, away from the slick-haired, loose-limbed youths who had taken over the area, to those few crowded streets of the new immigrants, where the Vietnamese held sway and Caucasian faces were duly pale and insignificant. It is a matter of always placing yourself outside the mainstream.

So never mind the emptiness of the Australian countryside, think instead of the empty cities, the empty Australian cities bristling with possession, the empty cities with their long grey

arteries stretching past neat houses set in private gardens, each dwelling separated from the road by a lowish fence but separated from its neighbour by two metre high palings. 'We love it here,' the residents say, 'everyone's so friendly,' and they fix a loose paling on their two metre high fence. Out in the green belts where the tidy brick dwellings line up side by side, televisions roar and custom-built kitchens purchased on time-payment and installed within the outer-suburban living memory, are cleaned three, four, five times daily, in order to preserve sanity. Sanity, sanitized, an unfortunate lexical connection.

And the weather doesn't help; the alienating blue skies of Australia suck the soul from you, drive people out of their minds into the great outdoors.

Amy looks up through the columns to the sallow London sky, breathes the heavy fumes, feels the dirt settling on her skin and knows she will always prefer this to the claustrophobic emptiness of her own country.

She glances at her watch, a quarter past twelve, and decides on an early lunch; better to confront the historian's smile with the courage of a full stomach. And starts off down the steps.

'And where do you think you're going when there's work to be done?'

Jeremy, a smile on his face and a cigarette in hand, is standing on the steps beside her. She gives him a peck on the cheek and laughs.

'You should talk! You're exactly,' she looks at her watch, 'four and three quarter hours early.'

'Ah, yes, but time with you will make me a better person, whereas if I'd stayed at work I might have turned to mush.'

'And what about your friend? What about Mim Drummond? Hadn't you arranged to collect her for our five o'clock drink?'

'I've just rung her, told her of the change in plans; she'll meet us at the pub instead.'

They linked arms and set off for a café where the coffee was Italian and the sandwiches made to order. As they walked, Amy asked about Victor, who had recently moved in with Jeremy.

'He thinks he's in heaven, and compared with the slum where he used to live, so he is.'

'And you?'

Jeremy smiled and shrugged, 'If he's in heaven, I guess I am too.'

They arrived at the café and were soon settled at a table. They placed their orders and while they waited for the food, exchanged recent letters from Philippa.

'Do you think she's all right?' Amy asked. 'She sounds a bit flat to me, hardly mentions Leo.'

'I'm sure she and Leo are fine, the problem is she's doing too much. If you read on,' he pointed to the middle of the last page, 'you'll see she had the children three times last week, and that's in addition to all her other commitments. You'd think Melanie and Evelyn would know by now that Philippa will take the kids whenever she's asked, so it's up to them to exercise some restraint.'

Amy nodded and sighed and continued to read. Since her arrival in London, she and Jeremy had dissected every aspect of Philippa Finemore's life. They were critical of Gray and Evelyn and Melanie and Selwyn who took Philippa for granted; 'They expect everything,' Jeremy said, 'and give nothing in return.' It was ironical, that they, the two members of Philippa's family ('You're just like a daughter,' Jeremy had said, much to Amy's delight) who did appreciate her had abandoned her; each of them had put their own needs ahead of hers, each shuffled in the shadow of a prowling guilt if they detected even a hint of gloom in Philippa's letters. Which explained the importance of Leo; his attentiveness, his admiration, his love for Philippa, eased their disquiet.

'Are you sure she and Leo are happy?'

Jeremy shrugged, nibbled on a sprout. 'As much as I ever know these things.'

Jeremy's uneasiness was compounded by what he described as the moral spinelessness of his brother and sister. 'It puts Philippa at risk,' he said to Amy, 'makes her ripe for exploitation.' He paused, was thinking and frowning. 'Melanie and Gray have changed, they used to be much more considerate, Melanie especially. These days they seem so mean, Evelyn and Selwyn too, although Selwyn always had a head start in that regard. None of them shows a jot of interest in other people, all that matters is their own comfort, their own immediate needs. Do you realize that despite everything Philippa does for them, they rarely give her a kind or appreciative word, and wouldn't even think to ask if she needed any help.'

Of her three children, Jeremy said, only he had Philippa's interests at heart, only he understood Philippa's true worth.

Which was a peculiar thing, Amy said, for many would suggest that Jeremy, the homosexual son, was his mother's greatest failure.

'I guess,' he replied, 'that neither Philippa nor I see it that way.'

Then there was Finemore's, which was another cause for concern. There had never been any suggestion of Jeremy's joining the business. From early childhood, his academic orientation had been clear, and, as time went on, it simply became a matter of which area of scholarship he preferred. George had taken a dim view of philosophy, to him it was sweet sherry to law's cognac or medicine's port. To please him, Jeremy had combined law with arts at an undergraduate level, but had never practised. He returned to the university for a masters degree in philosophy and then a PhD, by which time George had no option but to accept his son's decision. 'At least he gets the prizes,' George acknowledged, 'at least he's best at what he does.'

Which was an important quality for every man, but particularly his younger son who was a bit soft.

Now, with George gone and Gray and Selwyn at loggerheads, Jeremy felt obliged to offer his services to Finemore's, but didn't want to.

'And Philippa wouldn't want it either,' Amy said.

'Although after this morning, I'm inclined to think anything would be an improvement on academe.'

Amy ordered two more coffees and asked him what had happened.

He had spent the morning with his undergraduate seminar

class in modern aesthetics. 'I've been trying to interest them in the aesthetics of minimalism – with minimal success, I'm afraid. It's such desolate work,' he smiled at her, 'not that I want to dissuade you from your chosen profession, but at times it is less than satisfying. The students expect a performance, expect to be entertained; above all, they expect to be given the goods. So any attempt to provoke discussion is regarded as obfuscation, as somehow contravening the educational contract. They're there to learn, they say, and I'm employed to teach, which, by their account, I was not doing this morning. What they were wanting was argument A and opposing argument B, each summarized in a half page of simple statements. Which I refused to give.' He shook his head slowly, a wry smile across the fine, dark features that reminded Amy so much of Philippa. 'Instead, I decided to try another approach, resorted to the trusty video and slides – the modern undergraduate loves visuals – and just as we seemed to be making progress, I saw that one young punk, David Hume his name is, what a joke! was reading *Playboy*. Reading *Playboy* magazine in my class!

'I should have ignored him, teachers never win in these situations, but I was so incensed I couldn't stop myself. And what did the student do? Simply laughed, said *Playboy* was an aesthetic object, stood on his chair and displayed the centrefold to the rest of the class. Who laughed as well. "What's got into our tutor?" I heard one student say. "Perhaps he doesn't like girls," was the reply. And then added, "David wasn't disturbing anyone, so why pick on him?"

'Always,' Jeremy said, 'they defend their own, even when it's against their better interests.'

'There must be one good student in the class.'

'That's a myth if ever I heard one; a single good student can't save a class, the good student is quickly silenced by the rowdy certainties of mediocrity, or simply decides not to turn up. Anyway, fewer and fewer good students take philosophy these days. The trend here, in Australia too, is to garnish philosophy's drab reputation with seductive baubles, so one finds a new unit in the philosophy of sex offered alongside logic.' He picked up a piece of brown lettuce he'd discarded earlier in the meal and popped it in his mouth. 'Do you know what the fastest growing area in philosophy is?' Amy shook her head. 'Something called the philosophy of business. The philosophy of business! Can you imagine it? Perhaps we should offer a unit in the philosophy of business sex and really boost our numbers.'

'Your department actually teaches a unit in the philosophy of sex?'

'Sure does, by an ageing stud who wears leather trousers.'

They both laughed.

'Although it's no joking matter,' Jeremy said. 'What with the philosophy of sex and the philosophy of food and the philosophy of sport, philosophy bears little resemblance to the discipline I studied as an undergraduate. One need only attend a philosophy conference to see how the discipline has changed. At the last two national meetings, the sessions with the largest audiences - we now count numbers as if philosophy meetings were football matches - were devoted to the philosophy of business.'

'I'm surprised there's so much to say.'

'There's not, repetition plays an important part. I went along on both occasions - one should know the enemy - and heard speak a certain Keith Austin-Ward who's one of the British advocates of the area; he also happens to be the chair of Mim Drummond's department and, according to her, an intellectual newt. He's never published a book, hasn't written a refereed article for more than a decade, yet he's a full professor. Mim says he's a terrible teacher, and is forever harassing the female students, but he's managed to lure money to the department, and in the present climate nothing else seems to matter. Ask Mim yourself when she joins us later.'

Jeremy scraped the froth from the sides of his cup, licked the spoon, lit another cigarette and smoked; he was frowning slightly, his masseters were clenching and releasing; only when a waitress dropped a tray nearby did he collect himself.

'Want another?' He asked, indicating the empty cup.

But Amy's attention was elsewhere. 'Did you see that?'

'What?'

'Over there.' Amy nodded in the direction of three people squeezed around a tiny table.

A few minutes earlier, a woman had been sitting alone with tea and sandwiches and an open book, reading while she ate. A couple had entered, both of them big, bullish people, and the man had made for the single woman's table. His wife, a restraining hand on his arm, indicated the vacant tables on the opposite side, but he wanted the non-smoking area, he said, and without even a by-your-leave, sat down next to the woman. He huffed out of his jacket, stretched to another table, dragged over a spare chair and indicated his wife should join him.

Such a small table and such large people, Amy wondered whether the solitary woman with her book, her plate of sandwiches, her cup and saucer, her pot of tea, the pot of hot water, the milk jug, could hold her ground. But she did! She does! She pours another cup, leans her head on her hand to block out the brutes, and continues to read.

'Did you see that?' Amy says to Jeremy.

'What?'

'Over there.'

Now the waitress is greeting the couple, who wave the menu aside, they know what they want. The solitary woman, trying to maintain her solitude, continues to read; she refuses to be intimidated, eats slowly, sips her tea, turns a page. The waitress returns with the couple's lunch. The tiny table is crammed with food and tea and utensils. The man, so huge and grey, stares across the clutter to the wall; his legs, with parted knees and splayed feet, are stretched beneath the table, forcing the women to sit neatly, feet tucked under their chairs. He sits back, rearranges his crotch and waits. And then it happens. Reaching across him, leaning and twisting because her husband must not be disturbed and the table is precariously laden, the wife pours tea – not her own, she can wait – pours his milk, his tea, his drop of hot water, as she has always done, and hands him the cup and saucer.

'Do you think he can manage his own sugar?' Amy says.

'And there! Look there!' Jeremy indicates a young Japanese couple sitting two tables away. 'They're forty years younger and from an entirely different culture, yet doing exactly the same thing.'

The young man and woman are dressed in identical crimson jackets with hoods to protect them from the dithery London weather, she is stretching across the table with a spoonful of black forest cake. She feeds him, two mouthfuls for him, one for her, two mouthfuls for him, one for her. They do not talk.

Amy and Jeremy turn away.

'It's obvious we're made for each other,' Amy says with a squeeze of his hand. 'Most people don't notice such things, they don't want to bother with the ordinary, the details.'

'And you don't agree?'

'Of course I don't, and neither do you. Besides,' she smiles, 'if God resides in the details, so, too, does the Devil.'

'You've a touch of the philosopher yourself.'

Amy, still smiling, says, 'I'd prefer to call it caution.'

They did not return to the library as originally planned. From the café they made their way to the gardens at Lincoln's Inn where they sat and talked until a late afternoon breeze drove them back towards the museum and into the pub to wait for Mim Drummond. They found a corner seat and a clean table, and over half pints of cider continued to talk.

At half past five, Mim Drummond, a large, handsome woman with a burst of wild red hair, blew in through the pub doors, gaberdine coat billowing, satchel bulging, scarf sliding off her shoulders, emerald-green glasses slumped at the end of her nose. She paused, saw Jeremy and Amy, hurled herself in their direction, dumped satchel, scarf, coat and herself on to the leather bench, gave Jeremy a kiss, shook hands with Amy, drank vigorously from the cider Jeremy had waiting for her, lit one of Jeremy's cigarettes, and, with glasses still precariously balanced, smiled the most luscious, rousing and tooth-filled smile Amy had ever seen.

'I thought the day would never end! I hereby make a solemn vow, with you as my witnesses, that if ever another all-day meeting is called, I'll take a cut in salary rather than attend.'

'An all-day meeting?' Amy was incredulous. 'Do you mean a single meeting?'

'Just the one meeting.'

'For the whole day?'

'Since half past nine.'

'What about your classes?'

'All cancelled, our noodle in his wisdom judged the meeting to be more important.'

Jeremy laughed, turned to Amy. 'The noodle to whom she refers is that philosophy of business guru I mentioned earlier, Keith Austin-Ward.'

'He's also a fool with too much time on his hands, why else would he call an all-day meeting? Seven straight hours with my colleagues, the lot of us, from classical to contemporary, summoned to discuss the most intellectually vacuous proposals for increasing student enrolments I've ever heard. And,' she continued, 'no prizes for guessing which area of intellectual endeavour holds the solution to our numbers problem.'

'Wouldn't be the philosophy of business by any chance?' Jeremy lit a cigarette, handed the packet to Mim. 'My poor father would turn in his grave.'

'As well he might, but before he settles back into eternal rest he might tell us what in hell's name—'

'Now that's an apt choice of language when referring to the dead.'

She laughed. 'But as a once-lively business tycoon he might know what the philosophy of business is all about. I certainly don't.'

Jeremy suggested she ask Keith Austin-Ward.

'I'm not that desperate, although as a result of today's meeting, I could find myself teaching it; my department plans to offer an undergraduate major, plus a masters degree by coursework. The philosophy of business,' she sneered, 'how absurd.'

Amy bought some crisps, which were quickly demolished, and bought some more. Mim Drummond continued to talk: about her colleagues, the noodle, a book that had just been published in which both she and Jeremy had chapters, a recent journal article by an American philosopher written in the form of a cartoon. Amy was entranced, she had never before met such a person, never witnessed such *luxuriance*; the large hands punctuating sentences, the huge smile, the glasses travelling the length of the nose driven by the changing moods of the speaker, the lavish ideas, all created a person who was, simply, thrilling. Other people saw it too, other customers were watching this large woman with her resonant voice and huge laugh and extravagant gestures, and were smiling. She made you feel good; it was her lack of affectation and her air of being so utterly at ease with herself, that seemed, in turn, to put you at ease. And then there was the name, MIM DRUMMOND – Amy decided it should always be in capital letters – which, with its symmetry and rush of M's was the essence of stability and a startling contrast with the ebullience of the person. Watching Mim Drummond was like watching an engrossing film, you were lifted out of yourself, and forgot for the moment that the experience must, and would, come to an end.

Several minutes passed before Amy realized she had been staring, and even then she wondered if she might not stare a little longer. At the same time, she did not want Mim to think her rude, or, worse still, stupid, so, with a conscious effort, she let in the rest of the world, twisted around to include Jeremy in her view, and with a break in the conversation, asked how the two of them had met.

'It was about ten years ago,' Jeremy said, 'during my first trip to England, in Plymouth of all places.'

'Don't ever ridicule Plymouth. If not for Plymouth we wouldn't be sitting here now.'

'Plymouth, plus the fact that philosophy conferences are short on lesbians and gay men.'

'But long on ageing dons who hate physical exercise – '

'And cold winds – '

'And Plymouth does cold winds so well.'

Mim took Jeremy's hand, stared into his eyes. Feigning a Marlene Dietrich voice, she said, 'Didn't we have some wonderful walks around the ramparts of Plymouth? Didn't we darling?'

'And wasn't it freezing?'

'How can you say such a thing, when the fires of our friendship were burning so brightly.'

Jeremy laughed. To Amy he said, 'Can you see why I like her so much, and she's miserable today.' He turned to Mim, 'You *are* miserable?'

'Of course I'm miserable.' She took a hand to her brow, slipped into a semi-reclining position. 'After such a day, who wouldn't be.'

During the next hour, Amy learned that Mim Drummond, a PhD in philosophy and, like Jeremy, a specialist in aesthetics, had been born in Sussex, had attended school in London and university at Cambridge. She was now employed on contract at a new university which she described as 'part of the educational enthusiasms of the sixties.' At thirty-seven, she was one of the more junior members of a department in which the average age of faculty was 53.6, a department which was stifling under a hefty layer of dead wood, 'stagnant and stale, with hardly a publication between them.'

Mim, on the other hand, wrote regularly for the TLS, had published several papers, had a book on the politics of taste, and another in press, which, she said, would do nothing to improve her standing in the department.

Why was that? Amy asked.

'The book is called *The False Aesthetics,* it's concerned with the essential nihilism of postmodernism; it also tackles several of the intellectual fashions of the past fifteen years.' Her face crinkled with delight. 'Certain of my colleagues will think I'm being critical of them, while the rest will just hate me for having another publication. The only joy I give them is they're senior to me.' She lit one of Jeremy's cigarettes, smiled at Amy through the smoke. 'When it comes to hierarchies, the academy could teach even the army a thing or two.'

Most of 'the dead wood' had been founding members of the department, had last published a decade or two ago, drank too much, fiddled the figures to inflate their contact hours, regarded the World Cup as the cultural high point of the year, and were devotees of *The Times'* crossword. They avoided undergraduate teaching, and while they welcomed post-graduate students as 'cheap hours', the post-graduates invariably chose Mim or one

of the other junior faculty as supervisors, which was why, Mim explained, there was so much departmental support for a masters degree by coursework in the philosophy of business. 'Each piece of dead wood will teach a few classes in the proposed course and thereby claim post-graduate teaching hours.'

The departmental head was forty-nine year old Keith Austin-Ward who, if not for his dynamic body odour, would triumph as the deadest wood of all. He was the sort of man who, when asked to sign a document, perhaps a grant application or a leave form, would study it, exchange a full-stop for a comma, an indefinite article for the definite, insert 'had' to a verb that didn't need it, and with his signature duly applied, return the document to its owner, noting, modestly and seriously, that he had made a few improvements.

'For thirty thousand pounds a year he dots my i's and crosses my t's.'

'He has to piss on your work,' Amy said, 'like dogs marking their territory.'

Mim laughed. 'What an apt description and how very Australian.' And laughed some more. 'All those years when I thought Keith came to work only to do *The Times'* crossword, all those years when I would see him staring through his window, eyes closed, lips moving, all those debates with erstwhile colleagues about the weekend soccer, and I thought he was simply wasting time. But no, it seems he was actually thinking, or was occasionally thinking, and planning his foray into the philosophy of business. I always knew he read conference abstracts, nothing else mind you, just the abstracts, but it seems this was sufficient to show him how the winds were blowing.'

She was smiling no longer, shook her head slowly, removed her glasses and rubbed her eyes. 'I don't know why I'm surprised at what's happened, after all, it's simple enough, our office noodle has discovered late twentieth-century pragmatism and he likes it. And why not? It's easy, it's popular and it's mindless; all it requires is a few money changers in the temple, and there's no shortage of them.' She shrugged, replaced her glasses. 'I simply don't have the qualifications to be an academic these days; I don't lunch with the right people, my language isn't from the *Financial Review*, and my offerings to students are not sufficiently entertaining. Although, I must say, failure makes you very hungry. Are you two ready for some food?'

They moved around the corner for dinner at a Greek restaurant. Not that Amy wanted to eat; with excitement churning her stomach, she had little appetite, and merely fiddled with bread and dips while the others emptied huge plates of spiced lamb and vegetables. Over thick, sweet coffee Mim asked about Amy's dissertation. What was she proposing to study? Had she begun? Had the move to London been advantageous? With what she hoped was wit and erudition, Amy described her work, the novels she was studying, the thesis she hoped to write, even mentioned her growing disenchantment with literary criticism. After a few more questions, Mim suggested Amy might benefit from the library's collection of original manuscripts. 'I'm sure they'd give you some ideas, an infusion of energy at the very least. I think there's some Jean Rhys in the collection; certainly there's Virginia Woolf.'

As well Amy knew. Several times had she stood at the cabinet displaying *Mrs Dalloway*, just inches away from the unlined notebook, trying to decipher the bony handwriting in its purplish ink, while tourists rubbed against her, eager to see anything, just as long as it was famous and worth a fortune. 'Shocking writing,' says an American with shocking breath, resting his arm on the glass of the display case. 'Do you think she's the Virginia Woolf in that old film with Liz Taylor and Richard Burton?' says his companion; the man nods and mutters what a terrible film it was and how they'd do better to find the Beatles display which was 'somewhere round here.'

Mim shook her head. 'I don't mean just the manuscripts on public view, I mean the library of manuscripts.' And proceeded to describe a special pass that allowed people to study original works. 'It's the same system as in the Reading Room, although on a much smaller scale.'

Amy was incredulous. 'You mean you can actually read the manuscripts! Hold them in your hands, hold *Mrs Dalloway*, Virginia

Woolf's version, not Penguin's? In your hands?'

Mim was laughing. 'Although you're advised to use the book stands, for the protection of the manuscripts.'

Amy's reaction to the Manuscripts Students' Room was much the same as a believer entering paradise: she'd waited all her life for this. She had organized her reader's pass the very next day, and in the intervening month had spent as much time there as possible. It had been a month passed in a surreal landscape, one never before seen yet wondrously familiar, a complete, enclosed and marvellous world in which she was entirely at home. And a place of such treasures! Virginia Woolf, Jean Rhys, and E. M. Forster (who had nothing to do with her thesis but was one of her favorite writers) and Joyce, and numerous poets, and a huge collection of letters, and she knew if she were to study everything that interested her, never again would she know the haggard brain of the previous months.

She had begun her work in earnest with Virginia Woolf. The working draft of *Mrs Dalloway* was contained in three separate notebooks, each owned by Virginia Woolf, touched by her, and used by her – Amy would never adjust to the wonder of it all. She had finished the first notebook the previous day and was ready to begin the second. Now, as she came through the King's Library, she stopped at the Virginia Woolf display case wanting to see it empty, wanting to read the notice explaining that the exhibit, Volume II of the draft of *Mrs Dalloway,* had been temporarily removed.

For her. For Amy Vaughan.

Nothing, neither gift nor love, could give greater pleasure. Although, as she made her way through the early crowds, it occurred to her that if she had come to the British Museum as a visitor, just for a day, had seen the Virginia Woolf case empty and read the small notice 'temporarily removed' she would be desolate. And was determined not to dally over that particular volume.

She hurries past the crowds, through the door, shows her pass to the warder, on through the second door and into the Students' Room where she finds a seat at the end table adjacent to the windows; she sets up her book stand and goes to collect Volume II of *Mrs Dalloway*. As she walks back to her desk she feels again the reverence these manuscripts inspire. Always has she been moved by literature; sentences, pages, whole scenes can enter her thoughts and distract her from the nylon shimmer of every day. But there is something else with these manuscripts: to read the words the authors wrote, see their scratchings out, the margin jottings, turn the same pages they turned, hold notebooks they held, is . . . is what? Ever since entering here she has been searching for an apt description. Religious analogies trespass, which is not surprising, for reading these manuscripts takes one outside the quotidian, far beyond the sturdy well-springs of meaning; in the process of reading, Amy knows joy, satisfaction, fulfilment, and a profound awareness and total absorption she is sure believers find in their god.

She puts the manuscript on the reading stand, gently, so gently, lays out her own copy of *Mrs Dalloway* together with her notebook and pencil ready for work. She does not open the manuscript, wants to postpone the pleasure of the first glance, looks instead to the room, such an ordinary room, and the readers, such ordinary people, sitting at long, ordinary tables, five to a side, ten to a table, five tables in each of the two work areas. Ordinary, ordinary and not what she might have imagined. She smiles as she brings to mind ossified figures bent over mustardy pages, mussy grey hair and grey furrowed brows and nobbled hands snug in half gloves, smiles as she recognizes an image from childhood, an illustrated version of Dickens – *The Old Curiosity Shop*? *A Tale of Two Cities*? She can't remember which – that has seeped out of memory. The reality is very different; the readers are often young and smartly dressed in clothes redolent of a life not entirely devoted to the mind. They sniff and cough and acknowledge friends just like ordinary mortals, and itch their scalp and twirl their hair and wear shoes that squeak. Although such noises as do occur, even the sharp metallic tone of the modern telephone, are quickly absorbed by the hush of concentration that pervades here; which is not the precious hush that presages the entrance of someone famous, nor indeed the anticipatory hush that prickles with spectacular hopes, rather it is the hush of being occupied, of working without a fuss.

All so ordinary until you see the work, the manuscripts. The woman to her right has an illuminated volume, a Latin Bible, luxuriant pages bound between worn leather. She reads slowly, comparing the manuscript with a twentieth-century Latin Bible and a James I Authorized Version. She looks from one to the other, comparing and contrasting, occasionally frowning or smiling, making notes. Opposite is a man with a magnifying glass and a musical manuscript, intermittently he plays a phrase on the surface of the table, raising his eyebrows, inhaling deeply as if breathing on the melody. It is probably Handel he hears.

Amy cannot understand why people are not clamouring to enter here. Always there are empty seats, always she has no difficulty finding a space at the end table she has identified as her own. She wonders if it is different at other times of the year and resolves to ask Mim.

There are few students of the modern. As Amy passes between the librarian's desk and her own, she looks at the work of the other readers, sees that the manuscripts are very old, written in hands long consigned to history. They are glorious works, even the hasty scratchings on scraps of sallow paper – particularly these, as theirs has been the greatest struggle against the carelessness of time.

Finally she opens *Mrs Dalloway*, turning the pages as if on tip toe, not wanting to disturb nor intrude on a domain that is essentially private. Such a furtive business it is, for she must intrude, how can she not? as she swoops on each page, searches beneath the crossings out, studies the scenes tried and tried again, sees how the novel might have begun, how observations are constructed detail by tiny detail, sees all the wobbling and dithering that the writer never intended to be seen. And she wonders if she has chosen the wrong career, for what is driving her, what is binding her to these pages so that her eyes burn and her head aches, is a desire to learn how the novel was written, how Woolf arrived at the final published version. Amy knows she intrudes, but as she copies from Woolf's notebook, she cannot stop herself. She is conscious of a physical connection to the manuscript, as if she, or rather her head, is enclosed in a glass cylinder together with the manuscript. Down the tunnel she looks, and even though she is aware of her surroundings, the light from the windows, the other readers, the bleating telephone, her attention is rivetted to the page, to that spiny, uneven hand, the changing thickness of the nib, the scratchings out, the letters that lose their definition in a sentence composed in a rush. It's a different way of reading, like reading down a microscope; words are sliced from their sentences, perused and then collected together again, and in grasping the words, in prodding first this way and then that, there is a sense of being inside the language, of feeling its sound and rhythm. Never has Amy been so tensely animated, never will she understand why there aren't more people eager for this pleasure.

'Is it more crowded at other times of the year?' she asks Mim later that day.

Mim thinks not, certainly she's never had any difficulty in finding a place.

It is a late afternoon in June, the two women are seated on striped deck-chairs in St James's Park. They had to be striped, Amy said, because that's how they always appear in paintings and old photographs.

'So we're fulfilling a lifelong ambition, are we?' Mim said, after they'd chosen their chairs and sat down.

Amy laughed. 'Without a doubt.'

She wanted to explain how hiring deck-chairs in a park was symbolic of certain fundamental differences between English and Australian life, that to sit, as she was now doing, in a hired deck-chair was to feed a sense of liberation begun when she left Australia. 'There are no deck-chairs for hire in Australian parks, because there's no need for them, the Australian climate and the Australian attitude to space have seen to that. Space is cheap in Australia, there's so much of it and so few people, there's enough for everyone to have their very own piece, indeed, it's expected. So the great Australian dream of owning a home becomes the great Australian reality that most Australians do, in fact, live in their own homes. Not flats, not units but large houses set in large gardens.' She illustrated her words by carving up the air into huge square blocks. 'With all this,' she slashed the air, 'who needs public parks? Then there's the climate. People rush to the parks here at the first sign of spring, but in a warm climate, spring is hardly noticed. Which is not to say we don't have parks,' she continued, 'indeed, Melbourne has some of the loveliest parks in the world, but Australians don't need their parks in the same way as the English; Australians don't need parks to slough off winter's damp and cold, to breathe easily away from traffic, to relax out of the city's crowds. When Australians want to escape the city they go to the beach or the vast empty outback, otherwise they relax over a barbeque in their own back yard. Why sit in a park among strangers, when you can sit in comfort at home and watch the cricket on television at the same time?'

'And if it turned cold you could go inside.'

Mim was sitting all in a huddle, she looked freezing. Amy's jacket was lying on the ground, she picked it up and passed it to Mim. 'It'll be too small, but at least it's warm.'

'What about you?' Mim asked, slipping the jacket over her shoulders.

'Feeling cold is another pleasure of being away from Australia. Sun, sea and warmth play havoc with a life of the mind.' Amy started to laugh, 'Can you think of a single great work to have emerged from the tropics?'

Mim was laughing too, she couldn't off-hand, but she'd give the matter some thought. And sat quietly for a while. 'The more you tell me of Australia the more I understand your passion for grimy, damp and crumbling London. Understand too, the pleasure you take in the library, your tiny flat, your blustering through crowded streets.' She paused. 'Perhaps you've discovered the best way to live in London.'

'I think it's how one must live in the twentieth century.'

Mim smiled, reached across and took Amy's hand. The gesture

was spontaneous and warm, a Philippa Finemore gesture, and Amy did not pull away.

The two women sat in their deck-chairs, feeling the gentle nudge of the wind, watching the people stroll by. A duck with a glistening blue-green collar waddled over and then another; in the distance, beyond the hush of trees, was the roar of London streets.

'It's been years since I've done this; I'd forgotten how peaceful it could be.'

Amy's sensations, however, were of quite a different order. With her hand in Mim's grasp, her fingers were flushing, her palm was sending signals to other parts of her body, her knuckles felt like swollen bundles of nerve endings; Mim stroked the inner side of her wrist and the caress shot to her lower back. Amy shut her eyes, the sensations were intensifying, she should pull her hand away, but didn't. Always Mim had this bizarre effect. They had met several times over the past month, sometimes with Jeremy, more often without, and mostly at Mim's instigation. Amy was thrilled that Mim sought her out, but it created problems as well; instead of her usual control, her usual ironic detachment, Amy was all sensation with Mim. It was as if all her perceptions, all her feelings, were sharpened, so what was happening now to her hand could happen to any part of her. Everything was enhanced: the pleasure she felt in Mim's company as well as her anxiety that Mim might become bored; her excitement at Mim's ideas, and her misery over her own insipid offerings. She was a novice at strong emotion, her experience with Philippa had taught her that, but even Philippa was not much help in the present circumstances. For the crux of the matter was – it suddenly occurred to her that her hand had become a live wire – her feelings for Mim were etched with desire. It was a confusing discovery, and oddly distressing, not for any moral reasons, but because she thought she knew herself, thought she was in complete control of the person she believed herself to be. She was wondering what else she might discover, when her hand was released and Mim leaned forward to search the contents of her satchel.

'Hungry?' She asked.

Amy nodded, her hand suddenly freezing, the rest of her body bereft. Out came crisps, a bottle of wine, two glasses, two spoons, and a tiny container of caviar. 'Here,' Mim said, handing Amy a spoon and the caviar, 'it tastes better straight from the jar.'

From the jar or not, with a spoon or without, black caviar or red, it would not have mattered, Amy ate, and ate some more, wondering how she might engineer another touch from Mim's large white hand. Wondered too, what other women might do in the same situation. Certainly they'd try to remain calm, so Amy breathed deeply in and out and in and out and choked on a speck of caviar and started coughing. And here is Mim rubbing her back, firmly rubbing from shoulders to waist, and Amy knows she must stop coughing before she makes a fool of herself. Now there's an arm about her shoulders and, as the spluttering subsides, a hand rests on her thigh. 'Are you all right?' Mim is asking, 'You're not going to suffocate?' Not from caviar, Amy was thinking, and assured Mim she was perfectly fine.

When she was completely recovered she moved her thoughts and her deck-chair to safer ground. 'How was your day?' she asked, pleased her voice sounded so steady and the stampede in her stomach was so nicely hidden.

'Much the same as usual.' Mim leaned forward, Amy leaned back. 'Are you sure you're all right?' Amy nodded, and Mim continued. 'Much the same as usual, except I think the noodle's got something up his sleeve.'

'Deodorant?'

'If only. Although today the stench was not quite as overpowering as usual, and he was wearing a suit, a brown suit, but a suit nonetheless. A clean suit, too, no spots around the fly or dribbles down the tie.' She held up the bottle. 'More?' Amy nodded. 'Yes, our noodle is definitely up to something. A while ago he asked me for my course outlines and reading lists, all very suspicious, mumbled something about catching up on recent work in my area, which is somewhat hard to believe since he's never expressed an interest before. And he spent an age in personnel today, with much laughing with his cohorts when he returned to the department. If it were anyone but the noodle I'd say he had a new job, but the noodle's so comfortable in his noodledom I can't imagine he'd want to move, and besides, who on earth would have him?' She sipped her drink. 'And my mother rang. It's the parents' fortieth wedding anniversary and I'm expected home for the weekend. Do you want to come?'

Amy shook her head vigorously, and then, not wanting to appear rude, explained she was not much interested in family.

'What about your own?'

'Don't have one.'

'Everyone has a family.'

'No, everyone *had* a family; some of us have chosen to discard ours.'

Mim was eager to know more, but Amy not inclined to tell. 'Family, or rather my family aren't worth the time. We'd do better with another topic.' She paused for a moment and then smiled. 'How about whether the brain is in danger of becoming a vestigial organ.'

Mim laughed. 'What a grotesque idea, and yet horrifyingly possible.'

'If your students are representative of contemporary undergraduates, Jeremy's too, and the office noodle is typical of what passes for an intellectual these days, then we're in a lot of trouble.'

Mim was still laughing over the notion of a vestigial brain. 'Like the appendix. Of course, if the brain becomes useless then we'd be all body and the mind-body debate would be resolved once and for all.'

But Amy was wanting to be serious. 'When I was a student, what I hated most about my classes was the lack of curiosity. Everyone seemed to know everything, everyone was so opinionated, and while you'd expect this to promote lively discussion it never did. The other students seemed to think that everyone was entitled to a point of view whether it was informed or not, and that no point of view was superior to any other. So, for any one issue, while there might be several opinions, no opinion ever addressed another, and no opinion was ever asked to defend itself. And if you did try to argue, people would take it as a personal attack and accuse you of fascist tendencies. As bait, I would raise the Hitler argument: was Hitler entitled to eliminate whole groups of people just because it was his belief they were inferior? The other students were never impressed, some were openly contemptuous: only a fool would bring Hitler into a discussion of Shakespeare or Yeats or Dickinson, they would say, and advise me to stick to the topic in future.'

'What you're describing is the dominance of the present over the past. It's pragmatism by any other name and it's currently fuelling university policy.'

'I would have thought economics more than a neglect of history was to blame for what's happening in universities.'

Mim shrugged, 'Economic arguments invariably attach to the immediate. Economic rationalization of the humanities, for example, ignores that throughout human history, it's been the humanities, the arts and letters, that have been the major civilizing influences. Instead, we see a money value being put on classicists and philosophers and historians. Can they do anything for the nation's budget deficit? Can they help rectify the university's budget shortfall? Money has colonized culture, and, in so doing, has transformed it from something subversive and anarchic to a commodity as tame and bland as the pastel flowers on a greeting card. You complain about the lack of curiosity among students, but what else do you expect when people are committed to the strikingly predictable, when they avoid thought and reason, when they're happy to devote their entire lives to keeping their own houses in order?' She laughed, a hollow futile puff of noise. 'That the arts are being tamed in such an environment can come as no surprise. The arts have always sought to unlock the imagination, to drive us beyond ourselves. But no longer; the arts and humanities are being domesticated, packaged as commodities like any other, treated like any fashion item.'

'So culture becomes nothing more than a starter in the race of conspicuous consumption?'

'Exactly. Culture becomes artefact, values become artefact, and morality, if it can be said to exist at all, is only an opinion about what's right and what's wrong. Money is the godhead now; if it makes money then it must be good. And you can't get more concrete than that.' She shrugged. 'Perhaps our noodle has been smarter than I thought, perhaps the philosophy of business is in fact the new moral philosophy.'

There was little to say after that, besides, it was late, past five, and they'd missed the film they'd planned to see, and were too hungry to wait for the next session.

'Why don't I cook for you,' Mim said.

Amy thought it an excellent idea, offered her flat as it was the closest, as long as Mim could manage on a two-burner stove.

'Absolutely.'

They bought pasta, spinach, mushrooms, cream and pinenuts; Mim insisted on paying, it was her treat, she said, and within half an hour of arriving home had the meal prepared. They ate hungrily and with enjoyment, and afterwards lingered over coffee at Amy's green table. Mim asked about Amy's work, wondered if the manuscripts were making her a better literary theorist. 'Or are they changing your life's ambition?'

'Not so much changing as expanding it. What was once a vague inclination to write a novel is now a driving passion, but being the careful type, I know I should do my PhD.'

'So what's it going to be?'

'I think I can do it all.'

At which point, Mim leaned across and kissed her.

If the touch of a hand can play havoc with one's equilibrium, a kiss can wreck it entirely. Several hours later, Amy lay in the crook of Mim's arm wondering how much happiness a single person deserved. She was beset by questions, had propped herself on an elbow ready to talk, when the phone rang. She jumped out of bed, lifted the receiver and was greeted with the cloud of a long-distant call, a momentary delay, then Philippa's familiar voice. Was Amy well? Was her work coming along? Was the gas at the flat fixed? Did she receive the parcel Philippa had sent? Had she seen Jeremy? Were he and Victor managing in Jeremy's tiny flat? And Amy replied that she was well and the gas was fixed, although for how long was anyone's guess; the shirt was perfect and she had worn it that very day; Jeremy was in fine spirits and apart from having to clean up after Victor, seemed very happy with his new living arrangements; her work was fine, not the dissertation, but the manuscripts; and she'd been seeing a lot of Mim Drummond. Who now smiled at Amy, got up, wrapped a blanket about her shoulders and returned to the bed.

Amy asked about the Foundation, which, Philippa said, was running very smoothly; and Leo's cough? almost better, although he couldn't have complained more if he'd had pneumonia; the Pryors had gone up north for a holiday, a spur of the moment decision to try and break the cycle of infection that had plagued the children over the previous couple of months; Leo, too, had planned to go away, but had procrastinated so long over the destination, that when he finally came to a decision there was hardly more than a long weekend left to him, and while Philippa could have guessed this would happen, she refused to organize him; Lorraine Pascoe was back from her trip and she and Philippa were meeting that evening for dinner; there was a concert the next evening, and a book launch the one after.

A busy time, she said, but not the purpose of her call. She was planning a trip. 'Where?' Amy asked, not daring to hope but wondering how it could be otherwise. And of course it was to England, to see Amy and Jeremy, perhaps take Amy across to the Continent if she could leave her work for a few days. Philippa intended to be away about six weeks and planned to leave in about a month's time. 'Why not stay longer?' Amy asked. Philippa mentioned a particular project at the Foundation, a few loose ends at Finemore's Fine Wines and Spirits, and the family, Leo too. 'Of course, of course,' Amy said, 'I understand.' They continued to talk about plans for the trip, whether they would spend one week or two on the Continent, in one country or many; they talked of the enjoyment they would have, the pleasure of prolonged time in each other's company.

'And you can meet Mim Drummond,' Amy said.

At which point Mim left the bed and joined Amy under the blanket. The telephone call continued for a few more minutes, and with words of love, still so clumsy on Amy's lips, she hung up. Mim and Amy sat under the blanket talking for a while, and when it began to rain, returned to the bed and watched the water pour in heavy streams down the glass and the dappled streams dancing over the wall opposite the window. They listened to the rain, much as one might listen to one's own breathing. Which is a great comfort when you are dry and warm.

THIRTEEN

'You didn't give her my love.'

Leo rearranged the pillows, rolled on to his back, put his hands behind his head, and stared at the ceiling. 'Was it really so much to ask? And in such a long telephone call too.'

Philippa's irritation was immediate; it was Leo's tone that rankled, the whining accusation curling with disappointment that she heard increasingly often these days. She delayed answering, straightened the clock on the bedside table, recalled the pleasure of her conversation with Amy and soothed her growling nerves. Finally she spoke.

'Why don't you tell her yourself, Leo. Write to her, she'd love to hear from you.'

And sounded perfectly calm.

'You know I hate writing letters.'

'That shouldn't become my problem.'

'And neither it would if you'd let me add a few lines to yours.'

'No, Leo. No.' She reached for her dressing-gown. 'Why must you keep asking? Why force me to give the same refusal over and over again? My letters to Amy are private, they have nothing to do with you.'

He rolled to his side, raised himself on an elbow and took her hand; how she wished he wouldn't touch her when they were arguing. 'Things in them you don't want me to see, is that it?'

'Come now, Leo, that's not the issue. I just happen to believe that a person's letters are private. I don't read your mail—'

'But you could, I've nothing to hide.'

'Neither,' she continued, 'do I listen to your phonecalls. Certain situations are private.'

He shifted the weight from his elbow and she retrieved her hand.

'I suppose you tell her everything, or, at least, all the negative things. Like the time I fell asleep over dinner with those clients of yours, have you told her that in your private letters? And when I forgot we'd arranged to meet at the cinema, and was waiting instead at the shop. And of course you wouldn't want to forget my refusal to go to that charity thing.'

Suddenly Philippa was laughing. 'Leo, Leo, Leo, stop being so absurdly egocentric. My letters to Amy would be private even if they contained nothing more than my weekly shopping list.'

She gave him a friendly shove as if that would quieten her exasperation, but when he continued to lie there solemnly sulking, she decided to get up, and encouraged him to do the same.

'You'll feel better after a shower.'

Which experience had taught her to be true. It was almost as if Leo were two distinct people. There was the public, fully-clothed, active Leo, who was also the sensitive, responsive and appreciative man that Philippa had come to love, and the other Leo, the relaxed Leo, who, divested of the demeanour of public life, was a child, a wheedling, demanding boy, whom she did not want to bother about, and certainly not at her time of life. To send him to the shower was the best means of regaining the man. And when he appeared fifteen minutes later, washed and dressed and full of a film they had recently seen, which, he said, had had a criminally short season because audiences expected to be led by the hand through a linear, action-based narrative and could no longer appreciate film that required a degree of thought, and then moved on to electronic books, and from there to the future of small literary magazines, Philippa found herself once again very satisfied. He suggested they meet for lunch, and although she'd made a tentative arrangement with Beth, she decided to put her off until the following day, said she'd buy coffee and sandwiches and be at the shop around half past one.

'But there'll be no lunch tomorrow, Leo, nor dinner either,' she said, thinking to pre-empt another disagreement.

He looked annoyed, wanted to know why. She explained about lunch with Beth, that there were a number of issues they needed to discuss and sometimes the office wasn't the best place, and in the evening she was going to a concert. With her irritation clearly evident, Leo apologized, it was just that he liked to see her, wanted to spend more time with her.

'We wouldn't have this problem if we lived together. You could have your lunches and your concerts, and I'd still see you every day.' He started to laugh. 'And how your children would hate it. It would be the end of the civilized world, their mother living with a Jewish shopkeeper.'

Philippa laughed too, it would have been churlish not to, although she felt uncomfortable, wanted to spring to the defence of her children, despite having expressed similar sentiments herself. Just another of the claims of family, she supposed, that you could criticize your children as much as you wished, always knowing your fundamental allegiance was inviolate, but a stranger having no such loyalty, had no such rights. Although there were other relevant issues, and her mind turned back to the previous Sunday, issues of human decency and courtesy, which should override even the arcane bonding of family; if so, after the way her children had treated him, Leo was entitled to lead the attack against the Finemores.

There are certain situations you would prefer not to remember, yet they adhere to memory with every nuance, every inflection preserved. Last Sunday was one such occasion. Philippa had invited Melanie and Selwyn, Gray and Evelyn, and the five grand-children to lunch. She had also invited Leo, who had helped all morning preparing salads, arranging platters of cold meat and chicken, even making a pasta with a pesto sauce which none of the family had touched recognizing it as non-Finemore food, or, as Leo had joked afterwards, not quite kosher. It was not the first time they had met Leo, only the most protracted, and they had been awful. Philippa had watched her children with an anger that had paralysed her; that she had been unable to intervene, unable to deflect their insults merely fuelled her shame. And to make matters worse, her passivity implied she was colluding with them against Leo. 'Which I was not,' she said to him afterwards, but neither had she been able to censure her children, even though their behaviour had been appalling. Leo suggested, gently, kindly – indeed he was far too kind over the whole business – that in such a difficult situation, the coward that is in all of us, might have been to blame.

'Not so much the coward,' Philippa had replied, 'as the mother.'

For only a mother could love her children after what had occurred. Each had been rude to Leo after his or her own fashion. Melanie's approach had been the most forthright, she simply ignored him. For her, it was a matter of logic: Leo had no place in Finemore circles, this was a Finemore gathering, therefore, Leo was not present. Even when her youngest, Claire, was earnestly engaged with him, Melanie simply directed that the child be removed from his side. Claire had been crouched with Leo over Philippa's shell collection. When Leo encouraged the child to listen to the sea, hear the waves, Melanie's retort, 'What rot, that's the tram down Nicholson Street,' had been clearly audible to them all. 'I can hear it! I can hear the sea,' Claire had cried, 'but how did it get in there?' And Leo told a story that Philippa thought quite charming, of how the shell couldn't bear to be away from the huge pounding waves of its home, so some of the waves had made themselves very small and squeezed into the darkness of the shell, and after that it didn't feel homesick any more. The child was fascinated, wanted to know more, at which juncture Melanie asked Oliver to fetch his sister. 'Stay over here,' she told the girl. 'But he's Nanna's friend.' 'No darling,' her mother replied, 'Nanna's friends are over here, so stay with us.'

The others had been variously rude, disparaging and anti-semitic, employing a variety of tactics that ranged from direct verbal attacks through slurs and snide remarks to sly asides, all of them orchestrated by gestures and mannerisms that were rarely covert and always offensive. Fortunately, they had all left as soon as lunch was over, and Philippa resolved never again to repeat the situation. Several hours later, with Leo returned to his own home, and only Peach for company, her strongest feeling had been sadness, and her greatest desire that the situation had been otherwise. She also knew that while sorry for Leo, she grieved more for herself.

'So,' said Leo, his hand on her arm, 'what will convince you to come live with me and be my love?'

Philippa took his hand, turned it palm up, and kissed it. 'I'm too old to live in sin, and,' she added with a wry smile, 'have lost the habit of marriage.'

'But you do love me?'

How much easier it would be to say exactly what he wanted to hear, a tiny lie to give so much happiness. And struggled against the temptation. 'Most of the time.'

'You're a hard woman,' he said, not quite playfully.

'Just trying to be an honest one.'

There was little to say after that; he left the table, washed the breakfast things, kissed her and was gone.

With her first appointment not until half past ten, Philippa decided to walk to work. She was uneasy about Leo, and nagged by his brackish demands, yet knew from experience that dwelling on them brought little relief, so, once out in the street, with her short figure moving at its usual rapid pace, she deliberately replaced Leo with Jeremy and Amy and the prospect of several weeks in their company. For she missed them both, her talks with them, the laughter, the odd little cafés they frequented, and most of all, the particular way they made her feel. They brought out the best in her, or rather the parts of her that she liked best. Jeremy had always had this effect, probably because, from an early age, he had been much more in need of a sympathetic friend than a mother. When Jeremy had left, Philippa had felt his absence keenly, but he telephoned often, and she to him, which helped decant the ache. She knew he was happy in London, was pleased he had found someone, hoped Victor would be around for a long time. Not that Jeremy had ever expressed concern over his short-lived affairs, but it had worried Philippa who wanted him to be settled. It was different with Amy; despite her long and frequent letters, Philippa missed her greatly. In the months before she left, they had seen each other almost daily, then suddenly there was nothing, only the letters, which, with their trading of spontaneity for intimacy, revealed a different Amy, a more considered, more serious Amy. And a very settled Amy, too, although to discover the heart of London in a library, was certainly not everyone's idea of heaven.

Not for the first time, Philippa questioned her feeling for the girl. Was envy involved? Was she, at the age of sixty-three, attempting to borrow a life, buy another chance? Was Amy a convenient substitute for the omissions of her own youth? She thought not, the facts seemed far more simple: she liked Amy, was invigorated by her, challenged by her, and appreciated by her. Amy enriched her days, she portrayed the common happenings of a life anew; where Philippa had been accustomed to viewing the world front on, Amy took the oblique perspective. Which made the prospect of travelling with her so exciting.

Philippa had made a similar trip almost twenty years before when Melanie had finished school. In those days, it was accepted in Finemore circles that daughters, accompanied by one or both parents, would be sent overseas before commencing their tertiary training. Melanie and Philippa had travelled together (there had never been any question of George's going) and it had been perfect. The trip had occurred just prior to Melanie's change, before she had remodelled herself and sealed herself against unexpected pleasure, and she had been delighted by everything they did. There had been the canals of Venice, and the maze at Hampton Court, and eating pickled herrings in old Amsterdam, and the extravagances of Versailles. And there had been the two of them together. For three months, they were hardly out of each other's company and had thrived on it; they had talked and laughed and shared hopes and secrets to an extent that could never have happened among the habits of home.

Yet, how quickly had this time together become an oddity for Melanie, a piece of childhood, a moment in the distant past; in recalling the trip, she always assumed a slightly amused, detached air. But there had been serious consequences for Philippa, for, if not for those three months, she would not have suffered so severely the change in her daughter, if not for those three perfect months the loss would not have been so great. That she might be wanting to reclaim those days through Amy had occurred to her, but, she decided, life doesn't repeat itself so crudely.

She glanced at her watch and quickened her pace. The wind, concentrated by the huge city towers, tore at her clothes, worried her hair; she felt the touch of winter, a chill at the edge of the wind, and smiled to herself: far from reclaiming past happiness or seeking recompense for past failures, she was aware of a deep satisfaction at being Philippa Finemore at sixty-three years of age.

It was past midnight when Philippa returned home; her step was sluggish, her neck and shoulders were cramped and her head was screaming. Peach gave her an enthusiastic welcome, and although she must have been ravenous, allowed Philippa to cuddle her and nuzzle into the woolly coat - dogs always know when their owners need comfort - before galloping to her bowl to await dinner. And such a dinner it was, having been prepared at one of the city's finer restaurants. With Peach satisfied, Philippa made herself a cup of tea, stretched out on the couch and clasped a hand to her aching head. The pain was ruthless, gripping together in a pitiless assault, poor, demanding Leo with Melanie and Selwyn, her own wretched, dishonourable children.

If only Jeremy were around to supply some humour, or Amy, who had a way of dealing with problems without interference from the guilt and shame now hustling in Philippa's shadow. Amy would take the problems one at a time; she would begin with Leo because he was more familiar to her, would advise Philippa to forget the morning's disagreement and the lunch-time argument; she would remind her that as far as men went, Leo was a very fine specimen, that of course he wasn't perfect because the perfect man did not exist, and if occasionally his gentleness dissolved into passivity and his belief in an equal partnership disintegrated into a cloying dependence, these were preferable to belligerence and neglect. As to Philippa's complaint that sometimes he treated her like his mother, Amy would remind her that all men do, all men search for a mother in their partners. If you are going to bother with a man, Amy would conclude, then Leo was one of the best.

With Leo thus dismissed, she would pass on to Melanie and Selwyn and deal with them just as summarily, although, as past conversations had shown, far less persuasively. Families are dangerous and cruel, she would begin, and, as this embezzlement business shows, immoral too; you're better off without them.

But they're your past, Philippa would argue, your very self; you devote more than half your life to your children, they help form you, and equally you form them. Which only makes it worse when they go astray, because you doubt first yourself, not them.

'But that's ridiculous!' Amy had protested when Philippa first said this early in their relationship. 'You're not the only influence in their lives. Surely you wouldn't want to suggest that Gray's shallowness and Melanie's greed were learned at your breast. Be sensible, Philippa, your children went to kindergarten, went to school, they made friends, grew up, moved away, married; they watch television, read the newspapers, they learn what's valued this year, own what was valued last year, and will acquire what's on offer next year; you cannot claim sole responsibility for who they are, what they've become.' And went on to expose the absurdity of Philippa's position by referring to her own case. 'Would you ever suggest Estelle made me?'

'Well yes, in a perverse sense, she did, in that you were formed in opposition to her.'

'That's quite wrong. She provided only one way, in rejecting that, I had to develop others. I looked around, I read, I learned, I made choices. As to the nature of those choices, Estelle was irrelevant.'

Which, whether correct or not, did nothing to temper Philippa's pain and abhorrence over Melanie and Selwyn's choices.

'How can you be so sure Melanie is involved?' Lorraine had asked that evening.

Philippa explained about the monthly cheques, the parties, the extravagant renovations. 'And she still hasn't finished; not a week passes without a new ornament, a new piece of furniture. Of course she must have known what he was doing and did nothing to stop him.'

'But if George had been siphoning off money from the business, would you have been aware of it?'

'You know I wouldn't, but these days couples run their marriages differently.'

Lorraine shrugged, she wouldn't know about that, but irrespective of Melanie's involvement, Selwyn was indisputably implicated, a quick glance at the balance sheets had shown her that.

'It's simple,' she said, spreading the pages over the table as soon as they were seated in the restaurant, 'you couldn't balance the figures, Philippa, because they can't be balanced; the figures don't add up. What I think has happened is this: someone, and given Selwyn's location in the company it has to be him, has been diverting profits from here,' she pointed to Finwest, 'to—' she shrugged, 'I can't be absolutely sure where, but I can make a reasonable guess. There are substantial takings for Finwest, much of which has been lost between here,' again she pointed to the Finwest figures, 'and here,' she turned the page to total revenue. 'I assume the huge expenses, this figure here,' she pointed to a figure in the millions, 'is where the lost Finwest revenue has gone, but until I see a breakdown of the expenses, I can't be sure. What I suspect has happened is that when Selwyn set up Finwest—' Philippa looked up in surprise. 'Hadn't you realized? Finwest is a new company, wasn't there in George's day; I expect Selwyn started it for a specific purpose, say, revenue from liquor sales in the West, and he's been drawing on the account for his own personal use.'

'What? Stealing from the company? Engaged in fraud?' Philippa was feeling sick. 'But how could he get away with it? And what about the accountants? Surely they'd pick it up.'

'They'd be more likely to see a mistake than any deliberate attempt to defraud; they might, for example, query the size of the expenses this year as compared with previous years, but only someone who knew the business well would know that expenses couldn't have increased to such an extent. The accountants wouldn't have this knowledge, and nor should they. Besides,' she added, 'they're used to dealing with George whose honesty in business was beyond question.'

As Philippa well knew. How contemptuous he always was when businessmen were charged with cheating or stealing or some other illegality; deserved what they had coming to them, George would say, gave business a bad name. What would he think then, of his own family committing fraud? More to the point, what would he do? Philippa's own desire was to run, pretend none of this had happened, but even while she longed for flight, she knew someone had to stay and sort out the mess.

She stared at the columns of figures, so deceptively neat so deviously organized, and tried to think of something, anything, to change events. She stared until the numbers blurred and she found herself thinking of her mother-in-law, poor Dora, crippled by a stroke at the age of sixty-eight, her right arm and leg dead lumps of flesh, her drooping mouth with its trickle of saliva, and worst of all, by far the worst, the loss of language, leaving her unable to read or write, unable to utter the words she desperately wanted to say. When first it happened, Philippa had wanted to flee as if that could restore her mother-in-law, and throughout the next fourteen and a half months in daily care of that once fiercely independent woman, while she fed and bathed and dressed her, while she tried to plug the gaping holes where once a vibrant language had been, Philippa wished and wished with the idle fervency of a child that the tragedy had not occurred. But it had, the daily round of personal care was a consummate, if cruel, reminder of it, and while others defected, Philippa, a diligent and steadfast guardian of tragedy, endured. Always had she possessed this talent for tragedy, and while she might prefer to be differently endowed, you can't forget who you are and neither, at this late stage, can you change it.

She took a sip of wine, then another, and faced Lorraine.

'How much do you think Selwyn has taken?'

'According to these figures, somewhere in the region of one and a half million dollars.'

Philippa pushed her meal to one side, rested her head in her hands, pressed hard against her eyes. A distraught waiter, who remembered Lorraine from her days with George, rushed to the table, and, pointing to the two full plates, asked if there was something wrong with the meal. Lorraine assured him the food was, as usual, excellent, rather they'd been too engrossed in their conversation to eat. The waiter glared: no conversation was that important, and anyone who thought it was, had no right to come here in the first place.

Philippa raised her head, nodded at the food. 'I won't eat it,' she said to Lorraine, 'can't even bear to look at it.'

Lorraine asked the waiter to remove the plates and wrap up the food. 'Peach will love it,' she said, as the waiter strutted off.

Philippa turned the pages slowly. 'What will the accountants make of this?'

'They'll probably ask for a detailed breakdown of the expenses, not because they'd suspect any wrong-doing, rather they'll need to identify which expenses are tax deductible. George was scrupulous about this; he used to say that while under-paying the taxation department was unforgiveable, over-paying was stupid, and insisted that we make a note of all tax deductible expenditure as it occurred. That this isn't happening would, I think, be seen by the accountants as a small, but understandable omission given the huge upheavals following George's death.' She sighed and sipped her wine. 'Although you do realize the accountants won't be seeing these figures for quite some time, not until much later in the year when they prepare the books, so Selwyn's got a few months respite.' She shrugged, 'Perhaps he has a plan to pay the money back, perhaps we're being precipitous.'

Philippa shook her head, to her knowledge there was no way Selwyn could find one and a half million dollars without going into debt.

'I suspect it's more like two million by now. These figures,' Lorraine pointed to the sheets, 'stop at the 31st of March.'

'One and half or two million, Selwyn couldn't lay his hands on that sort of money.'

'But Melanie could.' Lorraine's voice was quiet and gentle.

At which suggestion the strait-jacket of family jerked tighter. Lorraine was right, through Philippa, Melanie could find the money, and Selwyn would have known this. The tightening in her chest, that sense of panic that leaves one gasping for breath, was still noticeable, even now, hours later, as she lay on the couch in the peace and quiet of her own home. She sat up, walked to the back windows and leaned her forehead against the cool glass; Peach trotted over and stood close by, her small warm body pressed lightly against Philippa's legs. Could Selwyn have assumed Melanie's co-operation without first divulging his plans? Could Selwyn, a man not known for taking risks, have acted alone?

The very next morning provided an opportunity to discover the extent of Melanie's involvement, but Philippa's courage failed. Melanie had phoned quite early. Nothing was wrong, she said in response to her mother's enquiry, and yes, they were still on holiday, or at least Melanie and the children were, Selwyn had been obliged to fly home for a meeting the previous day. Which was why she was ringing: the date had been set for the official opening of The Selwyn Pryor Business School of Australia, and she wanted Philippa to keep the day free.

'I'm so thrilled for him,' Melanie said. 'Everything he's worked for is bearing fruit. He's given so much time and effort to this project—'

'Not to say money,' Philippa interjected.

'Really Mum, sometimes you go too far. Why do you have to run him down all the time? What gives you the right to judge him? You might never have appreciated him, but there are plenty of people who do, and this tribute has nothing, do you hear me? nothing to do with money. It's an honour, pure and simple, for your son-in-law's service to education.' She drew in her breath, as if to continue in similar vein, then thought better of it. 'You make me so furious, but I won't let you spoil what everyone, except you, recognizes as a major triumph.' She supplied a late August date for the opening, hoped her mother's attitude would have improved by then, added that she would be giving a dinner afterwards at Hopetoun, and with a few words about the children ended the phonecall.

There could be no doubt where the money was going, neither was Selwyn the first nor would he be the last to buy his own perpetuity. And if he had been diverting funds to his business school, then it was possible that Melanie, with her 'honour, pure and simple', was not involved. That her husband and the centre of her life was a liar and a cheat, created quite a different set of problems, but at least Melanie would be innocent of fraud. The phone rang again; was her relief to be so short-lived? Philippa wondered, but it was Gray, ringing to invite his mother to the inaugural *Finemore's Faithful* Vintage Awards. Gray was so excited about his club, Philippa knew she had to try for his sake. Besides, the evening was not for a couple of weeks, and maybe the Selwyn business would be resolved by then. It was to be such a lively evening, Gray said, with some first-rate contenders for the awards, and a raffle in which the prize was as much wine as could be packed into the trunk of a BMW within a ten minute period, 'Single bottles,' he said, 'not cartons, we don't want to make it too easy. And we've organized a video link-up with the car-park, so everyone can have a front row seat and join in the fun. And we'll be donating a percentage of the proceeds to a worthy cause, that's Trevor's area, but one which I fully support, in fact, there should be more clubs like ours that acknowledge their social obligations.' There was a pause before he continued. 'Dad would have been so proud, I really wish he could have seen what I've done. But you'll see it, Mum, you'll come?' And of course she would, of course she would, wouldn't miss it for anything.

After finishing with Gray, she got up, showered, dressed quickly, and driven by a need to be out of the house and out of contact, walked to the coffee shop to take a breakfast amongst strangers. She had slipped a book into her bag, and although it now lay on the table, she ignored it, stared instead through the window at the street beyond. Despite the early hour, the café with its handful of round polished tables was nearly full; there was a comforting buzz punctuated by the hiss and gurgle of the coffee machine. Lucia brought her coffee and a croissant, and she sipped and nibbled and stared at the cars caught in the peak hour clutter, watched the drivers tapping their steering wheels, talking to or ignoring companions, combing hair, applying lipstick, singing along with the radio. And began to relax. None of the people here knew her as Melanie's mother or Selwyn Pryor's mother-in-law or George's wealthy widow, and, until her second coffee, she suspended the knowledge herself. Then she took pen and notebook from her bag and started to deal with the problems.

FOURTEEN

'This Foundation business of your mother's has gone on quite long enough,' Selwyn said to Melanie a few weeks after her return from holiday. 'If we don't take control of the situation, and do it soon, she'll be the ruin of us all.'

'Perhaps you should speak to her.'

Which was exactly what Selwyn had decided to do, that very afternoon, after the luncheon for the new dean. 'We've made an excellent choice for head of school,' he now said to Melanie, heaping Fortnum's best whisky marmalade on to his toast. 'He's a philosopher, a specialist in the philosophy of business.' Selwyn took a generous bite. 'Excellent marmalade,' he said, halfway through his mandatory twenty-eight chews per mouthful, 'excellent. He's exactly what we want. Charles - you remember Sir Charles Scurry? - was quite taken with him when he interviewed him in London. Not that the interview was anything but a formality, we'd already offered him the job. I don't think I've ever seen a more impressive written application: excellent academic record, good business connections, and I must say some very notable referees.' Selwyn started on another mouthful. 'Quite young too.' He swallowed, rinsed out his mouth with tea, swallowed again. 'I particularly like his being a philosopher, lends a certain prestige to the school. Business education is often regarded, quite erroneously mind you, as an imposter in the academy, and a philosopher at the helm will bring a scholastic tradition that many business schools are seen to lack. Not The Selwyn Pryor Business School of Australia,' he hastened to add, 'but prestige and tradition are two things of which you can never have too much.' He smiled at Melanie, patted her hand and finished his toast.

Before leaving for the office, he rang Philippa to arrange a meeting for that afternoon. She sounded distant, even a little nervous, almost as if she knew why he wanted to see her. She did, however, insist that the meeting be at her office rather than Finemore's, which, even taking into account the nuisance of mid-city parking, seemed a small enough concession.

Melanie, too, seemed nervous; Selwyn assured her he would be gentle,

'Gentle but firm. Your father would have wanted this, Melanie. I know he'd have opposed any idea of a charity; he worked so hard for you, for all the family, he'd be shocked to know that strangers were now the major beneficiaries of his labours.'

'Although he was a very generous man.'

'Yes dear, of course he was, but not a stupid one.'

Melanie was standing under the portico when he brought the car up from the garage. He blew her a kiss as he guided the car past her. She waved, was still waving when he reached the end of the drive; he sounded the horn, and after one last wave, saw her go inside. He swung the car into the street, slipped a tape into the cassette and thought about his wife. She had been the perfect partner, and if her ageing mother was proving difficult and one brother was an ignorant boor and the other a poofter, Melanie made it all worthwhile. She had placed him at the centre of her life, and whilst he believed this was where he rightfully belonged, a quick survey of his friends showed very few of them enjoying the same advantage; more common by far was the Gray-Evelyn arrangement, wherein Gray believed himself to be in charge but everyone knew Evelyn ruled their roost. But not so Melanie, she needed him but did not cling, she looked to him for advice but did not bother him with domestic details, she was happy with what he told her and never questioned further, she was, simply, perfect. In fact, between Melanie and old George could be found the best of the Finemores; as for the others, even their combined attractions amounted to very little.

It was Melanie's perfection, and the trust she had in him, which had made the Finwest arrangement so successful; unfortunately, Finemore's accountants would not be so obliging, which explained the urgency regarding Philippa's affairs. By Selwyn's calculations he had only three months in which to assume control of her assets, arrange for the necessary transfers from her personal holdings to Finwest, and thereby restore order to the Finemore books. He would rest easier then, not that his actions were purely opportunistic, for no one would deny that Philippa's nonsense had gone on quite long enough. Gray should have put an end to it right at the beginning, but Gray was incompetent even when his own interests were at risk, and now, with his energies concentrated on the new club, it was unlikely there would be any action from him. The situation was clear: Philippa had jeopardized the security of the family, Gray had shirked his responsibilities, so it was up to Selwyn to intervene.

He parked the car in his reserved bay and entered the office. Finemore's was bristling with end-of-month business. There was a pile of messages on his desk and an impatient Maureen wanting to see him. 'In a minute,' he said, when she buzzed from the outside office. 'In a minute,' he said, and leafed through his messages. There was one from Sir Charles that had come through within the last half hour. He dumped the other messages in one of the desk trays and started to dial, when Maureen knocked, entered, shut the door, walked across the room, and sat down.

'Not now, Maureen,' Selwyn said, making obvious his disapproval. 'I'll call you when I'm ready.'

'I'm afraid, Mr Pryor, there are a number of matters that won't wait.'

'Ten minutes, Maureen.' He gritted his teeth.

'*Now*, Mr Pryor.' She gritted hers.

This was not an incident to forget, he decided, as he signalled with a wave of a hand that she could go ahead, not to be forgotten at all. It might well be the case that good secretaries were hard to find, but efficiency, good spelling, and initiative were nothing if there was no respect.

'Have you read your messages?' she asked.

Respect, he thought again, if a secretary doesn't have it then she forgets who's boss.

'Well?' She said. 'Have you? Have you read your messages?'

He was deliberately abrupt: of course he had, and if she'd stop disturbing him he'd be able to attend to them. So, she continued, what did he plan to do? What about the complaints from the head storeman, the queries from the accountant, the dispute amongst the drivers, clarification for the marketing analyst?

'I cannot keep putting these people off,' she continued. 'I've had the drivers in here every day for the past week; as for the packers, unless some agreement is reached, you'll have a strike on your hands. The first, I might add, in Finemore's history.'

He didn't like her tone; she was blaming him, no, worse, she was criticizing him, something she would never have done with George. She might be efficient, but no one was indispensable.

'Have you referred these matters to Mr Gray?' Selwyn's voice was low, authoritative.

He watched her draw in her breath, suck in her cheeks, watched the slack skin pucker into deep intersecting crevices; he grimaced, and turned away.

'Of course I've spoken with Mr Gray, but he says these matters are your jurisdiction. And,' she added, 'most of them are.'

'I don't need you to tell me my job, Maureen.'

'Mr Pryor, I'm just trying to do my job, but I can't if Mr Gray is at his club and you're - well, I don't know what you're doing, but you're certainly not dealing with this.' Her sweep of an arm took in all of Finemore's - the executive offices, the packing-room, the warehouse, the loading bays.

'If, as you seem to be suggesting, Maureen, you're the only one on the job, why haven't you dealt with these matters?'

'I've done as much as I know how, and, believe me, Mr Pryor, if I hadn't, there'd be three times as much work waiting for you.' She stared at him without blinking, no movement of any kind;

a rodent, he thought, she looks like a rat, a cunning, evil, insolent rat. 'And where exactly have you put the messages?' she now asked, and almost immediately located them in the brimming in-tray. She snarled something about Lorraine Pascoe and the old days.

'These are not the old days Maureen—'

'You're telling me they're not.'

'—not the old days and we have to move with the times—'

'Exactly, Mr Pryor. So may I go ahead and arrange meetings with these people,' she pointed to the messages.

'I'm trying to talk to you, Maureen, and do not appreciate your interruptions.'

'Go ahead and talk all you wish, Mr Pryor, but I'd prefer it if we cleared away some of the backlog first.'

He was furious, could have hit the scrawny rat, instead he grabbed the messages and thrust them at her, making sure his skin was nowhere near hers. 'Do it, do it. But nothing for today, do you understand? Nothing.'

She left the room before he gave her permission to do so, and as she closed the door, he determined to get rid of her. He did not need to come to work to be insulted, and would not tolerate it. He should have let her go at the same time as Lorraine Pascoe, but kindness - Maureen was fifty-five and unlikely to get another job - had coloured his judgement. Well, no longer.

He looked up Charles Scurry's telephone number and dialled. It was nothing important, Sir Charles said, just rang to let Selwyn know that the dean's wife would be joining them for lunch. Sir Charles, wanting to leave nothing to chance, had decided to contact all the committee members as it was essential the new dean and his wife were given a warm welcome. Selwyn heartily agreed, although privately he was less hearty: a warm welcome was one thing, but the first meeting with the new dean was quite another, and most men never performed at their best in front of their wives.

He shuffled the piles of paper on his desk, wrote out a Finwest cheque, the last he hoped, swivelled his chair and stared at the skyline. He would have liked a cup of coffee but refused to ask

Maureen, although her apologies would come fast enough when she received her notice. He turned again to his desk. He could see there was a lot to do, but at ten-thirty and the lunchtime meeting at a quarter to twelve, there was little point in starting. He collected his briefcase, buttoned his jacket, and with Maureen absent from her desk, made a rapid exit.

He went to his club hoping for company, but there were few people about and none of them familiar, so he sat alone with a coffee and the *Financial Review*. The coffee sank straight to his bladder and he went to the toilet before leaving, but even before he reached his car wanted to go again. He drove the short distance to the business school, making it to the bathroom only just in time, and when a few minutes later he had the urge yet again, he started to worry about his prostate – although he would have thought himself far too young for such problems. But perhaps not, for his memory, too, seemed to be softening: in his breast pocket was the Finwest cheque he had meant to bank after the club. Premature problems of ageing men? Or perhaps the stress his mother-in-law had caused him? And as he strode down the passageway, as he stretched the long firm muscles of his legs, as he quickened his pace while his breathing remained deep and even, he put the blame firmly in Philippa's court.

With fifteen minutes before lunch, Selwyn decided to treat himself to a tour of the school. His school, The Selwyn Pryor Business School of Australia. He was not yet fifty and had achieved what more famous men have to die for. And what an honour it was! While not a large complex, it represented state of the art business education, all of it new, all of it shining in readiness. He inhaled the fresh paint – his paint, and slid his shoe across the polished floor – his floor; he read the benefactors' names on the honour board – his honour board, and nodded a greeting at his own freshly painted portrait. Leaving the foyer, he walked into each of the five lecture theatres, testing the acoustics in one ('It is my pleasure to welcome you here today to this, the inaugural lecture of The Selwyn Pryor Business School of Australia'), admiring the audio-visual panel in the next, taking the lectern in the third, trying the seating in the fourth, and in the last, pacing out his territory, up one aisle, across the room at the back and descent via the other aisle. From the lecture theatres, he crossed into the Scurry Building and entered one of the six multi-purpose rooms. Each of these had been designed, not only for school use, but for industry activities as well, and was equipped with a bar and comfortable furnishings; the catering service and the leisure centre - two squash courts, a fully-equipped gym and a pool - would also enhance the school's attractions to industry. Even the faculty offices could be made available to outside interests for limited periods if so required. Computer access, a priority of Selwyn's, was excellent and included a link-up with the Bureau of Statistics network, and a deal had been reached with JAYEFF electronics - Jonathon Forrest was a recent appointee to the board - for discounted laptops for faculty, students and associates of the school. Nothing had been forgotten in the creation of The Selwyn Pryor Business School of Australia.

Selwyn glanced at his watch, made a quick visit to the bathroom, and entered the conference room at exactly a quarter to twelve. All of the board members had arrived, but there was no sign of the guests of honour. And there remained no sign for another thirty-five minutes, which, given that the dean and his wife had temporary accommodation in a university flat not five minutes walk away, was difficult to explain. The board consisted of busy men unaccustomed to waiting, so when the dean and his wife did finally arrive, they found themselves greeted with a reserve they would not have thought possible in the amiable, carefree Aussies.

Keith Austin-Ward and his wife Gillian entered the room arm in arm and stood just inside the doorway waiting to be noticed. The conversation gradually wound down as the board members turned to face their new dean. Sir Charles stepped forward and there followed a brief and hushed exchange with much consulting of wrist-watches, at the end of which Charles turned to his fellow board members and explained that Keith and Gillian had understood that lunch was for twelve-fifteen not eleven forty-five.

Selwyn stood towards the back of the room and observed the

new dean as he was introduced to the various board members. Selwyn was a man who believed that appearance comprised, if not everything, certainly essential data from which almost all else could be deduced, and for the life of him he could not understand what Sir Charles Scurry had seen in Keith Austin-Ward. Dr Keith Austin-Ward, so impressive in his written application, was a grave disappointment in the flesh. He was a round-shouldered, poorly shaven, bank clerk sort of a man, dressed in brown sandals and dark grey socks, tweed trousers with stains about the fly, and a dun-coloured jacket that was desperately in need of a press. As Sir Charles approached with Keith and Gillian in tow, Selwyn automatically felt for the inside button of his dark, double-breasted jacket, checked it was fastened and everything was in its place, before extending his hand. Keith Austin-Ward's limp grasp was quickly forgotten in the strongest body odour Selwyn had ever known; that he was not particularly sensitive to smells – a regular source of irritation to Melanie whose nose was a finely tuned instrument – made him think that Keith Austin-Ward must smell very bad indeed.

Although these details could be fixed: smells, sandals, clothes. The public profile of the Pryor school, Selwyn would say to Keith at a private meeting in a week or two, demand a certain style, a certain code of dress. Perhaps a clothes allowance would help. Or rather two clothes allowances, for Gillian Austin-Ward at close quarters showed herself to be even more in need of intervention than her husband. She was a type of woman Selwyn found most unattractive, mousey plain – he thought immediately of ratty Maureen – facial hair, no makeup, thin-breasted and large-hipped. Indeed, she was one of the most ordinary women he had ever seen. Her accent was unashamedly north England, a shrill and opinionated resonance that cut straight through him. He did not want to touch her, and was pleased when she kept her hand to herself when introduced. But given who she was, he knew he must make an effort. He enquired about their flight, hoped the flat was comfortable, that they were over the worst of their jetlag—

'Far from it,' Gillian Austin-Ward interrupted. They had both been up at three o'clock that morning, and without their usual brand of tea – 'It's the small comforts you miss,' she said – it was hours before they could sleep again.

It would be better when they were in their own home, Selwyn suggested.

'Although when that'll be I can't imagine,' Gillian replied. One person tells us to live in this suburb, another recommends a quite different area, and without a car it's impossible to get a sense of the city, so you don't know whose advice to take.'

She continued to talk while Selwyn looked down from his height, intermittently nodding at the litany of complaint which had been composed in the two days since their arrival in Australia. She'd even sent a Sainsbury's shopping list to her sister in Manchester containing items she'd been unable to find at the university supermarket. Selwyn had hoped the dean and his wife would have been people to know socially, but as far as he could see, even with the clothes allowances, these were not the sort of people with whom Selwyn and Melanie would want to spend any time.

'Although I understand the weather here is very good,' Keith added, interrupting his wife's moaning.

'Only if you like the heat,' she said.

If there had been any doubt that Keith and Gillian Austin-Ward would ever enter the Pryor circle this was dispelled at lunch. As the beef was being carved, Gillian called to the waiter for well-done meat. 'We hate the sight of blood,' she said to the assembled company, and when offered wine, asked for something sweet. 'We like a sweet wine,' her husband confirmed. As Finemore's stocked the school's cellar, Selwyn knew there was no sweet wine on the premises, and suggested a flavoured mineral water instead. Which they seemed to enjoy.

At least Keith Austin-Ward's academic record was intact, Selwyn thought, as he cut into the tender, red meat; the list of publications and those remarkable references were, fortunately, immutable. He watched Keith shovelling food into his mouth, forkloads of meat and vegetables tossed through parted lips, and felt a wanton shiver of doubt. Even while he chewed, Keith was heaping potato and broccoli and meat on to the concave side of his fork, even while he chewed he was talking – about the soccer, the cricket, his interest in Australian Rules. Such impressive references from such well-known men, surely they couldn't be fabricated. A dribble of mustard escaped to Keith's tie; Selwyn watched it settle, watched as Keith rubbed it off with his sleeve.

He turned to Sir Charles. 'Is this how he came across in London?'

Charles was affronted. 'Of course not! Do you take me for a fool? We met at my club and he struck me as a thoroughly presentable fellow; Andrew Oldaker thought so too.'

Selwyn raised his eyebrows, what on earth was Andrew doing with the new dean?

'Andrew joined us for a drink, so did Ian Kirwan; they were both in London for that *Invest Australia* thing. Anyway, we all agreed that Keith was a likeable chap, a good talker, a man who enjoyed his Scotch.' Charles chewed slowly, thoughtfully. 'Perhaps something's happened in the interim, a death in the family, you know how that can knock one, or maybe illness. His wife doesn't look to be a well woman.'

No one, Selwyn decided, looked particularly well, but the fact of the matter was, the fellow had been appointed and they had to make a fist of it. From the very beginning, Selwyn had stressed that the business school must be top-drawer; when his own name became attached to it, Selwyn was even more determined that it would be a first-rate institution. He looked at Keith Austin-Ward who was spooning two, three, no, four huge dollops of cream on to his fruit salad, and realized there was much to do. Fortunately, the defining characteristic of appearances was their malleability, and Selwyn was a marketing man after all.

Selwyn drew up outside the bookshop beneath Philippa's office and looked around for a parking space. He shunned car-parks as a waste of money and would park illegally rather than use one. Besides, everyone knew that luxury cars were rarely booked. He smiled, for he planned to buy a Rolls after he'd taken control of

Philippa's affairs, and expected never to receive a parking ticket again. Despite the disasters that were Keith and Gillian Austin-Ward, Selwyn was feeling surprisingly good. It was not simply thought of the Rolls that accounted for his high spirits, he was convinced that, before too long, Keith and Gillian would be so changed as to occupy their places at the Pryor dinner table without embarrassment to anyone. During the short drive from the university, he had drafted an Austin-Ward Improvement Plan. He had decided to allocate the major part of Keith's training to himself, while leaving Gillian to Melanie and Maureen's replacement. Melanie would organize the location and style of house, the credit cards, the shopping expeditions, the beauty treatments, while Maureen's replacement would do the fetching and carrying. As for Keith's overhaul, a month should just about do it, clothes, grooming, memberships; improving his taste would take a little longer, the table manners too, but all would, in time, be fixed. It was more nuisance than anything else, and coming at the worst possible time. For Selwyn did not underestimate the work involved in taking over Philippa's affairs; the Foundation for a start - winding it down, closing the office, dealing with dozens of bludgers who would not take kindly to their handouts being cut - would be a complex and time-consuming business. And Philippa would need to be transferred to the other side of the city so the family could keep an eye on her, and, most important of all, Selwyn needed to lay his hands on one million nine hundred and sixty eight thousand dollars, plus the additional fifty that was still in his breast pocket, and return it to the Finwest account.

The receptionist at the Foundation invited him to take a seat as Philippa was still 'in conference'. Selwyn rolled his eyes: in conference indeed! How readily did people inflate their own importance, and decided to stand. If he were not so confident of success he would be extremely annoyed at being kept waiting, but as it was, he felt quite charitable towards the old dear and could shrug off her little displays of independence. For the first time since George's death, he thought of the consequences of losing a spouse, how utterly awful it would be. He could imagine no other wife but Melanie, which was not to say there hadn't been infidelities, particularly while at the university, but a wife was different, and no one would suit him quite like Melanie. If she were to die suddenly as George had done, there would be a long period of adjustment before he was himself again. Although Selwyn could never imagine himself so not himself that he would jeopardize a fortune as Philippa in her grief had done; but other oddities would be quite possible (moving away from home where there were so many painful memories, came immediately to mind) so he must not be too hard on her. And while Philippa had acted irresponsibly, he supposed she could have done a lot worse, like giving everything to the RSPCA – such travesties occurred if one were to believe the daily press. No, he decided, despite the difficulties of the past couple of years, things could have been very much worse.

He looked about the office; there were women seated at desks in the small glassed-in spaces, phones ringing, people going from here to there, a normal busy office. Which was not a bad achievement, considering that prior to George's death Philippa's organization skills had been confined to parties and fêtes and raising children and grandchildren. Not bad at all. The offices were, he supposed, quite attractive; the art, in particular, although not to his taste, added a distinctive, rather stylish touch. There were several paintings, modern, with an ethnic, mainly aboriginal, flavour. He had never seen the attraction of dots and squiggles and sleeping lizards, although he understood this type of painting was proving to be quite lucrative as an investment. He peered at a swirl of ochre tonings, aesthetically it left him cold, intellectually too – always something distasteful about the primitive, but if the investment potential were promising, he could learn to live with the stuff. He took out his diary, made a note of the artist, and continued about the room. He was aware of being watched, and he liked that; he was a tall man who knew the value of height, and a slim man with thick brown hair, who knew the value of those too. And he was happily married which meant he could show himself off without the self-consciousness of one who wanted something in return. Women, and those in this office were all women, tended to admire the strong blue of his eyes, delph blue was how Melanie described it, and he made sure to keep his head tilted slightly back so as to show the colour to advantage.

'Just a few more minutes, Mr Finemore,' the receptionist said, head bent over a pile of letters.

'Pryor,' he corrected, '*Dr* Pryor.'

She looked up. 'What was that?'

'Pryor, my name's Pryor, not Finemore.'

She nodded and smiled and returned to her letters.

Stupid bitch, he thought, and sat down. He leafed through a brochure about the Foundation, a surprisingly professional publication, he thought, although the venture itself was totally unacceptable. He unfastened the inner button of his jacket and sat back; a minute later he was sitting forward and refastening the button. He stood up and paced the room, determined to maintain an even temper, up and back, until finally Philippa appeared. There were three people with her, one of whom was very familiar. They all walked to the door, where two of them, including the familiar one, departed, after much vigorous shaking of hands. Philippa and a youngish woman approached.

'I don't think you've met Beth Saunders, our CEO. Beth, this is my son-in-law, Selwyn Pryor.'

After shaking hands, Beth excused herself, 'A mountain of work,' she explained, 'which won't wait any longer.' Selwyn watched her enter one of the smaller offices, a nice-looking girl with a pleasant manner; might make a suitable replacement for Maureen.

'Who were they?' Selwyn asked, nodding in the direction of the door.

'The woman is the permanent head of Industry and Training, and the other—'

'Of course!' Selwyn interrupted, 'Darcy Hawksworth.'

'I thought you must have known him, everyone does, he's not exactly media shy.'

'So what was he doing here?' The question emerged as a growl, a reluctant and resentful resonance from a man who, accustomed to having all the answers, rarely asked questions. But at the same time, a natural curiosity and a rich deposit of pragmatism, meant he must know what one of the country's best known businessmen was doing 'in conference' with his mother-in-law.

Philippa moved a folder from one arm to the other before she answered. 'At this stage, not much. Networking, information exchange, sounding us out on a youth employment scheme—'

'What youth employment scheme?' The growl had become a snarl; he heard his voice as he seldom did, less authoritative, smaller, but he had to know what business Darcy Hawksworth had with his mother-in-law. A couple of years before, at an Australian Industry dinner, Selwyn had sat at the same table as Darcy's younger brother and, not long afterwards, had been introduced, very briefly, to Darcy himself, but he was as far from having Darcy Hawksworth call on him as he was the queen, and if it were a choice between Darcy and the queen he would prefer Darcy any day. 'What scheme?' He asked again.

'An apprenticeship plan, quite brilliant really, that would see long-term unemployed young people acquiring work skills and, ultimately, a trade.' She paused, but he was wanting more. 'That'll have to do for now, Selwyn. It would take far too long to explain properly and,' she looked at her watch, 'I only have until 6.00. So, shall we begin?'

Selwyn walked ahead into Philippa's office expecting her to follow, but no, she had stopped off at Beth Saunders's office and was now in earnest conversation with her. Their voices were low, confidential, they referred to the file Philippa was carrying, and talked some more. Finally Philippa gave Beth's arm a squeeze, left the file with her and came into the office.

Such a rude bitch his mother-in-law could be, Selwyn was thinking, insult had followed insult ever since he had arrived, but still he remained calm, still he managed to resurrect a modicum of pity for the old dear, still, he reminded himself, would she be the loser. Although, in the long term, he hoped she would see it differently, in the long term she would thank him for bringing her back to her senses.

There was a coffee-maker in the room. Philippa poured herself a cup and offered him one. He refused, decided to get straight to the point.

'This Foundation business has got to stop, Philippa.' His voice was firm, his gaze direct. But so, too, was hers, she stared at him with a face of steel. 'Got to stop,' he said again, as if repetition would add weight to his message. He spoke about George, 'A wonderful man and an excellent husband and father, the sort of man you could lean on.' He referred to the pain they had all felt on his death, 'A great and deep pain, but nothing compared with yours, Philippa, nothing compared with yours, because unlike us, you were the major beneficiary of his strength and guidance for nearly forty years.'

'*Over* forty years.'

'Of course, Philippa, over forty years, more than half your life.' How he wished she wouldn't stare like that. 'Half your life,' he said again, but not even repetition was supplying the emphasis he needed. 'It's like a ship,' he found himself saying, 'with George the captain and you his first mate.' When pragmatism failed as it often did with women, Selwyn was not averse to trying other methods, and with a smile now on Philippa's face, he decided to stay with the metaphor. He talked about Philippa losing her bearings, running out of wind, plumbing the depths, the need for a new navigator - 'Not a captain, mind you, for we all know there could only be one George' - to guide her into harbour and help her find her land legs once more.

'And then what? Will the ship and the new navigator set sail leaving me alone on the shore?'

'No, no, not the navigator,' Selwyn hoped he sounded reassuring.

'Not much work for a ship's navigator on dry land. What's he - I assume it's a man - going to to?'

This was one of the problems with metaphors, they could so easily spill into absurdity, could also be used for deliberate obfuscation. Philippa was being rude and provocative, so he decided to dump the metaphor for his usual blunt approach.

'You need help, Philippa, help and guidance.'

'An experienced navigator?'

'Forget the navigator.'

'Now that my captain is dead?'

'Forget the captain.'

'Forget George!'

She seemed sincerely outraged; no longer sure whether she was trying to make a fool of him, he asked whether she found it useful to think in terms of captains and navigators.

'To be honest, Selwyn, I'm not sure.' She turned away and he heard her sigh. 'Why don't you continue and we'll see.'

Difficult conversations have turning points, moments which mark a shift in advantage, and Selwyn had long prided himself on recognizing these. With Philippa now leaning forward, apparently eager to hear what he had to say, the advantage was clearly his. He seized it.

'You're not your old self Philippa.'

She nodded.

'It's been two years since George's death and it seems you're still adjusting.'

She continued to nod.

'I know these things take time,' he watched as she stretched her neck and then rested her chin on the palm of her hand, 'and one cannot expect to adjust overnight to the loss of a companion of forty years standing,' he corrected himself, '*over* forty years,' and was pleased to see her smile. 'But now it's time you received some help.'

With her head resting on her hand the nodding was slower.

'You're not yourself.'

The nodding stopped, she sat back in her chair, she looked very serious, and he knew that augured well, so he was shocked when she spoke.

'And who exactly am I, Selwyn?'

He must be careful, must sound genuine, even though he wasn't sure what prompted her question. 'I think you know what I mean.'

'Yes, I think I do, but I'm not so sure you do.'

He clenched his jaw, swallowed his response; who was she to question his understanding, the fucking bitch? He smiled around his gritted teeth, steadied his anger with some easeful breathing, and when he spoke, was pleased to hear a quiet, gently modulated, well-controlled voice.

'Listen to me, Philippa, I came here with the best of intentions, I came here not wanting an argument, I came here to help you, and it makes me very sad to see how difficult you're making it.'

'Leaving aside the details of your help for a moment, what makes you think that you're the best to give it?'

Selwyn took his time; she could be a cunning bitch when she wanted, and he would not be trapped. What she really meant was, with three children of her own, why was Selwyn the one to take charge?

'Everyone's so busy,' he said.

'And you're not?'

'Of course I am, but you know me, I thrive on it.'

'And Gray doesn't? Melanie doesn't? And Jeremy, who after all is only at the end of the phone, doesn't?'

Selwyn wanted to say that Gray was a fool and Melanie did only what he, Selwyn, told her, and no one in their right mind would seek help from a poofter, but he kept the truth to himself. 'That's not the point,' he said. And suddenly it came to him. 'This family, the Finemore family, has been very good to me; when Melanie first brought me to your home, you and George welcomed me as one of your own; I think it's time to give something back.'

'And what exactly might that be, Selwyn? No ships, no captains, no navigators please, just tell me what you're wanting to do.'

He had won! When the other person asks you to spell out what you believe she needs to hear, then the fight is over. He sat back and stretched his legs; he had an urge to walk to her side of the desk, give the old thing a hug, but knowing she was just as likely to interpret his pity as gloating, he decided to stay where he was. He spoke softly, and, he believed, sympathetically.

'I want to help you wind up the Foundation, and once that's done I want to take the family interests off your hands. Gray and I want to,' he added hastily, knowing that Gray's contribution could be determined at a later time. He leaned forward, and with Philippa also leaning forward their faces were no more than twelve inches apart. Selwyn backed off. 'No woman of your age, even one as fit as you, should have such responsibilities; at your time of life you should be comfortable and carefree, you should be enjoying yourself.'

'While you look after my financial affairs.'

'Exactly. In consultation with you, of course.' The details of which would, like Gray's involvement, remain nicely vague.

'All of my finances, including my share in the business?'

'All of it, if that's what you want.'

'It's an interesting proposal, Selwyn.'

'I'm pleased you think so, although not surprised, you're an intelligent woman after all.'

'Interesting and perplexing.'

'A little confusion is understandable; you've been under a lot of strain lately, been doing far too much.'

'You want to manage my money?'

He inclined his head in what was, he thought, a modest movement.

'And yet it seems you've already done just that. And rather badly, I might add.'

He lifted his head slowly, tilted it to one side, raised his eyebrows, and kept silent.

'I refer to a matter of—' she paused a moment, 'it must be about two million dollars by now of my money, or, I should say, family money.'

His immediate response was violence, he wanted to punch the smugness from the old bitch's face, he wanted to plug her mouth with his fist, most of all he wanted to close those eyes, those arrogant, condemnatory eyes. And he knew he could do none of it, could do nothing that might betray him. For how could she know? She couldn't even balance her own cheque book, how could she understand a complex arrangement like Finwest? She might have a few suspicions, but facts? They were beyond her. Keep calm, smile, humour her, above all, give nothing away, just find out how much she knows. But it seemed she had no intention of telling him; she refilled her cup, stood sipping the coffee, staring at him, staring down at him.

He stood up too. 'Think I'll join you in a coffee.'

She invited him to help himself. As he poured and stirred and carried he felt a weakness deep in his limbs; she'd unnerved him, that much was clear, but there would be no damage. *For she could not possibly know.*

'Good coffee,' he said, and returned to his seat.

She nodded. And watched. And sipped from her cup. She was making him uncomfortable. He shuffled in his chair, his crotch was itchy, he scratched. The minutes limped by.

'One point nine million dollars? Two million? I want an explanation Selwyn, and I want it now.'

'I don't know what you're talking about. But seeing you know all about it, why don't you tell me?'

'I'm happy to, if that's the way you want it, although if you had any backbone at all, you'd own up to it yourself.'

She was a cunning old bitch, he was thinking, appealing to his pride like that, but she couldn't know and he would confess to nothing. He watched her open a file, recognized Finemore's monthly figures.

'Are you sure you don't want to speak in your own defence?'

'Defence of what, Philippa? I've no idea what you're talking about.'

'Oh yes you do, Selwyn. Let's begin with Finwest.'

An hour later Philippa stood up; she had another appointment and Selwyn must leave.

'What are you going to do?' He hated her, he had never felt such hate, it consumed him, took all his energy, he couldn't think clearly, could hardly stand up. He caught sight of the last Finwest cheque, his last fifty thousand, there on her desk, and he despised her.

'I've a number of options, and in due course I'll inform you. For the moment, however, I suggest, no, I order you to leave everything to me.'

FIFTEEN

Philippa entered the house, the dog at her heels and closed the door. The air was musty, unused, and very cold. Since her meeting with Selwyn, winter had taken hold; a mere two weeks, but the lead in her bones and the chill in the air made it seem longer. There are certain events, shocks, from which there is no recovery; they creep up on you, knock you about, leave you with a permanent limp. 'She became an old woman over night,' one hears people say, making mystery when in fact there is none. For if you are already poised on the brink of old age, it takes very little to push you over. It should also be said that one can be poised for a very long time, so long poised and so perfectly balanced that one forgets how very close to the edge one is. You practise the routines of a lifetime, rushing here, helping there, errands for children, minding grandchildren, baking for this one, shopping for that, moving *in order to* maintain your balance. Too busy to listen to cheerless entreaties to slow down, too busy by far to capitulate to aching joints, you deny and pretend. 'So young for her age,' people say, and you hear only the word 'young'. Then a tragedy occurs, some savage misfortune for which you are totally unprepared, and age, so neatly dissimulated, hurls itself at you. 'Aged ten years over night,' people will say, and even though you know they are wrong, even though you know that age has lurked in your neck and spine, your eyes, your feet, your once slender fingers these past ten years, your greatest fear now that age has materialized, is that you'll be unable to put it back in its place.

Philippa leans against the front door, her eyes are closed, the relief she feels is etched with nausea: never has she been this tired, never has she felt so old. It is very strange, almost as if she has stumbled into someone else's life, and she does not like it at all. She's not interested in being old, not ready to retire from life, neither does she want it said of her that she aged ten years overnight; she must restore herself, as she has restored the family these past weeks.

Peach is dashing up and down the passage. With a dizzying effort, Philippa bends down to rescue the mail from the dog's excitement, her pleasure at the sight of Amy's handwriting tempered by the knowledge that there'll be no trip now, or at least not for a long time. No Jeremy and no Amy, and can she be surprised at who are the losers?

She switches on the light in the living-room, sees the bundle of unread newspapers still folded in their neat cylinders, the dishes resting on the sink, a fine layer of dust on the woodwork, and prompted by that peculiar compulsion of the homemaker, brushes a ledge with her forefinger, inspects the track in the dust, wipes her hand. She ignites the heater and the solemn, stale air gradually transforms. Peach settles on her rug and is soon asleep. How Philippa envies the dog, for after two weeks of rushing hither and thither, of pleading here and placating there, of arguing and negotiating, Philippa would like nothing better than to curl up and sleep.

Such a brutal time it has been. Following the confrontation with Selwyn, there were meetings with Lorraine Pascoe, long conferences with the Finemore accountants, several middle-of-the-night conversations with Jeremy, who had offered to come home, but she would not hear of it, and Leo. During the first week, Leo had stood by, a quiet and wary observer, during the second, he had vanished.

Once, not so long ago, Leo had said he loved her, but not her family. 'Sometimes, though, it's hard to separate you.'

His comment had upset her. 'No one is free of responsibilities,' she had said. 'No one who has lived more than sixty years comes without ties.'

'But yours are chains, and I don't care for them at all.'

'Have you really tried?'

He had shrugged: probably not, but could she blame him for that? He was accustomed to a peaceful life, one free of family. 'You want to live in a vacuum,' she said, 'just the two of us.' He nodded, slowly and sadly: perhaps, he said, she was right.

His absence over the past few days seemed to suggest he had chosen his vacuum, and it did not include her. She picked up the flowers he had given her when last they met. They were hothouse roses, pinched and perfect, identical blooms deprived of the haphazard joys of nature. She had never cared for such flowers, and even as she thanked him, told him how lovely they were, knew that as small a deceit as this was, it would only increase her dissatisfaction. Now, with the shine gone from the flowers, and the crispy knot of petals drooping on the stem, she knew that the moment she stopped speaking her mind was when honesty had been most needed. She sighed and sighed again, six blooms, one for each decade of her life, ten years for each dead flower. Lives so important as they are lived, she thinks, amount to very little in the long run; the details that give passion to an event, that supply its distinctiveness, are so easily lost. And we are accomplices, for what is regarded as a failure of memory is often the need to forget.

She puts the kettle on and walks around the room; despite the mess, the film of her absence, it is good to be home. She walks slowly, carefully, touching as she goes - an ornament, the spine of a book, an embroidered cushion, the carved wood of the mantelpiece - she touches as one might a forgotten flower found pressed between the pages of a book, or a handkerchief buried for years at the back of a drawer, touches in order to remember, to reconstruct a life.

Can two weeks alter a person's existence? A mere fourteen days unravel sixty-three years? She would have thought not, would have thought that one's grasp, *her* grasp on the essentials of being was firm enough to withstand most challenges. As indeed it was. For she *had* withstood Selwyn's challenge, and dealt with Gray's wounds and Melanie's dissatisfactions, and set Finemore's on a sound footing once more. But still there remained a sharpened anxiety, as swift and sure as an arrow in flight, that pronounced her life as fundamentally changed, and in its wake was a sense of loss, of having faced facts, harsh realities of that there could be no doubt, of which she'd long been aware but had managed to ignore. To pay off Selwyn's debts, to make Gray feel like the son and heir, to safeguard Melanie's happiness, she had first to concede Selwyn's moral bankruptcy, to attest to Gray's incompetence, and admit to her daughter's greed; to help her children she had been forced to see them as they truly were. And had lost something in the process.

She stands before the photographs on the mantelpiece, all her family smiling for the camera, lying for the camera - revisionist history as history's first document - and knows that the trust is missing, amputated, gone, together with a long-held, although rarely questioned belief in her children's basic goodness; her love remains, but it has lost its legs. So, when Melanie thanks her as she did last night for saving Selwyn, and apologizes for her outbursts of the previous days, Philippa knows that no matter how appealing this behaviour, more genuine by far is the invective of the preceding two weeks. 'It's your fault,' Melanie had shouted at Philippa day after day. 'Selwyn would never have resorted to something like this if you hadn't taken Dad's money. You expect us to live like paupers, but why should we? It was not what my father brought us up to expect, and it's certainly not what he intended. If Selwyn acted wrongly, he showed a concern for my welfare at a time when you were not.'

It's your fault, it's your fault, once, twice, sometimes three times a day, providing a far more authentic account of her daughter than the gratitude with hug and kiss that came last night. Ages ago, Amy, in talking about the reappearance of her own mother, referred to the touch she craved even though she knew it could do her no good; 'toxic' was the word she used. So it was with Philippa, who longed for her daughter's love. But love had not been on Melanie's mind the previous evening; her apology had been no more than an expression of relief that Hopetoun would not have to be sold, Selwyn's reputation was intact, and their style of life had been preserved. Relief, not love. And a brief relief at that, for last night Melanie knew only that Philippa had agreed to pay off Selwyn's debts, she had not yet learned of the new arrangements at Finemore's.

Standing in front of the family photographs, Philippa wonders how much forgiveness a mother can muster. She knows that memory is partly to blame, memory is a double agent when it comes to mothers. It protects so carefully the good times using, among other things, family snapshots as cheap preservative, while into the maternal trough of forgetting go all those damaging acts that provide a truth about your children you'd prefer not to know. To forget is always easier than being disappointed.

And so it was with Melanie. Philippa selected from the display a photograph of her and Melanie taken on their European trip. Behind them was Lake Como, and behind that, the Italian Alps; they must have asked one of the other hotel guests to take their picture. They were standing with arms linked, leaning against the balustrade. It was April, the Villa d'Este not long open after the winter, the air fresh, their hair teased by the wind, and, half-turned to each other, they were laughing. It was a precious time, set against the novelty of a European spring, the beautiful hotel, the calm of pre-season guests, a time that had slipped into memory with all its facets intact. Forever would they stand on that balcony in front of the lake in front of the mountains arms linked and laughing. And if Melanie had, in later years, reduced their relationship to a brittle, instrumental affair, selective memories, the insurance of a mother's love, would always pardon her.

Although, this time there had been a flaw in the process, as if memory itself had grown dry and brittle, and the photographs, formerly such loyal accomplices, had lost much of their mnemonic power. It was an agony: the faded memories, the jaded present, the loss. Philippa replaced the photograph with the others. She blinked hard, tears flowed over her cheeks to fall in purplish patches on her blouse. The dampness went through to her skin.

Amy's letter lay on the table; Philippa checked the postmark, written a week ago, she might not, at the time of writing, have heard about Selwyn from Jeremy. A glance at the first page showed she had not. The usual typewritten letter had been replaced by four pages of excited scrawl, mainly about Philippa's trip and what they might do together: museums, libraries, galleries, trips to Cambridge, Oxford, Kent, perhaps a day down in Brighton. They would go to the theatre, and hire deck-chairs in the gardens, and feed croissants to the bourgeois ducks in Regent's Park and attend lunchtime concerts at St. Martin-in-the-Fields. They might go to Edinburgh for a few days, or Paris, or maybe Amsterdam. And she'd found the ideal place for Philippa to stay, a sort of guest-house, clean and cozy, midway between Jeremy's place and her own. Philippa closed the letter, Amy would be devastated about the cancelled trip, but with the new management at Finemore's and the smouldering in the family, Philippa could not possibly leave.

These past several nights, riddled with anxiety, the worst kind of wakefulness, Philippa had grasped the unwanted thoughts, scooped them up one by one and dumped them at the margins of consciousness; she had then set about filling the space with images of Amy: Amy in the bookshop, Amy across the table at dinner, Amy in her leopard skin tights and aqua hat, Amy taut and white after meeting her mother, Amy talking and listening and laughing and arguing. Images plucked from memory, but also scenes from imagination; for Philippa also saw her in London, in the library and the manuscripts room, saw her striding the Bloomsbury streets, squinting in the metallic light as she stopped to read the blue plaques; saw her in the park watching the ducks as they fought for their portion of pond; saw the college where she taught, its dowdy passageways and grimy lino floors, the acoustic tiles stained with nicotine, the scarred vinyl furnishings. Imagined her in her flat, a single rectangular room with a kitchen behind a partition and a shared bathroom out on a landing seven steps down. 'Get yourself a proper flat,' Philippa had said. 'At least find something with your own bathroom.' But Amy had refused; she was perfectly comfortable, had lived in far worse places. 'That's exactly the point,' Philippa said, 'it's no longer necessary.' Which was not the point, Amy replied, and closed the conversation.

The flat suited her well, and, in time, through her letters, Philippa understood why. It had everything she wanted, yet could easily be abandoned: a home for the moment, a home for the homeless. Philippa could picture her, a week from now, seated in her chair, the one with the wooden arms on which a previous tenant had carved a swastika, the one from which Amy had, with her nail file, gouged out the offending symbol, a cup of coffee by her side, reading Philippa's letter and learning that the trip had been postponed. And would she understand? Would she know the change was not because Philippa cared any less for her than she did her own children, but rather she couldn't turn away from her family when she was needed?

'You've reduced the dynamics of family to need,' Amy would write. 'You're at their beck and call.'

'She's at their beck and call,' Amy would say later to Jeremy, 'and it's simply not right.' Jeremy would reply that a different set of moral imperatives operated when it came to the family, not speaking in his mother's defence, rather stating a fact. That Amy would have none of it, Philippa knew perfectly well, but would she understand? Would she forgive?

Perhaps it is easier to reject something you've never had. Perhaps it is more difficult. What is, however, unequivocal, is that having assembled the ribs and girders of a life you cannot dismantle it without risk of being crushed. Until the family problems had eased, Philippa could not possibly leave the country.

She knew Jeremy would understand, but would Amy? Would she be forgiving? And not wanting to upset her any more than was necessary, Philippa decided to ring her in the morning. She leaned forward, resting her head in her hands, Amy would lose and yet, loving Philippa, would probably understand. But what of her own daughter? What of Melanie? Once she heard the whole story, as she undoubtedly had by now, would she withdraw even further? Would anything remain of the girl she once had been? Would Melanie, such a fierce supporter of her husband, ever forgive Philippa for what she had done? Gray had not been much impressed with his mother's plans for Finemore's, but at least he had been forewarned, at least he had known what to expect from this afternoon's meeting. Selwyn had not. When it was all over, he accused Philippa of being a 'vindictive old bitch' who had deliberately set out to humiliate him.

Had she set him up? Had she been vindictive? She thought not, which was not to say she did not resent him, for she resented him mightily. Most of all, she resented his refusal to admit to any serious wrongdoing, indeed, as far as he was concerned, the blame lay entirely with George and Philippa: George, because he should have known better than to leave control of a fortune to an ageing wife, and Philippa, whose actions had forced Selwyn to seek funds elsewhere. Now, to add to all his other grievances, was Philippa's failure to warn him of her decisions regarding Finemore's. That she had not, had been a deliberate choice: her decisions were final, she knew Selwyn would not like them, and was not such a fool as to provoke one of his ferocious attacks. Self-preservation not vindictiveness had caused her to act as she did.

Besides, she had felt under no compulsion to speak with him, for hadn't she said when last they met, 'Leave everything to me'? Hadn't these been her very words? Only now, with decisions made and dispensed, did she stop to think how Selwyn might have interpreted her injunction. He would have known she wouldn't allow the family name to be dragged through the courts, so could be sure that what he referred to as his 'indiscretion' would not be made public. He would have shuffled through the available options and culled satisfaction from the obvious: she would bail him out and restore financial order at Finemore's; she would do this discreetly and quickly with a minimum of damage to the business and the family. Then, to safeguard the family interests and knowing that Gray lacked all leadership qualities, she would appoint Selwyn as managing director of Finemore's. From Selwyn's point of view the outcomes would have been self-evident.

'What can I do?' Philippa had asked Jeremy two weeks ago. 'What options do I have?'

And Jeremy, who knew his mother well, answered, 'Abbreviate

your suffering and do what you already know you must: bail him out.'

The next night, Jeremy had rung back. 'What will happen to Finemore's? What's to stop Selwyn from doing it all over again? What if the business school needs to be expanded or the house requires another round of renovations?'

The obvious solution was out of the question. 'Gray is incapable of running the company,' Philippa said.

'I know he is, but you're not. You'd have a good deal to learn, but you'd manage it, and there'd be people around who'd be only too willing to help. Lorraine Pascoe for a start.'

Which gave her the idea.

Poor Gray, pink and quivering, had been horrified. It was fortunate, he said, he'd not confined his interests to the company, it was fortunate, he said, he had *Finemore's Faithful*.

'And the investment properties, too, I thought you might like to manage them.'

And he did, he liked that very much. In fact, Gray liked the idea of investments even more than he liked being managing director of a large liquor company. Property, so solid and reliable, complemented the image he had of himself. Yes, he said to his mother, he would be happy to manage the properties.

'What harm can he do?' Philippa said to Jeremy when she discussed the idea with him. 'Besides, I can't reduce his standing in the business without giving him something in return.'

'A sort of consolation prize?' Jeremy suggested.

'If you like. Although he can't get into any trouble. The properties will remain under my control, my signature will be required for all significant business. All he'll manage is the day-to-day affairs, which should suit him very well.'

So Gray had arrived at the afternoon meeting forewarned about the restructuring at Finemore's but satisfied with his consolation prize. Not so Selwyn. He had stood in the doorway, five minutes past the hour, the last to arrive, dark, double-breasted suit sitting exactly as it should on his tall, thin body, silk tie hanging perfectly straight, head tilted slightly upwards as was his wont. Stood in the boardroom doorway, a deliberate tardiness she was sure, in order to provide Finemore's executive staff with a fine view of the man who would be, or so he must have thought, their next managing director. Stood and posed, not bothering to look at those assembled for he knew who would be there, and in not looking, not seeing Lorraine Pascoe next to Philippa. And did not see her until he was about to take his seat. He stopped; a shadow of confusion crossed his face, and, after the confusion, a sequence of thoughts that carried him from anger through annoyance and lastly to some explanation that clearly satisfied him, for he smiled at the gathering and sat down. He remained calm, almost smug, during the first part of Philippa's speech. He already knew the outcome and knew that success demanded a measure of generosity. Even when Philippa dwelt on the halcyon days of George's leadership and the magnificent contribution of Lorraine Pascoe, he nodded a courteous acknowledgement, and when she passed on to the difficulties since George's passing, the fall in figures and the soggy morale, still his facade was congenial; he knew where all this was leading. So when Philippa announced she had appointed Lorraine Pascoe managing director of Finemore's Fine Wines and Spirits, he probably heard his own name, heard the words he had rehearsed so often in his imagination, and it was only when people rose to congratulate Lorraine, that he must have replayed Philippa's announcement and heard what she really had said.

The smile left his face slowly, so slowly, dragging downwards as dollops of wet sand slide down the sides of a child's castle, and when the movement stopped, what remained was an expression of pure violence, and it was directed towards Philippa. But barring sale of the company, what else could she have done? Selwyn's self-interest put Finemore's at risk just as much as Gray's lack of ability. More. The two of them working together may have succeeded in running the company, but each had shown that to be out of the question.

'They manage to get along in the family circle,' Jeremy said on one of his phonecalls.

Only because the goals of domesticity were so different to corporate goals, Philippa had replied. There had been a long pause before she continued. The family, she said, was going nowhere, it was a matter of maintaining the status quo, of ensuring that so little occurred, nothing unexpected could happen. 'The family,' she continued, 'is, unfortunately, allergic to change. But not so a business; it must welcome challenges, even create them. A successful business is dynamic, a successful family is in a state of hibernation. That the boys manage to get along in the domestic sphere,' she said, 'is because nothing's required of them.'

The boys could not run Finemore's but Lorraine Pascoe could. Initially, Lorraine had rejected the idea. So many reasons, she said, not the least being the boys' animosity. But there was also her age, and George's absence.

'George used to run Finemore's and I ran it with him.' She smiled at Philippa. 'You see what I mean?'

Philippa had taken her objections and wrestled with each in turn. Four days ago Lorraine had relented.

'But only for two years, only a two year contract.'

'In the first instance,' Philippa replied, 'and then we'll talk some more.'

'The boys will hate it.'

'But you're used to that, haven't they always opposed you?'

Now it was over, Philippa wondered if she had done the right thing. Usually when one made decisions one was rewarded with a sketch of the future, but not in this instance; Philippa was beset by doubts and questions, fears too. She wanted things to be right, and everyone to be happy; she wanted to keep her family, wanted too, to keep Amy Vaughan, wanted to keep the life she had made, the Foundation, her little house, new friends, might have wanted Leo but was no longer sure, and indeed wondered with his recent absence whether she still had the choice. As a girl, she thought life would be easier when she grew up; as a young mother, she assumed life became easier when the children left home; now, as a widow with adult children, she was resigned to the truth: this was how it was.

She wanted her children to be happy, but didn't want to worry about them. She was pleased about Jeremy, had thought he might never settle down; and while he complained about Victor, who

kept the oddest hours and had an abhorrence of housework, Jeremy seemed happy. She would have preferred it if he were not so far away, but would visit, visit often, once the family was back to normal. Her thoughts turned to Melanie, whose idea of happiness had turned out to be so different to Philippa's. Melanie had made her choices years ago, not Philippa's choices to be sure, but then neither was it Philippa's life. She sighed, perhaps it was time for her to accept that. As for Gray, he seemed well-pleased with his tightly-packaged existence, particularly now he had *Finemore's Faithful*. And Trevor Potter as well, in whom Gray seemed to have found not only a business partner but his first real friend. Of all her family, only Evelyn seemed less than happy, and it was difficult to know why. Certainly Gray had been busy with his club, but then he'd always been busy with something, and he now had Trevor to talk to, when formerly he'd only had his wife. Evelyn said she needed something of her own, not cake decorating, something weightier, something more transcendent. 'I feel empty,' she confessed to Philippa one night as they were stacking the dishwasher, 'empty.' And then a couple of months ago, without any warning, she had announced she was returning to university. 'Plenty of women my age do a degree, plenty of older women join the work-force.' Gray was unimpressed: she didn't need to work, and if it was an interest she was wanting, there was always *Finemore's Faithful*; but no, Evelyn said, she needed a new direction.

Philippa wondered if Evelyn had heard yet from the university, rose from her chair and made a note to ring her in the morning. Peach stirred, went to the back door, and Philippa followed the dog outside. There was a frost in the air, the sky was a perfect, clear, winter's dark. Philippa shivered; she thought of Melanie and Selwyn, Gray and Evelyn, she thought of Jeremy and Amy, Leo, too, and she continued to shiver, her whole body shaking, teeth chattering. And then, just as suddenly, as if warm arms had grasped her and held her close, she was quiet. As quiet as the night and just as calm. She was too old to suffer defeat and too young to surrender to it, and while she missed Leo, missed him greatly, she was also past the age of compromise. Once, not so long ago,

Amy Vaughan had said that in living a life one of the hardest tasks was defining what you wanted; it required you to know your limits and accept them, but not continually to suffer them. And when you know, she said, so you can act.

Philippa went back inside. She pulled the chair closer to the heater and reached for her diary. She turned the pages, turned over the days of winter on through the months of spring, she turned and turned until she came to Christmas. Never had she known a European Christmas, a winter Christmas, but she would, this year she would, and leaned her head against the back of the chair, closed her eyes, and thought of the future.